i

'This is Police business, Sarah,' Nick said again. 'Don't you have enough on your plate right now with running the farm?'

'Not you as well,' she said under her breath, then responded briskly, 'I'm perfectly capable of doing more than one task at once, you know.'

He smiled. 'I wouldn't suggest otherwise. You know I only have your welfare at heart.'

'Of course you do.' She came out of the herb garden and closed the gate behind her. 'As you've pointed out, I have a lot of things to see to, so I'd better make tracks for the farm.' She hesitated. 'Will you let me know how things go with your investigation?'

He nodded. 'I will.'

She was conscious of his gaze on her as she walked away, but her mind was elsewhere, in complete turmoil. Something dreadful had happened to Jenny and she didn't believe it could be simply put down to misadventure or suicide. Somebody had set out to kill the Estate Agent and he or she was trying to lead the police into passing it off as an accidental death, but Sarah vowed she wouldn't let them get away with it. She would do her very best to find out exactly who was behind the horrible deed.

Dear Reader,

Welcome to the first book in a Murder Mystery series about Sarah Marshall and Sweetbriar Farm, the property she has inherited from her beloved grandmother.

I hope you enjoy being alongside our heroine as she struggles to keep things from falling into ruin, and that you'll want to cheer her on in her efforts to find the truth about her friend's unexpectedly sudden death.

Happy reading!

Joanna

SWEETBRIAR FARM MYSTERIES

Book One

Deadly Medicine

by

Joanna Neil

ISBN13:9781731038418

Reviews of Joanna Neil's Books

A Cotswold Christmas Bride – (www.goodreads.com)

'I've never given a romance novel five stars before, but I loved this one.'

The London Consultant's Rescue – (Coffee Time Romance Review - 4 cups)

The author does a good job of combining this medical romance with a little bit of mystery, making it a cut above the usual.

The Doctor's Longed for Family - (Coffee Time Romance – 4 cups)

I really enjoyed this one. Abby and Matt are both very attractive and intelligent characters, dedicated to their careers and their patients. I liked the development of their relationship amidst the drama of the emergency room and the confusion of the filming of the series and Matt's niece and nephew added a lot to the story. The author pulls off a really nice ending.

Dedication

To my family, with love, always

Acknowledgements

Many thanks to my daughter, Kerry Bates, for her wonderful artwork and to Mark and Liam for all their technical help and their endless patience.

CHAPTER ONE

SARAH Marshall stood in the cobbled yard and looked around at the farm she'd inherited just a month ago from her grandmother, Grace Marshall. What was she to do with it? Her green eyes clouded, troubled by memories of the kind and loving woman who had passed away and left an empty place in her heart. It seemed to Sarah that the inheritance was a mixed blessing, and she was in a quandary.

It was Saturday, on the Easter weekend, a fine April morning, with a pale sky and a watery sun, but there was a faint breeze blowing, causing her to pull her light jacket around her, cupping it to her with her forearms. The wind gently played with flyaway tendrils of her long, honey blond hair.

'So, do you think you might want to sell up?' Jenny Carter was brisk and straight to the point, as usual. She was a woman in her mid-fifties, immaculately dressed in a stylish pencil skirt and jacket as befitted her calling as the local Estate Agent. Her hair was chestnut coloured, salon maintained in a carefully layered cut. She wore make up, applied with a delicate touch and finished off with lipstick in a muted coral shade.

Beside her, dressed in faded blue jeans and with a pin-tucked button through shirt beneath her jacket, Sarah felt that perhaps she ought to have made a bit more of an effort. Her skin was nude except for a touch of moisturiser.

'I'm not sure,' she replied. 'That's really why I wanted you to come over and take a look at the place and hopefully advise me as best you can. It's good of you to take the time to do that for me.'

She and Jenny had come to know one another from meeting up by chance every now and then when they used the Post Office, or the Bank, or found they needed last minute bits from the village shop. They'd become friends over the last few months.

'I've taken a fortnight off work so that I can give it some thought,' Sarah added. 'It's not an easy decision to make - I'm not sure what Gran had in mind when she left it to me. I know she loved the farm - it meant a lot to her - but over the years as she got older and started to become a bit frail I felt it was becoming too much for her to handle. I don't know if I'll be able to do it justice.'

Jenny nodded. 'I can see it's a tough one. A farm is a lot to take on, when you already have your work at the solicitor's office in town, and that's something you enjoy doing, isn't it? Whenever we've chatted you've been enthusiastic about it.'

'It is.' Sarah smiled. 'I love being a paralegal. It's all I've known since leaving Uni five years ago. The work's varied and interesting, I like the people I work with, and I get to research into cases, and even go to Court on behalf of my clients, sometimes – mostly people who can't get legal aid, so I feel I'm really doing something to help.' She made a face. 'I'm really not sure I'm cut out for running a farm, albeit a small one.'

'Hmm - it's a dilemma, there's no doubt about it... I do understand your problem, how it is that you're at a crossroads. As it stands, the farm won't fetch a great price on the open market. Things here are looking a touch dilapidated, to be frank. The paint's peeling, some of the hutches and stalls are showing signs of rotting, and generally it could do with tidying up. I know your Gran left money in trust for someone to go on looking after the animals and so on for a couple of months, but there needs to be somebody in charge to sort things out. That fence, for instance, needs some urgent attention if you don't want the sheep straying.'

She waved a hand in the direction of the field and they walked over to the fence in question to take a closer look. It was a fact... several posts were beginning to decay at the base. Sarah examined them for a moment and then looked around. From here the hillside rose gently, providing ample grazing for a couple of dozen woolly, black-headed sheep. The lambing season had almost finished, and several ewes were feeding their offspring. Before too long it would be time to start the shearing.

'You're right, of course,' Sarah admitted, as they walked back to the farmyard. 'There are so many things I need to attend to.' She smiled. 'I shall have to start making lists.'

Jenny acknowledged that with a brief curve of her lips. 'Definitely. I wish I had your energy. I can see you've done so much here already, tidying up the kitchen garden and harvesting the broccoli and cabbages from the field. Not to mention rounding up most of the hens.' Her gaze followed a Rhode Island Red that had determinedly evaded Sarah's efforts at capture and was now wandering around the yard pecking indiscriminately as they talked.

Sarah felt a slight pang of guilt. She'd guessed from comments the Estate Agent had made about other farms she'd visited that she wouldn't be too keen on chickens, and had done her best to get them back in their run before she arrived. 'There are still more winter crops to be harvested,' she said, 'and I need to make a start on sowing crops for the summer season.'

Jenny sucked in a slow breath. 'It makes me tired just thinking about all that work.'

Sarah gave her a concerned look. Jenny's features were slightly pinched, as though she was under a bit of a strain. 'Are you okay? You look quite pale all of a sudden. I'm sorry for mentioning it, but I know you have some kind of heart problem... word gets around in a place like Woodvale!' Most of the locals knew that Jenny became breathless every now and again, though she did her best to disguise it.

'Oh, that's all right.' Jenny frowned. 'It's nothing. It's been a difficult morning one way and another – not while I've been here, you understand, and nothing to do with work – but otherwise - problems I really could have done without.'

'If you'd like to come into the house and sit down for a while... I could make us a drink...'

'No, no... thanks, but I'm okay, and I really need to get on - I was late getting here - I must apologize again for that... and I still have other calls to make.'

'If you're sure?'

'I am. It's kind of you, but there's no need to worry about me, Sarah.' In an absent gesture Jenny laid a hand lightly over her chest. 'The truth is I have a heart valve that doesn't work quite as well as it should, but it isn't too serious.' She frowned. 'Which reminds me, I must pop into the pharmacy when I leave here and get my prescription filled. I only have a few days' supply left... digoxin,' she confided. 'It's not prescribed a lot these days, but it suits me better than other medications - it helps to keep my heart rate steady.'

As though embarrassed by the disclosure, she took a quick breath and straightened her shoulders, coming back to the matter in hand. 'Anyway, back to more important matters... if you do decide to sell, you'll need to think about whether you want to spend money on doing the place up to get a better price, or make a quick sale for less than the market value.'

'I will. I'll give it some serious thought.' Sarah glanced at Jenny, wondering if she should leave well alone... but once the bit was between her teeth... 'These problems you had this morning – I can see they must have upset you. You don't seem to be your usual self today.' Now that she gave it some thought, Jenny had been quieter, less driven than normal. Up until now, Jenny had always given the impression that she was a hardy, determined woman, who could deal with whatever came her way. She was certainly ambitious, coming to this Cotswolds village a couple of years ago, a few months after her husband died, and taking over the Estate Agency in the nearby town of Caulders Lea. Yet perhaps she had her own inner struggles that few people knew about.

'Oh, I'll be fine. My stomach's giving me some gyp, to be honest - heading for an ulcer, I suspect - I've had a few set-tos with a man who lives in my neighbourhood, and that hasn't helped. Ben Reed - you probably know him?'

'Ben? Yes, I've seen him rolling home from the Horse and Groom a few times. He's a bit of a loner, I think.' Ben was around forty years old, not given to making friends easily. 'I think he has a drink problem, but I heard he does odd jobs around the village, building work, plumbing, and so on. I can't say that I actually know him, though. What's he been up to?'

Jenny pulled a face. 'It's his dog, Lexie - she was constantly barking and howling, and a few weeks ago when I couldn't stand it any longer I went to see him about it. He lives several houses away from me, on an adjoining road, but the sound carries. He kept the dog outside all the while, chained up amongst loads of junk, and he left her for hours, whatever the weather, so she was wet and cold and covered in mud when I saw her. She can't be much more than a year old, and she's pregnant, poor thing. I had it out with him, told him he had to look after her properly, but all I got was a load of abuse from him for my trouble. I told him I'd call in the RSPCA if he didn't sort things out.'

'It's upsetting to hear something like that. I hate to hear about animals being harmed.' Sarah frowned. 'So, did he put things right?'

Jenny pressed her lips together. 'No, he didn't, so I warned him again and when he still ignored me, I called the authorities. The RSPCA officer came and took the dog from him, but in the end I said I would look after her, because they were full to brimming over at the kennels. I took her home and gave her a bath and a good feed. Underneath all that dirt she's a beautiful Boxer - very thin, and her coat's in poor condition, but I hope I've rescued her in time.' She sighed. 'It's a worry, because I have to go away to a seminar the day after tomorrow, and I really don't want to put her in kennels after all she's been through. I suppose I'll have to, though. I'm going to be away for about three days.'

'Is there anything I can do to help?' Sarah considered the matter briefly. 'I'll be staying at the farmhouse instead of my flat for the next two weeks, and I have all these other animals to care for, so I can't see that one more will make much difference.'

'Are you sure it wouldn't be too much trouble?' Jenny looked doubtful and relieved at the same time. 'Oh, I'd really appreciate that, Sarah.'

'Yes, I'm positive. I expect she'll be company for me of an evening.' She glanced at Jenny, who was frowning and rubbing her midriff. 'Do you have anything you can take to ease your stomach pain?'

Jenny nodded. 'I make a tea from comfrey leaves. I know the herb's used more as an external salve these days, but my mother used to swear by an infusion of the leaves in water, and when I tried it I found it helped.' She smiled. 'So now, with the appropriate cautions about reading up on it for themselves, I recommend it to anyone willing to listen. I go home at lunchtime most days and generally I'll make up a brew.'

'Well, I hope it helps today.'

'It will, I'm sure. As you know, I'm a firm believer in herbal remedies.' She smiled. 'Just ask anyone at the hairdresser's, or around the village. I'm always trying to gather converts.'

As she walked with Jenny along the wide farm drive to where her car was parked, Sarah suggested, 'Perhaps I ought to come over to your place sometime soon and introduce myself to Lexie if she's going to be staying with me? What do you think?'

'That's a brilliant idea, Sarah. Why don't you come this evening, if you're free? I could make you a spot of supper, if you'd like? Nothing fancy - macaroni cheese, maybe? It was always my husband's favourite.' She smiled, as though she was recalling a happy memory.

'That sounds lovely. I'll look forward to it.'

'Good. See you later, then.' Jenny slid behind the wheel of her black Toyota and Sarah opened the farm gate and waved her off. She had a lot of thinking to do, and lists to make, but perhaps she would take one more stroll around the farm while the sun was high in the sky. The light made everything look brighter, the colours more vivid, and maybe she could get some inkling of what her grandmother would have wanted her to do.

She went back along the drive to the cobbled yard where the buildings were arranged along two sides. There was the old stable block, now unused, attached to the farmhouse that was built from mellowed, honey-coloured Cotswold stone. On the other side were outbuildings, feed stores, animal stalls and pigsties. There were more buildings in other parts of the farm, a couple of barns and more storage sheds.

In the distance she could see fields, marked out from one another by the sweetbriar hedgerows that were filled with buds ready to burst into pink May blossom. The neighbouring

Manor House nestled at the foot of a lush, green slope, and much nearer, on her grandmother's land, her gaze settled on the beautiful leafy copse she remembered from her childhood. On warm, lazy days she used to play among the trees with her friends, and in the autumn they would pick apples from the nearby orchard. There was a narrow brook flowing across one side of the land, and in summer they would stand on the wooden bridge that fed the duck pond, and dip their fishing nets in the water in the hope of catching a stray tiddler.

Both the copse and the pond, along with a couple of the fields, belonged to her now, and although it was a privilege it was at the same time something of a liability. She didn't know what she was to do with her inheritance. She was torn. How could she cope with running the farm and doing her day job?

'Hello, there. Is it all right if I come over?' She turned at the sound of a heavily accented male voice.

'Oh, Mr Sayed, I didn't hear you coming.' She smiled at the tall Asian man in greeting. 'I was far away in my head just now.'

'Call me Raj, please. I apologize for interrupting. I do not mean to intrude.' He looked at her quizzically. 'They were good thoughts, I hope?'

'Mostly.' Her mouth curved fleetingly. She had loved her grandmother dearly and there were so many fond memories attached to this place. But how could she take on the responsibility of looking after it? 'What can I do for you, Raj? Do you want to come into the house for a cup of coffee?'

'That is most kind, thank you.'

He acknowledged her offer with a nod of his head and followed her through the wide oak door that led directly into the farmhouse kitchen.

Raj Sayed was a gentleman, in the old-fashioned sense of the word. He was courteous, and respectable by all accounts, and he had very recently taken up residence with his wife in the Manor House after it had come up for sale. Sarah had been to the house to introduce herself and welcome them to the neighbourhood when they moved in. He was in his fifties, she guessed, with strong, angular features, black hair with strands of grey, and a small, dark goatee beard. He was dressed in smart casual clothes today, dark trousers and a light jacket worn over his open neck shirt.

'I have been meaning to come and see you, hoping that we could have a chat,' Raj said, as she set the coffee maker to brew. 'I have been so taken up with moving into the Manor House this last week that it has been difficult to find the time. I hope I am not keeping you from something?'

'Nothing that won't wait for a while,' she answered softly. She slid a cup towards him. 'Help yourself to milk and sugar.'

'Thank you.' He added brown sugar to the dark liquid and stirred the coffee slowly, as though deep in thought.

'Are you settling into the house all right?' Sarah asked, coming to sit opposite him at the large oak table. This was a true farmhouse kitchen, with a wood-burning stove in one corner and a set of fire irons nearby next to a basket of logs. A large range cooker – an Aga – was set into an alcove where the old fireplace would have been, and there were lots of golden oak cupboards all around, with glass fronted cabinets and open shelves displaying her grandmother's fine crockery. There were original wooden beams overhead, restored over the years, but harking back to a different era when the farmhouse had first been built.

The beams continued on, into the dining room, which was reached through a wide archway. The ancient inglenook fireplace still had pride of place in there, complete with an iron trivet for the old copper kettle, another set of fire irons and a large bucket stacked high with logs.

'Yes, it is everything I had hoped for,' Raj said. 'I have always wanted to own a Manor House and this one suits me very well. It has everything I want. The house is perfect, exactly what I dreamed of, although there is not much land attached to the property. That is the only flaw. I have long had this ambition to own horses and ride out over my Estate.' He gave a rueful smile and took a sip from his coffee cup.

Sarah chuckled. 'That sounds like a dream a lot of people would share.'

'I am sure that is true.' His mouth curved. 'However, that does bring me to something that I wanted to ask you. If you will permit me?'

'Yes, of course.' She was a little puzzled. What could he possibly want or need from her? 'Please, go ahead.'

He nodded fleetingly. 'Thank you. Then, forgive me if I am being too... direct here... but in my dealings with Geoffrey Hollins from the Meadows Estate Agency, I came to understand that you might be thinking of selling this farm?'

'Ah, I see... I think.' Geoffrey was Jenny's Associate, her second in command, a colleague she'd recruited soon after taking over the agency, when she'd realized the work was too much for her to handle on her own. 'Yes, I did pay a visit to the office, and I mentioned to him that I wasn't sure what I was going to do about it. He said Jenny Carter knew more about the farm than he did, and asked her to come over and advise me. I haven't made up my mind, yet, what I'm going to do. I thought I would give myself a couple of weeks to spend time here and think it through.'

'Of course. I understand.' He drank more coffee. 'But if you should decide to sell, I wonder if you might consider me as a buyer? I would be more than willing to take the farm off your hands at a reasonable price, and you wouldn't even need to advertise the property. I am sure we could come to some mutually satisfactory arrangement.'

'Well, thank you, Raj. That's certainly something I'll keep in mind.' Sarah was flummoxed by the offer, coming out of the blue like that. It sounded like the answer to all her problems but still she was cautious. She wasn't going to rush into anything. For her grandmother's sake, and for all that the farm had meant to her, she had to be sure she was doing the right thing. 'I'm a little surprised,' she said, 'after all, you've only just bought the Manor House. Are you certain this is something you want to do?' How could he afford it? He must be a very wealthy man to even consider it so soon.

'I am absolutely certain,' he said firmly. 'There is no doubt in my mind this is what I want. I have been in business for many years, but now I want something different. I want to invest in property and, as I was saying, land is everything to me. Here it is right on my doorstep. I sincerely hope you will consider my offer.'

'I will, definitely, I promise.' She would have to talk to Jenny about Raj's suggestion and let her deal with any subsequent negotiations, should they get that far.

'That is good.' He finished off his coffee and they talked for a while about the Manor House and how it had changed over the years, with the extension of the living accommodation and renovation of the courtyard and outbuildings. 'But I have taken up enough of your time,' Raj said eventually, glancing at his watch, 'and I have to meet with a friend at the golf course.' He smiled. 'It is an informal way to conduct business, you understand.'

'I can imagine,' she murmured. 'I hope you enjoy your afternoon and that it proves to be a fruitful one for you.'

After he'd gone, Sarah made herself a late lunch and then busied herself with jobs around the farm. She made a temporary repair to the worst part of the fence that Jenny had mentioned, and made sure that all the smaller animals had been fed and watered. A couple of young farm workers had been in earlier to make sure the rabbit hutches were clean and that the goats' supply of hay had been topped up. The goats had plenty to eat and foraged all day long on the grass around the farm, but Sarah was concerned about the ewes on the hillside. Those who were feeding lambs needed the grazing supplemented with grains from wheat, barley, corn and oats. She went out to the field with a sack of grain and added it to the feed troughs.

Coming back to the yard, she reflected on how lovely the farm looked on this spring day. There was a lot of work to do around here, but perhaps she ought to count her blessings. She'd come across a carpet of bluebells in the copse this afternoon, and there were delicate pink cuckoo flowers blooming by the pond. The meadow was bright with yellow cowslips, whilst here and there, in grassy tufts and in the shade of trees, she'd come across pretty little dog violets.

Feeling her spirits lift, she walked back to the house, where she showered and changed, getting ready for the evening. She put on a fresh pair of jeans and a soft cashmere top and was just pulling a brush through her silky hair when the phone rang. It was probably her mother, wanting to chat, or possibly Jenny might be ringing to cancel. She laid down her hairbrush and answered the call.

'Ah, Miss Marshall, I'm glad you picked up,' a man's voice said. 'It's Geoffrey Hollins here, from the Meadows Estate Agency. I wondered, is Jenny there with you?'

'No, Mr Hollins, she isn't.' Mr Hollins was obviously working late if he was still in the office. She frowned. 'Jenny left here several hours ago. Is something wrong?'

'I'm not sure.' He sounded perplexed. 'She's not answering her phone, and she didn't turn up for her mid-afternoon appointment, which isn't like her. She was supposed to be viewing an old house out by Bourton on the Water, but the client rang me to ask where she was. It's not like her to miss a viewing without phoning in.'

Sarah frowned. 'That's strange, isn't it? It's no wonder you're concerned.' She hesitated. 'I hate to say it, but could she have had an accident, do you think?'

'It's possible, I suppose. I'll look into it.'

'Actually, I was just getting ready to go over to her house – we're having supper together this evening - I'll drive over there now and see if I can find out what's happening. She was feeling a bit under the weather earlier, so perhaps she just decided to take the afternoon off.'

'Hmm, maybe. But I'm sure she wouldn't do that without letting the client know if she wasn't going to keep the appointment.'

'Yes, that's probably true... though it's possible she might have decided to lie down for a while, and then she could have fallen asleep. I'll see what I can find out and I'll ring you as soon as I know anything.'

'Thanks. I'll be waiting for your call.' There was a worried note in his voice as he rang off.

Sarah left the farm a short time later and drove her baby blue Fiat the couple of miles to Brackley Close where Jenny lived. Her house was set back in a quiet cul-de-sac, a collection of detached, modern homes in a relatively sheltered spot, screened by mature trees. Across the road from the cul-de-sac was a main road and an adjoining short street made up of half a dozen houses. One of them, the corner house, was a bit run down, with an overgrown front garden, and she wondered if that was where Ben Reed lived.

Jenny's house, on the other hand, was an elegant detached property, with a tidy block paving frontage and a smart, modern front door fitted with a brass knocker. There was a garage attached to the house, set back further along the drive, but Jenny's black Toyota was neatly parked in front of it, so most likely she was at home. Sarah rang the doorbell, and instantly a dog started to bark inside the house. She waited a while, and then knocked, but when no one came to answer, she decided to go and look around the back of the house.

Glancing around fleetingly, she noticed the garden here was neat, carefully tended, with wide, colourful borders full of rhododendrons and bright pink azaleas, tall irises and fragrant orange wallflowers arranged around a curving lawn. To one side, nearer the kitchen, was a herb garden, where rosemary, mint and parsley were ready to be harvested.

Sarah knocked on the back door, calling Jenny's name. Lexie barked again, sounding closer this time, and she guessed the dog was in the kitchen. There was still no answer from Jenny, so she shouted out once more as she tried the door. It was unlocked, and she stepped inside, standing still as the Boxer bounded towards her.

'Hi there, Lexie,' she said softly. Uncertain how the dog would react to a stranger, she stayed where she was and let her sniff her hand. Lexie's coat was brown, patchy in places as a result of being neglected, but her head was golden brown with black markings around her nose, and her chest and paws were white. 'Good girl,' she murmured, shutting the door behind her. 'Where's Jenny, I wonder? Perhaps she's upstairs - that might explain why she hasn't heard me knocking.'

She was beginning to worry, though, that Jenny might not be well. Straightening, she spoke in a firm voice as Lexie fussed and whimpered. 'Now, I want you to sit, and stay, while I go and look for her.' She repeated the commands, her tone deeper and more authoritative this time, and Lexie dropped to the floor, whining anxiously. 'It's okay... that's good.' Sarah lightly patted the dog's back and took a quick look around the room.

The kitchen was large, well equipped with a pleasing array of cream coloured cupboards and dark marble effect worktops. An island bar stood in the centre of the room, with a wine rack built in at one end and two bar stools to one side. It was finished in the same dark marble surface as the rest of the worktops, and on it Sarah noticed a tall latte glass that held the remnants of a pale green liquid. Was this the comfrey tea that Jenny had mentioned? A wicker basket filled with oval shaped green leaves stood on the worktop alongside a blender that had a residue of chopped leaves and a small amount of liquid in the mixer jug.

Sarah walked around the island bar heading for the open door that she guessed might lead to the hallway and the stairs. Perhaps Jenny was asleep in her bedroom.

Only, she didn't get as far as the door. Before she had even taken three strides she saw something that made her gasp in horror.

Jenny was lying on the floor, one arm beneath her, while the other was stretched out as though she'd tried to stop herself from falling. Concerned, Sarah knelt down beside her and checked the pulse at her wrist. It was barely discernible and Jenny was hardly breathing. How long must she have been lying here? What had happened to her?

CHAPTER TWO

'**JENNY... Jenny...** can you hear me?' Sarah dropped to her knees beside the woman lying on the floor and quickly felt again for a pulse in her neck. The woman wasn't responding to her in any way, but Sarah could feel the faint flutter of a heartbeat beneath her fingers. 'I'll get help,' she told her, not knowing if Jenny was even aware of her presence.

Pulling her phone from her jacket pocket, she called for an ambulance. 'I found Jenny - Mrs Carter - lying on the floor in her kitchen,' she told the operator in response to his questioning. 'I think she must have been here for several hours. I know she has a heart condition, but I've no idea what happened.'

'The ambulance is on its way,' he said. 'Keep her warm and keep checking to see if she's breathing. I'll stay on the line and talk you through what you need to do.'

'Okay. Thank you.' Keep her warm, he'd said, but there was nothing here to help with that. 'I'll go and see if I can find something to wrap around her.' Sarah took her phone with her and quickly went upstairs, going in search of a light duvet. She found one on Jenny's bed and hurried with it back to the kitchen.

'This should help a bit,' she said quietly, kneeling down and wrapping the duvet around the sick woman. 'Can you hear me, Jenny?' She was still unresponsive, though, her skin clammy from shock, with faint beads of perspiration breaking out on her brow.

Lexie crept up alongside Sarah and began to whine softly. 'I know,' Sarah said, patting the dog. 'I know you're upset.'

She anxiously watched over Jenny while she waited for the paramedics to arrive. What could have caused her to collapse this way?

Jenny's handbag was open on a chair nearby and Sarah could see a prescription packet from the pharmacy in there, the paper bag still sealed. If she had come here straight from the pharmacy it meant she could have been lying here for anything up to five hours without being able to phone for help.

When the paramedics arrived, they quickly assessed their patient, connecting her to an ECG monitor, giving her oxygen via a face-mask and initiating intravenous access. Sarah showed them the pharmacy package and they opened it up and noted down the contents before giving it back to her. 'Does she have any other tablets in the house, do you know?' the paramedic asked.

'I'll go and check the bathroom - there may be something.' She hurried away, leaving them to work, and swiftly checked the bathroom cabinet. There was a bottle of digoxin tablets in there along with a second container that held a different type of medication. Then she looked in the bedroom, checking drawers and cupboards, but there wasn't anything in there.

'There are four tablets in here,' she said, going back to the paramedics and showing them the digoxin bottle. 'According to the instructions she's supposed to take one a day. This other bottle has different tablets in it, but it's almost full.'

'Thanks. Those others are diuretics - water tablets – they were probably given to her to help relieve congestion on her lungs caused by the problem with her heart valve. We'll tell the emergency team.'

'Okay, good.' By now, Jenny was on a stretcher, and as they wheeled her into the ambulance, and closed the doors behind their patient, Sarah watched from the pavement and debated what she should do. It was clear Jenny was very ill, and she wanted to be there for her if she should regain consciousness on the hospital ward. It must be frightening to wake up in a hospital bed surrounded by strangers, albeit well-meaning ones. She would hate it if it happened to her. But there was Lexie to consider, too. It wouldn't be right to leave her on her own for much longer. The dog wasn't altogether fit and healthy and she was heavily pregnant, too. Sarah was deep in thought as the ambulance moved away, its siren starting up as the vehicle gathered speed.

'All right, Lexie,' Sarah said, going back into the kitchen and searching through the cupboards for dog food. 'I'm going to give you your dinner and some fresh water and then send you out into the garden for a few minutes. Then I'm going to go to the hospital, so you'll have to wait here until I get back. I'll try not to leave you for too long, but I will come and fetch you, I promise.'

She realized it would have seemed odd to anyone who might come across her talking to the dog this way, but Lexie tilted her head on one side, and genuinely seemed to be trying to understand what she was saying. The poor dog must have been distressed, knowing something was dreadfully wrong, and yet unable to do anything for her new mistress.

Half an hour later, after phoning Geoffrey Hollins, Jenny's colleague, to update him on the situation, Sarah settled the Boxer in her bed in a corner of Jenny's kitchen and left the house. She slid behind the wheel of her car and drove to the hospital, taking the road through the village and heading for the local town of Caulders Lea about six miles away.

The whole incident with Jenny had her mystified. Jenny had said her heart condition wasn't that serious. Apart from a stomach problem that she'd put down to stress, and perhaps feeling a little tired, Jenny had seemed reasonably well able to cope this morning as they'd looked around the farm together. There was nothing to suggest that her condition was so critical that she would suddenly suffer from such a dramatic collapse.

At the hospital, Sarah hurried to A&E reception and enquired after Jenny. 'Mrs Carter was brought in by ambulance a short time ago,' she said. 'Can you tell me how she is? Has she regained consciousness yet?'

'Are you a relative?' the receptionist countered.

'No, I'm a friend,' Sarah replied. 'I found her and called for the ambulance. I don't know if she has any relatives living locally. She's a widow. I understand she moved here from Chesham a couple of years ago after her husband died... there was a friend back there that she mentions occasionally, but I've never heard her speak of any family close by.'

'I see.' The receptionist made a note of the information. 'We'll check up and try to get in touch with her former neighbours to find out what we can.' She scrolled through the text on her computer before glancing at Sarah once more. 'Apparently Mrs Carter's in Resus at the moment. You'll need to speak to the A&E nurse to find out more.' She pointed along the corridor towards double doors marked Resuscitation. 'You'll see the nurses' station through there.'

'Thanks.' Sarah walked swiftly along the corridor and approached a Senior Nurse who was filling out forms at the central desk.

'There's not much I can tell you at the moment,' the nurse told her. 'We're doing everything we can for her, of course, but her heart rhythm is unstable and I'm afraid so far she isn't responding very well to our efforts.'

'Is it her heart condition that's causing the trouble?' Sarah asked worriedly. 'She told me she was taking digoxin for a heart valve problem.'

'We're trying to find that out right now. We've done blood tests and it does seem from the preliminary results that she might be suffering from an overdose of digoxin... but as soon as we have any more information we'll let you know.'

'I don't think that's possible,' Sarah said, shaking her head. 'To have overdosed, I mean. She was only taking one tablet a day, and she still has an unopened bottle in her bag. As far as

I could tell, the only thing she had at lunchtime was a herbal drink made from comfrey leaves. She was a great believer in herbal remedies.'

'We'll need to look into that,' the nurse said, frowning a little. 'It's certainly a mystery.' She gave Sarah a reassuring smile. 'We have our medical team working with her right now - they'll do whatever's necessary to take the very best care of her. I can't guarantee we'll have anything more to tell you any time soon, but in the meantime, if you want to stay, there's a visitors' waiting room along the corridor. You'll find a tea and coffee machine there, too.'

'Thank you.' Sarah pulled in a deep breath and realized she could do with a caffeine intake right now. She'd had a busy and ultimately upsetting day, and she needed to take some time to think about what had happened.

Armed with a polystyrene coffee cup a few minutes later, she went and sat down on an upholstered bench in the waiting room. How was it possible for Jenny to have overdosed on her tablets? It didn't make any sense. Jenny had said she didn't have many tablets left, and she needed to collect her prescription. From what Sarah had seen of the kitchen there was no evidence of any medication being taken, except perhaps for the herbal drink, and how could that have harmed her? Surely, there must be some other explanation?

From time to time, Sarah went along to the nurses' station to ask how Jenny was doing, but even after three hours of waiting, no one could give her any positive information. 'Her heart went into a chaotic rhythm and we had to resuscitate her again,' a nurse said. 'We're giving her an antidote to the digoxin, but it could be some time before we can say she's out of the woods. It would probably be for the best if you go home and try to get some rest - maybe ring in later for an update.'

'Oh, I see. Okay, thanks... perhaps I'll do that.' Sarah was disturbed by what had happened to Jenny, and she wanted to stay, but she also had to keep Lexie in mind. It was late in the evening by now and the dog was badly in need of some cosseting after her previous bad experiences. It was more than time to get her home to the farm.

Outside, darkness had fallen. The sky was grey and overcast, the moon hidden behind cloud, so that the country lanes cast long shadows as Sarah drove to the village. Back at Jenny's house some half an hour later, she set about gathering together everything that she would need to take home with her for Lexie - the rigid oval dog bed and cushioned mat, food and dishes, along with some chew toys that Jenny had thoughtfully provided. She carried them out through the front door to the car and stowed them in the boot.

'I'm sorry about this, Lexie,' Sarah said, coming back to the kitchen and bending down to stroke the Boxer's head. 'It must be very confusing for you right now, but I'll look after you, I promise.' She studied Lexie thoughtfully, and the dog looked back at her with an intent expression, ears cocked. 'I do understand how you must be feeling,' Sarah murmured. 'You've not been doing too well and you're not in a good condition with patches of fur missing, which can't be good - I'll have to talk to the vet about that - and about those pups you're carrying. But we'll get things sorted out, don't worry.'

Even as she spoke, she suddenly became aware of muffled sounds coming from outside the house... a kind of scuffling followed by a sharp rapping on the window that made her jump and catch her breath in dismay. Lexie began to bark loudly and Sarah swivelled around, dry mouthed, looking to where the noise had come from. Alarmed, she saw the shadowy figure of a man walking by the window. Who would be lurking outside at this time of night? Her mouth went dry and her heart began to pound.

'Miss Marshall - Sarah,' a man's deep voice said, 'I need you to open the door. Let me in, will you?'

She stared, wide eyed as the man's features became clearer, and then breathed an inward sigh of relief as she recognised the interloper. She'd had dealings with him from time to time in the course of her work at the solicitors' office. Recovering her equilibrium, she went over to the door and pulled it wide open. 'Detective Sergeant Holt,' she protested, 'you frightened me half to death. What on earth are you doing creeping about outside at this time of night? I expect to see you in Court, or at the office, not skulking about in a strange back garden in the dead of night.'

'Skulking! That's hardly a word I'd use,' he said, walking into the kitchen and glancing around. 'And I could say the same of you, couldn't I? It's a bit late for you to be here, isn't it?' In his early thirties, Nick Holt was tall and lean, with dark hair that had a tendency to kink, and steely blue eyes that held a keen intelligence and took everything in.

Lexie was still barking. 'Quiet, Lexie,' she said. 'He's a friend.' Turning her attention back to the detective, she explained, 'I told Jenny I would look after the dog while she's away at a seminar, so I'm here to take her home with me.' She frowned. 'Only, Jenny's been taken ill, so I suppose now it means I'll be taking care of the dog for a bit longer than I bargained for.'

'That's going to be difficult, isn't it, if you're working?'

'Actually, I'm technically on holiday from the office for the next two weeks. I'm staying at the farm to sort things out.' Her mouth made a rueful shape. 'Perhaps I'll have to ask my mother to lend a hand.' It was an irony, because with the farm she had more than just a dog to worry about over the next few weeks.

'Ah, I heard about your Grandmother passing. I'm sorry. This must be a difficult time for you.'

She nodded. 'She left the farm to me, so I have to decide what to do with it.'

'That must be something of a quandary for you.'

'Yes.' She studied him. 'Anyway, what are you doing here?'

'A nurse from A&E called the station. The medics want to know why Mrs Carter has a serum digoxin level that is way beyond the norm. I need to check the house for any kind of medication, but they're also asking about any herbal remedies she might have taken.'

Sarah mulled that over for a moment. So, they were still putting her collapse down to digoxin toxicity and not to any decline in her original heart problem. 'Is there any news about her condition? Is she starting to come around?'

He shook his head. 'No, not yet, I'm afraid. Is she a particular friend of yours?'

'We've become friends over the last few months. My mother knows her from the village Fellowship group.' Her brow creased as a worrying thought struck her. 'I'll have to tell Mum what's happened.'

'I'm sorry. The doctors are very concerned, because she's not responding to treatment, and what's happened to her appears untoward. So, I'm here to gather up any items that might fit the bill and take them back to the lab for testing... if there are any to be found, that is.' He sent her a hard stare. 'You haven't touched anything, have you?'

'Well, of course I have,' she retorted. 'I've fed and watered Lexie, grabbed a duvet from the bedroom to keep Jenny warm, and I've collected together all the things I'll need to take the dog back to the farm. If you mean, have I touched the blender and the comfrey leaves, then no, I haven't. I assume they're what you're looking for?'

'Hmmph.' He obviously didn't appreciate her mild sarcasm.

'There are no tablets she could have taken,' she added, 'except for those in her bag, and the ones in the bathroom cabinet. I already showed them to the paramedics. There were no empty containers in the kitchen waste bin.'

'I'll take the ones that are here... but I'll need to do my own search, anyway.' He looked at the island bar and the wicker basket. 'So, the leaves in the basket are comfrey, is that right?'

'I assume that's the case. Jenny sometimes buys them from a health store in town - but she grows herbs in her garden, so they've could possibly have come from there.' She peered at the basket. 'They look fairly fresh.'

'I'll bag them up and take a look around.'

'All right.' She hesitated. 'I should go. I need to get Lexie bedded down for the night. She looks exhausted with all the stress.'

'How can you tell?' He glanced at the dog, his expression dubious as Lexie returned his look with a suspicious stare.

Sarah sent him a withering look. 'Haven't you seen the size of her? She's expecting a barrow load of pups to arrive any time now - she's bound to be worn out. What she needs is peace and tranquillity.'

He grinned. 'Oh, I see. Woman's intuition, is it?' He appeared sceptical, adding, 'I expect it's that same intuition that makes you believe the likes of Daniel Richmond will make good. Seen anything of him lately?'

Her shoulders went back, her spine stiffening. Now and again they clashed over youngsters who came to Court for various offences. Nick believed she was too sympathetic towards one or two of the youthful tearaways they came across from time to time.

'I know you think I'm too soft in my attitude to some of the lads - Daniel in particular,' she said defensively, 'but I believe youngsters can be led astray and get into trouble – it doesn't mean they can't change their lives for the better, given the right help. Anyway, it's a long while since he was in the magistrates' court - and I've heard he's staying out of trouble these days.' She glared at him. 'Just because a teenager falls into bad company and makes silly mistakes, it doesn't mean he has to be branded for life as a ne'er-do-well.'

Annoyingly, he smiled at that. 'You're a pushover for a tale of woe,' he said.

She scowled. It was clearly time for her to leave before she blew her top. 'I have to go,' she said. She turned to the dog. 'Come on, Lexie, we'd best be off.'

'Be seeing you,' Sergeant Holt said, still grinning, and acknowledging her with a nod of his head.

'Not if I can help it,' she muttered, heading out of the door.

Lexie climbed dutifully into the back of her car and settled down on the upholstered seat. Sarah eased herself behind the wheel and started the ignition. 'Okay... home,' she murmured.

Back at the farm a short time later, she unloaded the boot of her car and set the dog bed and equipment down in the kitchen. Then she filled a dog bowl with fresh water and put it down to one side of the door.

It was very late by now, so she let Lexie have a mosey around the yard, and then settled her for the night in her bed in a corner of the warm kitchen. At one end of the room the wood-burning stove was still alight, the embers of the logs Sarah had been burning earlier giving a faint orange glow to the room.

Realizing she was hungry, having missed out on a meal, she made herself some supper, a crusty baguette filled with bacon, lettuce and tomato, along with a hot mug of tea. Then, after half an hour or so, feeling replenished and a little more able to deal with things again, she picked up her phone and called the hospital.

'I know it's late to be ringing,' she said to the nurse she'd seen earlier, 'but I wondered if there's any news on Jenny Carter's condition?'

There was a pause on the other end of the line. 'Oh, I'm sorry,' the nurse answered, 'but I can't really give you any information over the phone. Perhaps you could come in to the hospital and we could talk?'

Sarah caught her breath. The nurse wouldn't have said that unless something was dreadfully wrong. She'd had no problem talking to her before. 'It's bad news, then, isn't it?' she said. 'What's happened... has... has she died?'

The nurse hesitated. 'Are you alone – are you sitting down?'

'I'm okay. Please tell me.'

'I'm so sorry, but I'm afraid Mrs Carter suffered a cardiac arrest and passed away a few minutes ago. We did everything we could, but unfortunately she didn't respond to treatment and we weren't able to resuscitate her.'

'But how could it happen?'

'We won't know exactly until after the post mortem, but it seems the high level of digoxin toxicity caused heart arrhythmias, leading to a cardiac arrest.'

Shocked and distressed, Sarah spoke to the nurse for a little while longer, before ringing off. She sat in her grandmother's armchair by the wood-burning stove for some time, not moving, just thinking, trying to take in everything that had happened that day.

It didn't make any sense to her that Jenny had died. She'd been talking to her only that morning, walking with her around the boundaries of the fields and inspecting the farm buildings. She'd managed all of that without any difficulty, and there was absolutely no indication that only a few hours later she would be dead. Nothing about her collapse added up. How could she have overdosed on digoxin? Something was very badly wrong, Sarah was convinced of it.

CHAPTER THREE

'**HI, MUM**.' In the morning, a few hours after Sarah had learned that Jenny had died, she walked into the kitchen of the house that had once been her childhood home, and straightaway found herself enveloped in the warm, loving memories of family life.

'Hi, sweetheart.' Her mother looked up from where she was seated at the table in the corner of the room and gave Sarah a smile. Hannah Marshall was an attractive woman, with golden brown hair that fell in soft waves to complement her fine features. She had a trim figure and today she wore a rose-coloured dress that swathed her body and accentuated her slender curves. 'Oh, you've brought a friend with you.' She sent the Boxer dog an assessing glance and frowned. 'She's in a sorry state, isn't she? Some of her fur's missing. Is this Jenny's dog? She told me she'd acquired a dog from somewhere, but she didn't go into too much detail, except to say her coat was in a poor state. We were a bit rushed the other afternoon at the meeting. There was someone there to show us how to do flower arrangements and Jenny left early to go and see a client.'

'Yes, this is Lexie, Mum. Lexie, meet Mum.'

As though she sensed a new friend, the dog's tail began to wag. Sarah unclipped her lead and draped it over the back of a chair. 'She's been neglected for some time, according to Jenny Carter, and I think it's left her feeling a bit under par and out of condition. Ben Reed had her, but he left her outside all the time and neglected her.' She looked around for the percolator. 'Is there any coffee in the pot?' Answering her own question, she peered into the jug on the kitchen worktop and poured herself a drink, topping up her mother's cup as well. She added cream and brown sugar crystals, and then stirred the hot liquid. 'I've made an appointment at the vet's surgery for when I leave here. Matt says he'll look her over and advise me - on the pups, as well. She must be due to have them soon.'

'Heavens, yes.' Hannah abandoned the laptop she'd been working on and stood up to go and inspect the dog more closely. 'She's big with them, isn't she? How is it that you're looking after her?'

'Jenny had made arrangements to go away for a short time and didn't want to put her in kennels. That's understandable, I suppose, because she could do with some special care right now, so I offered to help out.'

She paused to take a deep breath. 'Then, yesterday, Jenny was suddenly taken ill.' Her mouth twisted painfully with the recollection. 'It was awful, Mum – I found her unconscious on her kitchen floor and had to call for the ambulance.' Her voice quivered slightly. 'They did what they could for her at the hospital, but in the end it was no good... she died this morning, in the early hours. I can't get over it. It all happened so quickly.'

'Oh no... that's terrible...'

As her mother absorbed the shock, Sarah explained the situation, adding, 'The police are looking into it, to see what could have caused her to be taken ill like that. Nick Holt came to the house to collect things to take to the lab. There'll be a post mortem – I went to the hospital first thing this morning and the consultant said he believed it was digoxin toxicity that caused her to die, but he can't explain it.'

'That's such shocking news.' Her mother was troubled, having difficulty taking it in. 'I can scarcely believe what you're telling me. Poor Jenny. I was only talking to her the other day, and she seemed fine. She was telling me I'd get a good price for this big, old house if I wanted to sell any time, but I told her I wasn't ready to up sticks, not yet, at any rate. I've always run my catering business from here and I feel comfortable with my lovely kitchen, where everything's to hand.' Her blue eyes clouded momentarily. 'I admit, I did toy with the idea of selling up, after your father died, but this is our family home, where we brought you up - you and your sister and brother. You may have your own places now, but you all come back here on a regular basis to see me, and I'm glad of that.'

'Me, too, Mum. This is our base, where we come to recharge ourselves.' Sarah sat down at the table and Lexie flopped to the floor beside her. 'I think Lexie is pining for her mistress,' she said, idly fondling the dog's ears. 'I phoned Jenny's number last night to see if Nick Holt was still there - I wanted to tell him the news from the hospital, but he must have left, because instead Jenny's voice came over the answer phone. As soon as she heard it Lexie's ears pricked up and she started to whine.'

She sighed. 'So, as of yesterday afternoon I was all set to have Lexie with me for just a few days, but now - well, everything's changed. I told Matt all about it when I phoned the veterinary hospital because he wanted to know what I was doing with a dog.' She lifted her hands in a helpless gesture. 'I'm still trying to come to terms with Jenny passing like that. It was so unexpected.' She frowned. 'Anyway, now she's gone... and it looks as if I'm going to have to keep Lexie with me. It's certainly not what I bargained for when I said I would look after her, but I don't see that I have much choice. I can't believe Jenny's not with us any more.'

Her mother nodded, her golden-brown hair drifting lightly with the movement. 'She'd only looked after her for a week or so, but she probably gave the poor dog all the attention she'd been missing over these last few months. I can imagine Ben would have soon grown tired of looking after her. I've often seen him around the village and he always strikes me as being a hard type. Do you think he'll try to get her back - after all, if the pups turn out to be pedigree, they could fetch quite a substantial sum?'

'I hadn't thought of that.' Sarah pulled a face. 'It's possible, I suppose, but I don't know her history. I don't know how he acquired her in the first place.'

'Whatever you do - be wary of him, if you see him. Ben's a volatile character. He can become aggressive if he's had too much to drink and in that case he's best avoided - you never know where you are with him. He was always having run-ins with Jenny over something or other. She used to tell me about it whenever we met up at the village hall. She passed by his house every day, and I think she told him on more than one occasion that he needed to do something to tidy up the outside because it was pulling property values down in the area. The front garden was overgrown with weeds, she said, and there were always old timbers stacked up or left lying about to rot. Lots of junk, as well, cluttering up the place.'

'Yes, I saw some of it when I was on my way to her house to collect Lexie.' That was only yesterday, but she was still struggling with the fact that so much had happened and all with no adequate explanation. It was bothering her. Perhaps she ought to phone Nick again and ask if the results of the lab tests that he'd ordered had come through yet. She was pretty sure she had his mobile number in her contacts list on her phone. Would he tell her? Probably. The problem, as she saw it, was how had Jenny overdosed? The comfrey leaves wouldn't have hurt her, would they?

In the meantime, she leaned forward to flick a quick look at the laptop computer her mother had been working on when she arrived. 'What are you busy with today? Am I interrupting something important?'

'Nothing that won't wait,' her mother answered, coming to sit down once more and sip her coffee. 'I was just trying to sort out a menu for a client. The Griffiths are hosting a dinner party in a few days and they want me to do the catering for it. Natalie's left the selection of food mostly to me. I thought I might try a vegetarian option, maybe a puff pastry tart with feta cheese and roast vegetables, and as another choice perhaps bundles of asparagus, tomato and rosemary, wrapped around the middle with pancetta. I could add a pasta dish on the side. I haven't made up my mind about a main course yet.'

'I'm sure you'll come up with something wonderful - you're a great cook, Mum - and a professional, that's why you have so many appreciative clients.' Sarah glanced idly through the collection of recipes on screen, asking, 'Is this dinner party for a special occasion - an anniversary or some such?'

Hannah shook her head. 'Not as far as I know. I think most of the guests are contacts Lewis Griffiths has made through his engineering work, and the dinner is an opportunity to get them together and perhaps conjure up some new business. I don't know how much trade he drums up locally, but all the work is done in his engineering workshop in the village. You'll have seen it.'

'Yes, I drive by it on my way to work. It's been a bit quiet there, lately, I think. I've not seen as many comings and goings as usual — there haven't been many cars on the forefront or vans being loaded up. Perhaps his trade fluctuates.'

'Could be.' Her mother's brows drew together briefly. 'I was a bit surprised they were having this dinner party, actually, because they're in the process of putting their house up for sale. I'm not sure where they're planning to move to. Jenny was handling it for them - though I recall there was a bit of an upset over something - I'm not sure what... Jenny only hinted that things weren't going as well as she would have liked and their relationship with her had soured somehow. We always chat - ' She stopped, the colour draining from her face momentarily, and she quickly corrected herself. 'We used chat at the weekly meetings of the village Fellowship group, and she'd tell me all sorts of things. She was working, but she would organize her schedule so that she could come at least once a fortnight. She was a great believer in taking an active part in the community.'

Sarah nodded. 'You wouldn't really have known she had a heart problem, would you? She was always so active and involved with village life.'

'That's true... I'd heard her heart valve was giving her some problems, but I wasn't aware of exactly how serious the condition was. I know she believed in keeping busy - she made us a lovely lemon and thyme drizzle cake for our

Fellowship's anniversary celebrations earlier this year.' She sighed, then glanced back at the computer screen and scrolled through a series of pictures. 'You know, I think I might go with crispy pork chops and a spinach and Roquefort salad. What do you think?'

'Sounds good to me. Whatever you cook tastes delicious.'

Her mother smiled. 'That's settled, then. I'll run those ideas by Natalie Griffiths and see if she'll give me the go-ahead.' She reached for a notepad from a nearby shelf and started to scribble a list. 'It means I'll need a selection of vegetables, fruits, and herbs, of course.' She made a wry face. 'Grace always used to supply most of what I needed from the farm. Do you think there might be some things you could tick off my list?'

Sarah studied the notepad for a moment. 'I should think so... I'll see what I can rustle up. I know we have asparagus and spring greens, and there are onions in the barn, along with potatoes... spinach in cloches... and there are all sorts of different herbs in the kitchen garden. I'll have a look through what we have and make up a box for you.'

'Thanks, Sarah, I'll drop by and pick them up on the day.' She appeared preoccupied for a moment or two. 'Actually, Natalie mentioned she could do with some table decorations -

something unusual, she said, with a rural or rustic feel, just to add a talking point. I told her Grace used to do a lot of really lovely craft work and there might be something up at the farm that she might like to borrow. I said I'd ask you.'

'Yes, that's fine. I'll see what I can find. Right, then...' Sarah glanced at her watch. 'It's time we were off to take this young lady to see the vet.' She got to her feet, clipped the lead on to Lexie's collar, and walked to the door with her mother, stopping to give her a quick hug. 'I'll see you later.'

Lexie jumped into the back of the car, and Sarah sent her mother a quick backward wave as she set off for the vet's surgery. Arriving at the car park a few minutes later, her phone began to burble just as she pulled up into a space and cut the engine.

'Hi Sarah, it's Nick here... Nick Holt. Do I take it that you've heard the news from the hospital about Mrs Carter?'

'Hi, Nick.' Her voice took on a serious note. 'I did, yes. I'm still reeling from the shock.' She hesitated. 'Did you get the results from the lab? Did they test the comfrey leaves and the contents of the blender and the glass?'

'Uh-huh, I did. It seems there weren't just comfrey leaves in the basket on the worktop - there were a whole lot of foxglove leaves mixed in there, too.'

'Foxglove?' Sarah gasped. 'No... surely not - how is that possible?'

'They're quite similar to comfrey leaves, apparently, according to our pathologist, and when they're not in flower they can quite easily be mistaken for each other if you're not looking at them too closely. Unfortunately, foxgloves are highly toxic. It seems they're a potent source of cardiac glycosides like digoxin – I'm told digoxin comes from the foxglove plant. And it turns out that the remains of the drink in the cup and in the blender contained a high concentration of these glycosides, so the conclusion has to be that Mrs Carter was poisoned by the foxglove leaves.'

'But that's dreadful - I don't see how on earth that could have come about.'

'That's what I need to find out. I wondered if you knew the name of the health shop where Mrs Carter obtained her supplies - we need to check it out to make sure there's no problem with the product the Company is selling.'

Sarah searched her memory. 'It's something like "The Health and Well-being Centre," I think, in Caulders Lea. She used to talk about all the different herbal remedies they stocked. But I'm pretty sure Jenny has comfrey plants in her garden at the moment, so I can't see why she would need to go out and buy them.'

'I dare say, but we have to make enquiries, all the same, to be certain we've covered all the possibilities. Thanks for your help.' He paused momentarily before adding, 'I realize all this must have been very upsetting for you, Sarah. I'm sorry it turned out to be such bad news.'

'Thanks. Yes, it was, and I was stunned when I found out, but I'm okay, really. It's just that it came out of the blue. I never imagined anything bad could happen to her.'

'I know. It's hard to deal with something like that.'

He cut the call, and Sarah pondered their conversation for a minute or two before sliding out of the car and letting Lexie out of the back. From the sound of things, Nick was working on the assumption that the foxglove leaves happened to be in the basket through some kind of mistake. Surely that was unlikely? Jenny knew all about plants – herbs and flowers. She would have been able to distinguish between the two types of leaves.

For her own peace of mind, she needed to find out for herself where Jenny obtained the comfrey leaves, and the only way to do that would be to go back to the house to thoroughly check out the garden. But first things first... Lexie needed to be given the once-over by the local vet, and Matt would be ready for them any time now.

Lexie clearly didn't like being at the veterinary surgery. She panted and fussed and whined in the waiting room until it was their turn to be called, and no amount of soothing words from Sarah, or gentle stroking, would calm her. After a few minutes, though, Matt came out to greet them. He was a long, lean man in his early thirties, with a tidy crop of black hair, and grey eyes that crinkled at the corners when he saw Sarah.

'Good to see you, Sarah.' He greeted her warmly and gave Lexie a quick glance as he led the way along the corridor. 'Ah - this is the dog you've just acquired - that was all a bit of a rum do, and no mistake. It was a shock to hear that Mrs Carter has died. She brought Lexie in just under a fortnight ago, so we already have her notes on computer. Come on through to the surgery.' He ushered them in to his room and shut the door, dropping down on to his haunches to greet Lexie and run his hands over her in a gentle, but thorough, examination.

'Do you think she's going to be okay?' Sarah asked worriedly. 'She's heavy with the pups, but she's quite thin in herself, isn't she?'

'Well, she's not had the best start to gestation, but we'll keep our fingers crossed that she's on the mend.'

51

'I was also a bit concerned the unborn pups might have been harmed in some way because of her poor condition.'

'Hmm... usually what happens is the pups take any nutrients they need from the mother, basically at her expense – which is why she's lost some of her fur - but she's certainly looking better than she did when I first saw her a few days back. I suggested to Jenny that she should give her puppy food rather than adult dog food - it has more protein and nutrients in it and it provides more energy to keep up with demand in pregnancy.'

'Ah... so that's what the opened bag of puppy food was all about! I wasn't sure if Jenny had made a mistake when she went shopping!'

'No, no mistake, and it definitely appears to be helping. Feed her little and often. Even after this short time you can see that her fur is beginning to grow back.' He ran his stethoscope over the dog's chest and then finished his examination. 'I'd say she's ready to have these pups any day now. You'll probably find she goes off her food a few hours before whelping starts. She'll most likely become restless and try to find a quiet place where she can settle down for the birth.'

'Do I need to do anything when she starts to give birth?'

Matt shook his head. 'Just leave her to it, but keep an eye on proceedings. If she's like most dogs she'll instinctively know what needs to be done.' He got to his feet and straightened up. 'If you think there's a problem, if she seems to be struggling or one of the pups is taking a long while to appear, then give me a ring and I'll come out to you. If I'm not available for any reason, we'll ask someone else to come instead.' He glanced at her. 'Are you at the flat, or are you staying with your mother while you have Lexie with you? You don't have a garden at the flat do you so it would make things a bit difficult if you have a dog there?'

'No, I don't, but I'm not staying at either of those places. I'm at Sweetbriar Farm for at least a fortnight while I'm taking a holiday from work - my grandmother left the farm to me and I have to decide what to do about it, so I'll be staying there with Lexie for a while.' She chuckled. 'There's plenty of room for her to exercise there at any rate!'

His mouth curved. 'Too right! And she'll have plenty of other animals to keep her company.' His expression sobered. 'I was wondering what was going to happen to the farm after your grandmother passed. I must come and take a look at the ewes and their offspring as soon as I get the chance, to give them a quick check up. Your grandmother was always happy at lambing time - she said she liked it when the local children came around and volunteered to help to feed the little ones if need be.'

'It's true. She loved the farm and she liked children to share in any special event. I spent a lot of my childhood there with my friends, running around the fields and the copse.'

He acknowledged that with a nod. 'Have you any idea, any gut feeling, what you'll do with the farm?'

'No, not yet.' She pressed her lips together fleetingly in indecision. 'I do have someone who's very interested in buying, but I'm torn both ways because I'm pretty sure my Gran would have wanted to keep it in the family. My father died some years ago, so she couldn't leave it to him, but for some reason she lighted on me to inherit it instead of my brother or sister. They were provided for in other ways - a cottage by the sea, and a small trust fund that my grandfather set up - which they're happy with, so it's down to me to make up my mind about the farm. I don't know what to do. For one thing, there'll be a lot of expense involved. And I have my job in town - it's what I trained for. I really don't see how I can do both.'

'I agree, it's a major decision to make. Even though it isn't large, as farms go, you'd be taking on a huge responsibility, and I think you might find it's more than you can handle. Farming isn't a nine to five job, as you'll discover... it's tough work, you're out in all weathers, and you have the added burden of having to manage staff. It's not what you're used to, Sarah. You've not been brought up to it.'

'My grandmother seemed to manage well enough,' she retorted.

His mouth made a wry shape. 'She had a husband and son to help her for a good many years. It was her way of life.'

She sniffed. 'Hmm. I see. I guess you're saying I'll have to get myself a man, then, if I want to have any kind of success at running a farm!' She wagged a finger at him. 'I don't think so, Matt! I'm quite capable of working out how to do things for myself, thank you!'

He laughed, holding up his hands in submission. 'All right, that came out wrong. I wouldn't dream of suggesting you couldn't achieve anything you set out to do!'

'Hmm... it's okay, I'll forgive you.' She grinned back at him. 'Thanks for looking Lexie over for me,' she said, 'and for the advice, but I need to be going now. There are a few things I have to sort out before I go back to the farm. Give me a ring when you're ready to come out to look at the sheep.'

'I will.' He walked her out along the corridor and called for his next patient as Sarah went outside to the car park with Lexie.

'We're going back to Jenny's house for a little while,' she told the dog as she settled her in the back of her car. 'I need to check up on something.'

It seemed strange to be going back to Jenny's house, knowing that the older woman would never again be there, but Sarah parked up, took a deep breath and stepped out of her car. She left the windows wound down a bit to give the dog some air. It wasn't a hot day, so she would be all right in there for a short time. 'You can stay in here while I nose around in the garden, if you like,' she told Lexie. 'I shouldn't be too long.'

Lexie showed no inclination to move, staying motionless on the seat, her head resting on her paws, and Sarah hurried around to the rear of the house. Jenny's small herb garden was separate from the main garden area, situated close by the kitchen, so that she would only have had to step out of her back door and walk a few metres to gather any produce. It was neatly enclosed with a rustic fence about forty-five centimetres high and there was a gate for access. Sarah opened it and walked on to the random stepping-stones that ran through the centre of the garden.

There was a whole collection of plants available for harvesting right now... among them Sarah recognized crops of thyme and parsley, along with a large rosemary bush in one corner.

A bed of mint straggled in among the taller chives, which in turn were growing alongside a patch of garlic cloves. New leaves of lemon balm were beginning to show, and next to them there were several comfrey plants, with their rosettes of oval green leaves.

Sarah studied the garden thoughtfully, looking around for any signs of foxglove plants. In the far corner of the herb garden, there was a solitary, presumably a self-seeded foxglove, not yet in flower, but with leaves very similar to those of the comfrey, green and oval, but with tiny serrated edges. It was too far away from the comfrey plants for Jenny to have mistaken it, Sarah was sure. Besides, from what she could see at this distance, the leaves of the foxglove were intact, whereas several of the comfrey plants had been harvested recently.

'Ah-hah... I might have guessed you wouldn't be able to stay away! You're determined to find out how Mrs Carter came to overdose on digitalis, aren't you?'

Sarah turned to see Nick Holt stride into the back garden and come to stand on the patio close by. He made a wry smile.

'You know me so well!' she answered. She straightened, abandoning her inspection of the foxglove plant. 'Actually, I can't help it,' she added with a shrug. 'I feel I owe it to her somehow. She doesn't have anyone else to watch her corner.'

He studied her thoughtfully. 'You do know this is police business now, don't you?'

'Police business?' she echoed. 'Does that mean you're treating Jenny's death as suspicious?'

'That's rather a strong word,' he murmured. 'Let's say it's more a case of misadventure that we're looking into right now.'

'Hmmph.' There was a hint of scorn in her voice. 'I'd say it was virtually impossible for her to have overdosed herself accidentally. There's a solitary foxglove plant, untouched as far as I can tell, in the herb garden.'

He frowned. 'Have you been treading on the earth around here and disturbing the soil?' There was a hint of admonition in his tone.

'No, I haven't. Don't worry, I haven't messed up your territory. I haven't moved from the stepping-stones. You should have a little faith, Nick.'

'I only wish I could.' His handsome features made a faintly mocking expression. 'And yet... here you are.'

She ignored that and looked around, her gaze focussing on the flower borders across the other side of the lawn. 'She does have foxglove plants over there, but she's hardly likely to have harvested leaves from the flower beds, is she?'

'I think you might be getting ahead of yourself, Sarah. You don't know that there weren't any other foxglove plants in the herb garden. She may have cut the leaves and then thrown the plants on the compost heap. We'll look into it. You should leave the police work to us.'

'But you think her death was accidental?'

'I'd say it was a strong possibility. Either that or suicide.'

She shook her head. 'Then I have to say I think you're wrong. Jenny was meticulous in everything she did. She wouldn't make a mistake like that and pick the wrong leaves. And there's no way she was suicidal. She was planning on going to a seminar, and she certainly wouldn't have abandoned Lexie.'

'But you were going to have Lexie for a while, so she knew she would be safe... and she might have changed her mind about the seminar.'

'I don't believe that for even a minute. I only spoke to her about it on Saturday morning when she was at the farm.' She studied him briefly. 'Did you get in touch with the herb company?'

'I did. The lab's examining their product right now, though Jenny hasn't bought any comfrey from them recently.'

'See, I told you so.'

'Police business, Sarah,' he said again. 'Don't you have enough on your plate right now with running the farm?'

'Not you as well,' she said under her breath, then responded briskly, 'I'm perfectly capable of doing more than one task at once, you know.'

He smiled. 'I wouldn't suggest otherwise. You know I only have your welfare at heart.'

'Of course you do.' She came out of the herb garden and closed the gate behind her. 'As you've pointed out, I have a lot of things to see to, so I'd better make tracks for the farm.' She hesitated. 'Will you let me know how things go with your investigation?'

He nodded. 'I will.'

'Okay. Bye, then.'

'Bye, Sarah.'

She was conscious of his gaze on her as she walked away, but her mind was elsewhere, in complete turmoil. Something dreadful had happened to Jenny and she didn't believe it could be simply put down to misadventure or suicide. If Jenny hadn't put those foxglove leaves in the wicker basket, someone else had to have done it. Somebody had set out to kill the Estate Agent and he or she was trying to lead the police into passing it off as an accidental death, but Sarah vowed she wouldn't let them get away with it. She would do her very best to find out exactly who was behind the horrible deed.

CHAPTER FOUR

'**THESE HUTCHES** are in a sorry state,' Sarah commented, glancing at her teenaged helper as she lay down fresh wood shavings for the rabbits and added hay for warmth. 'I'm going to have to do something about them, but I can't really afford to buy new ones just now, not with all the other work that's needed around here.' She spoke to him, but her mind was elsewhere – she wanted to be out and about finding out who might have wanted to harm Jenny, but the work on the farm had to be done, come what may.

'My mate, Danny, could probably help out,' Rob suggested. He was busy cleaning out the hutches so that Sarah could renew the bedding but now he paused, straightening up. He was a strong lad, nineteen years old, with muscular arms outlined by the short-sleeved white tee shirt that he was wearing atop blue jeans. His hair was brown, clipped short at the sides and slightly longer on top. 'Maybe he could repair them for you. He's finishing off a two-year course in carpentry and joinery at the College, and he's pretty good. Came top in all his exams.'

'Do I know him?'

'Danny Richmond. He lives down by the Post Office.'

'Oh,' Sarah exclaimed, recognizing the name. 'Yes, of course, *Danny,* not Daniel.' She and Nick had talked about the lad recently. 'I remember him... he must be about nineteen or twenty now, I should think.' She frowned. 'I got to know him a few years back. As I recall, he used to be up to all sorts of trouble in the village, didn't he?'

'Yeah...' Rob pulled a face. 'Not any more, though. He went through a bad patch when his Mum and Dad split up, but he's calmed down a lot and I think he's found his way - he really likes what he's doing now.'

'Yes, I'd heard something to that effect.' She nodded, filling the feed bowls with nutritious nuggets. There were more than a dozen rabbits and guinea pigs of all descriptions that needed to be housed, all the result of her Gran taking in unwanted pets over the years. Grace Marshall had a soft spot for any vulnerable animal, and here at Sweetbriar Farm they had the best of everything. They were well looked after.

'Maybe I'll give him a call,' she said. 'Do you have his number?'

'Sure. I could give him the heads up, if you like? Let him know you need some work doing.'

'Yes, that'll be good. As long as he knows I don't have a lot of money to spare.' She smiled, pulling her phone from her pocket and inputting Danny's number. 'I think I might have to reinforce their enclosure as well,' she said, making a mock frown as she watched a long-haired, fluffy grey rabbit hop around on the grass. 'I had to chase this little feller out of the kitchen garden this morning. He'll probably have a giant tummy ache after all the greens he managed to munch his way through before I caught him.'

'Oops!' Rob laughed.

'Yes, oops, definitely!' She put the bag of feed to one side. 'I have to go out in a while, Rob, so perhaps you could keep an eye on Lexie for me... she was off her food this morning? I think she'll be okay sitting outside in the yard - she seems to like watching what's going on, but you can keep the kitchen door open for her in case she wants to go back inside. And will you keep a weather eye on the hens? I'll give them a feed before I set off. I'm not sure how long I'll be gone - maybe a couple of hours. But you can ring me if you need me.'

'That's fine. Leave it with me.'

'Thanks.' After a lot of soul-searching last night, she'd made up her mind to try and find out more about the circumstances leading up to Jenny's death. In Sarah's opinion, the older woman hadn't been remotely suicidal, nor would she have made the mistake of gathering the wrong leaves for her herbal drink, so someone else must have put them in the basket. The leaves had been mixed in with the comfrey in such a way as to be unnoticeable to someone casually preparing a brew. Safe in her own home, with lots of things on her mind, Jenny probably hadn't even looked closely at the contents. Why would she? It was surely reasonable to assume that someone must have set out to cause her harm and Sarah was keen to discover who would want to do that.

But how was she to find out what she needed to know? Maybe the best way to start would be to retrace Jenny's steps on that last fateful day, which meant a visit to the Estate Agent's office was in order, just as soon as she'd fed the hens.

Sarah left Rob to clear up and went to get a bucket of food pellets. Mostly, in the daytime, when she could guarantee there would be people about, she allowed the hens to roam freely across the farm yard, but at night she brought them inside the chicken house which had a secure, covered wire run attached to it. Now, as they roamed, she scattered the pellets across the cobbled yard and immediately they gathered around her and began to forage hungrily. After a while, satisfied she'd done the bulk of her chores for the morning, Sarah went back into the farmhouse to tidy herself up before setting off for the local town of Caulders Lea where Jenny had her Estate Agency.

Geoffrey Hollins greeted her in a friendly way as she walked in through the main door some half an hour later. He was a stocky man, with a slightly expanding midriff, and hair that was beginning to show signs of grey. He wore a suit and tie, and had on dark brown leather brogues. His hazel eyes beamed a welcome. 'Miss Marshall, it's good to see you. I'm so sorry our last conversation had to be about poor Jenny.'

'Yes, it was upsetting to have to pass on such bad news.'

He became business-like. 'So, are you here because you'd like to talk to me about that... or maybe you've had some more thoughts about selling the farm?'

'Ah...' She hesitated. 'Actually, I haven't made a lot of headway there, I'm afraid. I'm still trying to work out what I should do about it. Jenny did say that it might be advisable to spruce the place up a bit before it went on the market, so I think I'll concentrate on doing that for the time being.'

'I know you asked Jenny for her thoughts about it, and she prepared a file on the property.

She knew her stuff, and that's wise advice she gave you - although, you should know, someone has expressed an interest in buying the farm. The gentleman came in and said he was looking to purchase land and that he'd heard the owner of Sweetbriar Farm had passed away. He wanted to know if it might soon be coming on the market.'

'You're talking about Raj Sayed?'

He nodded. 'That's right. Have you spoken to him about it?'

'Yes, he's my neighbour, and he came to see me... but I told him I'm not sure yet what I want to do.'

'That's quite all right. I'm sure he understands, and if you should decide to sell I'll be only too glad to help if that's what you'd like. I'm sure we can negotiate a good deal.' He studied her thoughtfully. 'So, if it isn't the farm that brings you here, is there anything in particular that I can do for you? Did you want to talk to me about Jenny?' His expression was sombre. 'It's dreadful that things turned out the way they did.'

'Yes, it was awful, and Jenny's death was totally unexpected. I'm trying to work out how on earth it could have happened.' She glanced around the office, at the two desks arranged at a welcoming angle so that clients would be immediately made to feel at home. Jenny's beech wood desk was still as it must have been a couple of days ago when she left the office to come to the farm. There was a computer monitor and keyboard on there, a wire tray containing a bundle of files, a pot of pens and pencils, and a small vase of sweet-scented wallflowers that had probably come from her garden. Sarah noticed a mug, too, embossed with pictures of herbal remedies. 'It must be even worse for you, after you've worked with her so closely this last couple of years.'

'It's been very hard to accept,' he agreed. 'I'm still trying to take it in, trying to find a way to come to terms with it.'

'I can imagine,' she said on a sympathetic note. 'What will happen now - about the business, I mean?' Sarah's expertise as a paralegal was coming to the fore. 'I know from my experience at work that sometimes people don't make proper provision for these kinds of eventualities and that can cause a lot of problems. Will you be able to carry on running things without a hitch now that she's no longer here?'

'Oh, ah... um... yes.' Her question appeared to have thrown him off balance for a moment or two. 'We had a formal partnership agreement drawn up - we... uh - we finalized things only recently, as it happens.'

'Oh, I didn't know that.' She was surprised. 'That should make things go a lot more smoothly for you.'

'Yes.' He seemed embarrassed, his mouth making an apologetic slant. 'I admit, I had been a little concerned about what might happen if she should be taken ill and I was left to carry on alone.'

'I suppose that's always a worry when there are only two people running things, especially if there are signs that one of them might be unwell. You don't know what's going to happen and you don't want to be left with your affairs in a mess.' Sarah was suddenly alert and curious to know more. Geoffrey Hollins appeared to have been caught off guard by her question, and clearly hadn't been comfortable revealing the details of his new ownership of the firm. But why would it matter if he had nothing to hide?

'Well, yes, I was feeling a bit anxious about it,' he answered. 'Jenny was having treatment for a heart valve condition and there was some talk about her possibly needing surgery at some point in the future, so I confess I began to wonder if I needed to tidy any loose ends to do with the business. We didn't discuss it for a long time. I didn't know how she would react to my bringing the matter up - it was a delicate subject and she was always keen to show she was on top of things and could soldier on.'

'I think most folk in the village who met her knew she had to pace herself sometimes, despite her determination to go on with all her activities.'

'It's true, she was quite open with people - but she had a positive attitude to life, so she would make light of it and enthuse about the herbal remedies she was keen on, as though they kept her going. Clients would comment on her hand decorated mug and she would explain about feverfew for headaches, and lemon balm for colds, and so on. And about comfrey, of course...' His voice trailed away.

'Yes, she was a great believer in natural remedies.' Her brows indented a fraction. 'So, in the end, she was willing to talk to you about formalizing the partnership?'

He nodded. 'Eventually. She wasn't sure at first. It's never nice to have to think about these things, but we had a chat about our shared responsibilities and how we should deal with the financial side of things. There were friends back home where she came from - but I don't think there is any close family - certainly there was no one who would be there to take over the business.'

'That would have made her decision easier, I expect.'

'Yes, and of course, the agency was always her prime concern. That's why I thought something was wrong when her client rang to say she hadn't turned up on Saturday afternoon. She was also supposed to have called on the Griffiths, before going to Bourton on the Water, but when she didn't arrive they assumed she'd been delayed elsewhere.'

Sarah gave him a probing look. 'So, the Griffiths weren't annoyed about her not putting in an appearance, then?' According to her mother, Lewis and Natalie weren't too happy with Jenny. Something had soured their relationship, she'd said, so what had gone on?

'Oh, I wouldn't say that.' Geoffrey pulled a face. 'I didn't hear from them until the next morning — it was on the Sunday when Mr Griffiths rang my mobile number. I think he was about to complain... he certainly sounded brusque. You can imagine, I wasn't ready to deal with anything like that, so I told him what had happened to her. He said he was sorry to hear that and he would talk to me in a day or two about their sale and rang off.'

'At least he gave you some breathing space. I know how frantic everything can get when you're involved in the property market. Everyone's on edge and nerves can get frayed. When I bought my flat I wanted everything to go through smoothly and, most of all, I wanted the transaction to be done fast. No hanging about, no getting caught up in chains of buyers and sellers. The whole procedure can be draining.'

She hoped by revealing a little of her own emotional experience he might be coaxed into telling her more about the Griffiths' plans, but Geoffrey was circumspect. He was a professional and it seemed he wasn't about to divulge anything of his clients' business dealings.

'They just want to sell up and move on, like everyone else.'

Sarah nodded agreement. She would have to go and call on the Griffiths. That was the only way she would be able to find out more about the problems they'd been having with Jenny. In the meantime, she had to get back to the farm and see how Lexie was doing.

'Thanks for giving me your time, Mr Hollins. I'm just trying to get my head around what happened - I'll let you know what I decide to do about the farm.'

'Thanks, I'll look forward to hearing from you.' He saw her to the door and watched her walk to her car.

Sarah was deep in thought as she slid behind the wheel. Was she any nearer to finding out who would have wanted to harm Jenny? There was Ben Reed, of course, angry and resentful because she had taken away his dog and hassled him by complaining about the state of his property, but would he have reacted by trying to poison her? Maybe.

Then there was Geoffrey Hollins, a seemingly respectable businessman, who had everything to gain from her death. He had phoned Sarah to ask if she knew Jenny's whereabouts, but that could simply have been a way of covering himself. He was now the sole owner of the Company... but would he have killed to get what he wanted?

And what of the Griffiths? What grievance did they nurse over their dealings with Jenny? She would have to find out.

Rob was at work with Jason, another young farmhand, in the kitchen garden when Sarah arrived back at the farm some time later. They were weeding between the rows of herbs and salad vegetables, and she called out to them as she approached the kitchen door. 'You're doing a great job there, lads. I'll put the kettle on for a brew.'

'Thanks. That'd be great.'

Lexie had wandered in from the yard while Sarah was out, and had settled herself in her bed in a corner of the kitchen. Usually when Sarah came into the room the dog would wag her tail and come to greet her, but this afternoon she stayed where she was.

Sarah went over to her and stroked her soft brown fur. 'Are you okay, Lexie? How are you doing?'

Lexie was straining and licking herself and was generally restless, so Sarah guessed it wouldn't be too long before she went into labour. 'I'll stay with you,' she told the dog, conversationally. 'There are loads of jobs I need to get on with in the house, so you don't need to worry, I'll never be too far away.' She flicked the switch on the kettle and set out mugs and plates on the table, then made sandwiches for the boys, using bread fresh from the local bakery and thick slices of ham and cheddar cheese. She took a bowl of salad from the fridge and placed it next to the sandwich platter, adding a dish of coleslaw and a selection of sauces to the table.

'Tea's ready, boys,' she called, dipping her head out of the back door. 'Time to clean up.'

Rob was first to appear, having washed at the sink in the outhouse. There were sanitizers and paper towels provided for the workers - something her Gran had been very keen to promote. Jason followed, slightly diffident, fairly new to the farm and not knowing how to go on.

'Sit down, and help yourselves,' she told them, waving a hand towards the oak table.

'Aw, that looks good,' Rob said. 'I'm starving. Cheers for this.'

'You're welcome.'

'Thanks, Miss Marshall.' Jason sat opposite Rob and followed his lead, selecting a couple of sandwiches and accepting the mug of tea Sarah offered.

'Call me Sarah,' she said. 'We're not formal around here.'

'Okay.' He smiled, relaxing a little, and began to eat. He had a good appetite, stoking up on energy for the jobs he would be doing around the farm. Like Rob, he was a muscular lad, used to handling sacks of grain or hoeing between the rows of crops growing in the fields.

When they'd satisfied their hunger, the boys went back to finish up their work outside, getting the hens back into the compound and making sure the goats were bedded down for the evening. They would stop work at five and then head off home, leaving Sarah alone at the farm. She was still getting used to that, being on her own here at night.

She cleared the table, stacking the crockery into the dishwasher and then turned her attention back to the dog. 'Is something happening, Lexie? Has it started?'

Lexie was panting heavily and then as her labour advanced she concentrated hard on delivering her first pup, licking and gently biting at the sac that surrounded him until he was free. She went on licking vigorously at his wet fur and stimulating him to breathe. When she was finally satisfied he was okay, she rested awhile until the second one started to emerge.

'You're doing so well!' Sarah said softly. Lexie was a good mum, constantly checking her babies to make sure they were healthy and strong, and then letting them feed.

After the fifth pup was born she rested again, and Sarah wondered if it was all over, but soon she started to strain and she guessed the process was beginning once more. Only this time the pup didn't appear and after a few minutes Lexie seemed to be distressed.

Sarah was starting to feel anxious. This couldn't be normal, could it? She couldn't let anything happen to Lexie or the puppies after they'd come so far. She had to do something to help her.

Worriedly, she called Matt, relieved when he answered right away. 'Lexie's having her puppies, but I think something might have gone wrong,' she told him. 'It's been too long between pups and I don't know what to do to help her.'

'I'll come over,' he said. 'I'm only a couple of miles from the farm, so I'll be with you in two ticks.'

'Thanks.' She cut the call and turned anxiously back to Lexie. 'It's all right,' she murmured in a soothing voice. 'Help's on the way.'

Matt was as good as his word and turned up a few minutes later. 'How's she doing?' he asked, putting his leather medical bag down on the floor beside the dog bed and rolling up his shirtsleeves.

'I think she has another pup in there, but nothing's happening.'

He put on surgical gloves and knelt down beside Lexie. 'Let's see what's going on here, shall we Lexie?' he said softly. 'We'll find out what's causing the problem.' He examined her carefully and finally he told Sarah, 'There's definitely another pup in there, but the uterine contractions have stopped... I'll give her an injection to see if we can get them started again.'

Sarah crouched down beside him, stroking Lexie and murmuring encouragement. Eventually, when the contractions started once again, Lexie started to deliver her pup, only for it to become stuck in the birth canal. Sarah held her breath in apprehension, but Matt gently eased it on its way. Lexie seemed exhausted, but once the birthing process was complete, she began to carefully lick her new-born pup.

Sarah gave a sigh of relief. 'Is that all of them, do you think?'

Matt nodded. 'Six healthy pups - all of them pedigree from the looks of things.'

'Pedigree?' she echoed.

'If I'm remembering correctly... I dealt with Lexie's previous owner when Lexie and her siblings were born – it would be something like a year ago, I imagine – and he told me about the dog's history.'

'My mother wondered if that might be a possibility. We didn't think Ben knew that - he didn't seem to care about her welfare, but surely he would have been a bit more cautious if he'd known?'

'We can only guess. Either way, it's a good thing Lexie was being looked after properly through this last stage of whelping, or things could have turned out disastrously.'

'My mother thinks he might try to get her back once he finds out about the puppies.'

'That's not going to be an option, is it?'

'No.'

She heard the uncertainty in her own voice and Matt studied her thoughtfully for a moment. 'Are you worried about him turning up here?'

'I don't know. He bothers me because he gave Jenny so much trouble - she said it was making her stressed, and I'm not sure just how aggressive he was towards her.'

He frowned. 'Are you thinking he somehow made her heart condition worse?'

'No, not that, exactly. Her heart condition wasn't the cause of her death - it was an overdose of digitalis from ingesting the poison from foxglove leaves.' There was no reason Matt shouldn't know – Sarah had been in Jenny's house and might have noticed the leaves herself if she'd looked carefully. 'I just feel that it warrants more investigation. I'm trying to find out who might have wanted to hurt her.'

His dark brows lifted. 'Someone like Ben Reed, you mean?'

'I'm not sure. He's a possibility, don't you think?'

'I don't know.' He screwed up his mouth a little. 'But I do know you, Sarah, and I suspect you'll be delving into things with that paralegal mind of yours, when really you should be leaving any enquiries to the police. Isn't Nick Holt looking into Jenny's death?'

'Word travels fast around here, doesn't it?' She gave him a sceptical look. 'Nick Holt doesn't seem to think there are any suspicious circumstances, and once he's made up his mind to something, he's not easily persuaded otherwise.'

'Are you speaking from experience here?'

'Oh, we've had our differences of opinion before, over various cases that have come to court. Not in the verdicts,' she hastened to add, 'but in our interpretation of character. He sees things in black and white, whereas I see the grey areas.'

Matt smiled. 'Well, if I can help in any way...'

'Thanks.' She grinned back at him. 'You've been brilliant, Matt, coming over to help with

Lexie. Look at her, she's doing so well and the puppies are all feeding.'

'She's probably worn out, so keep her quiet and give her plenty of nourishment and keep fresh water on hand. She should do fine.'

'I will.' She got to her feet. 'Coffee, I think. Would you like some?'

He unfolded his long limbs. 'I certainly would. And then maybe I should go and take a look at the ewes and the lambs while I'm here. It's still light enough to be able to see outside.'

'That's a good idea, thanks.' She made coffee and they chatted for a while about this and that, reminiscing about the time when her grandmother ran the farm.

'She loved this place,' Matt said, 'but I think it probably became too much for her towards the end. She wasn't able to keep up with all the maintenance that needed doing.'

Sarah's mouth turned down a fraction. 'I know. I feel guilty that I wasn't able to do more to help out. I came here whenever I could, at weekends and sometimes in the evening after work, but there was only so much I could do. And there wasn't an endless supply of money to keep up with repairs. She didn't want to sell the holiday cottage to pay for things because we all loved staying there by the sea whenever we had the chance.' She cleared the cups away and added, 'Shall we go and see to the lambs?'

He nodded and went with her to the door. 'You did what you could, and I know she appreciated that,' he said, resting a hand lightly on her shoulder. 'Anyway, your Gran's priority was always the animals, and she made sure they were looked after properly.'

'Yes, that's true.' They walked together to the field where the sheep grazed and Sarah stayed with him as he tended the flock.

'They're all doing well,' he said, eventually. 'You can go ahead with the sheep shearing in a couple of weeks. The lambs won't need to be touched. They'll keep their coats.'

'Okay. I'll get that organized.' The wool wouldn't bring in a lot of money by the time she'd paid the shearer, but every bit would help.

She said goodbye to Matt a few minutes later and walked back to the farmhouse. Dusk was falling as she went into the kitchen and for a moment or two she found the eerie silence of the house unsettling. Then she saw Lexie and the puppies snuggled up in their big bed and immediately brightened.

She set about making herself some supper, a quick snack of pasties and a side salad, and just as she was about to sit down to eat she heard a car come to a halt on the drive. Who would be calling on her at this time of the evening?

She went to the door and saw Nick walking towards her. 'Hi there,' she greeted him. 'I wasn't expecting to see you. Is everything okay?'

He nodded. 'I just came to keep you up to date,' he said, following her into the warmth of the kitchen as she ushered him inside.

He saw Lexie and the puppies in the bed and smiled as he went to look at them. 'So, how many does she have?' He stroked Lexie as he counted them. 'She did well – they're perfect, aren't they?'

'Yes, they are,' Sarah said, smiling.

He sniffed the air appreciatively.

'I just heated up some pasties,' she told him. 'Would you care to join me?'

His mouth widened appreciatively. 'I'd like that very much, thanks. I've been on duty since early this morning and I missed out on a meal.'

'Well then, you can sit down and help yourself.' She put two more pasties into the Aga to heat up and poured tea, coming to sit down at the table opposite him. 'So, what's happening? Have you found out any more about how Jenny came to die?'

He made a faint grimace. 'You're not going to like it,' he said bluntly. 'The Chief Inspector is convinced her death was suicide or at the very least accidental. He wants it recorded as such and he thinks the Coroner will agree with him. There was a foxglove plant in the herb garden and that's enough to go on as far as he's concerned.' He put up a hand to ward off her protest. 'I know... I know how you feel about it, and I do sympathize with you, believe me.'

He bit into the flaky pastry she offered him and sighed with contentment. 'Mmm, that's good.' He munched for a moment, then added, 'The problem is, there's been a spate of burglaries around the village lately - three of them in properties that Jenny was selling. The boss says we need to concentrate on those.'

Sarah raised her brows. 'Since when were burglaries more of a priority than a suspicious death?'

'The Superintendent was one of the victims. He has a big house, two or three miles from here. They took a load of stuff from inside and even removed the garden furniture from on top of his new decking.'

'Huh. Even so...' Sarah was shocked. 'I can't believe they can just ignore something as serious as this. Jenny's death can't have been accidental.'

He nodded briefly. 'Between you and me, I'm inclined to agree with you, but officially I'm not allowed to spend time on an investigation. My superiors argue that there was no sign of a break-in, and it was well known that she'd been having trouble with Ben Reed. They believe the stress of that situation, along with her heart problem, and the fact that she was a widow who only moved to the area two years ago could have led to her taking her own life.'

'She lost her husband over two years ago, and she came here to make a new start. She has friends in Caulders Lea.'

'Even so, it can take some time for stress to build up. And once it reaches a peak it wouldn't take much to tip a person over the edge.'

As she opened her mouth once again to make an objection he said quickly, 'I'm only repeating the arguments that have been put to me, Sarah. I'll do what I can, on the quiet, but I can't make any promises.'

'I guess it's down to me, then,' she said, her green gaze darkening and her mouth taking on a firm line. 'I need to talk to a few people.'

'Now let's get this clear,' he said, shooting her a stern look. 'I don't want you to go playing the sleuth... that can get you into all kinds of trouble.' His jaw tightened. 'And most definitely keep away from the likes of Ben Reed. You could end up getting hurt.'

'Hmmph! I would have thought he was a prime suspect - although Geoffrey Hollins could also be on the list, since he had something to gain from Jenny's death.'

'You've been to see Geoffrey Hollins?'
She nodded.

His blue eyes took on a flinty edge. 'I'll tell you again, Sarah, leave the detective work to me. You don't know what you could be getting yourself involved in.'

'Well, of course, if you're going to give the investigation your full attention, I won't need to do anything, will I?' she said sweetly. 'Would you like another pasty?'

CHAPTER FIVE

'**I DON'T** like to have to tell you this, Sarah, but I think you may have a leak in the barn roof,' Rob said next morning. He and Jason were busy stacking boxes of spring cabbages and cauliflowers on to the farm truck, ready to be taken to the local shops, when Sarah came by to see how things were going.

Her jaw dropped a fraction. 'What makes you think that?'

'Some of the greens were a bit wet - we've put them to one side for composting, but I think you might need to take a look for yourself.'

'Okay, show me.' She went with Rob to look in the big barn where they stored winter and early spring vegetables. It was dark in there until they flung open the wide doors to let the pale sunshine flood in.

Rob strode across the barn to where some hessian sacks were stacked against the wall. 'I don't know how long it's been going on, but these sacks are wet and there are a couple of large puddles on the floor.'

Sarah looked around in bemused silence, turning her gaze up to the rafters, but it was impossible to see from here where the leak was coming from. 'Thanks for telling me, Rob. I suppose I shouldn't be surprised – this barn's really old. I think maybe I'd better talk to Daniel about it when he comes over this morning, just in case it's anything to do with the woodwork.'

'Ah - you called him, then?' Rob looked pleased.

'I did. He said he'll be free around lunchtime so he'll come and have a look at what needs to be done.' She glanced around once more. 'In the meantime, we'd better dry out these sacks and cover the rest with plastic sheeting. You'll find some in the store shed. Would you and Jason see to that when you come back from making the deliveries? And any produce that you can save will need moving away from that part of the barn. We'd better keep it clear.'

'Yeah, sure.' He went to turn away and then said as an afterthought, 'I told my little brother and sister about Lexie's puppies. Would it be all right if they come along to see them today with some of their friends? They're off school this week 'cos of the Easter holidays.'

'Yes, of course - as long as they make sure Lexie stays calm and peaceful and doesn't get disturbed in any way.'

'I'll keep an eye on them. Thanks, I'll give Mum a ring to let her know it's okay.'

He went back to loading produce on the truck with Jason, leaving Sarah to ponder the new predicament that had presented itself. A leaking roof was the last thing she needed right now. She'd prefer a straightforward day-to-day running of the place so that she could concentrate on finding Jenny's killer. But when had anything in her life ever been simple? Still, at least she'd arranged to go and see Natalie Griffiths this afternoon. It was Natalie's half day off from the salon, so that might give Sarah the opportunity to gain a bit more insight into the problems she and her husband had been having with Jenny.

'Oh dear. That could turn out to be expensive to put right,' her mother commented when she stopped by the farm a little later that morning and heard about the leaky barn. 'Roofs can be tricky. Do you think it might be wiser to sell Sweetbriar as it is, rather than pay out for repairs?'

Sarah pulled a face. 'It probably would make more sense, but every time I think that way I see Gran in my mind's eye, gently telling me how much effort she put into this place and how it has been handed down through the generations. It's hard enough as it is for me to come to terms with selling up, and I don't think I can bring myself to let it go for a pittance after all her hard work.'

'Ah...' Her mother gave her a quick hug. 'You and your Gran always were two of a kind. Despite the fact that you have a career planned out, she must have sensed something in you that drew you to the farm. You were always here every chance you got when you were younger. I think that's why she left it to you.'

Sarah sighed. 'You're probably right, but I've been looking at the finances, and the way things are I'm going to be struggling to keep my head above water...' Caught out by the irony of that, she chuckled. 'And that could be literally, if the barn roof's anything to go by!'

Her mother grinned with her, and they went into the house to check on the pups. They found a small group of children assembled in the kitchen with Rob, watching, awestruck, as six brown and white puppies suckled hungrily at their mother.

'They're so greedy! Are they all boys?' Rob's sister asked excitedly. She was about ten years old, Sarah guessed, and the boy would be about eight.

Sarah laughed. 'No, there are four boys and two girls.'

'They all look the same - they're...' Rob's little brother hunted around for the word. '*Six*tuplets!' he pronounced triumphantly.

'I guess they are!' Sarah examined the puppies carefully. 'They all have brown fur with white socks and white chests, and four of them have white markings down the middle of their faces. The two with black faces are girls.'

'They're squeaking!' The children were thrilled by the experience of seeing Lexie and her puppies, but after a while Rob gently reminded them that it was time to go home. 'And Lexie needs to rest,' he added.

'You can come and see them another day,' Sarah promised, seeing them back down the drive and safely on their way.

'I must go, too,' her mother said. 'I'm baking cakes for a charity tea in the village hall.'

'Okay. Good luck with that - and remember to save a few for me,' Sarah said with a smile, waving her off.

'Will do!' her mother called back.

Sarah went into the house and started to sort out the table decorations her mother had asked about the other day. They were her excuse for paying a visit to the Griffiths' house.

It wasn't long before the weight of her responsibilities began to bear down once more, though. Daniel Richmond arrived some half an hour later, parking his old Ford Transit van on the drive. His presence here reminded her all too sharply of the numerous repairs and renovations that were needed around the farm.

'Hi, Daniel,' she said, going to meet him as he walked into the cobbled yard. 'I'm really glad you could come over.'

'That's okay. College is closed this week for the holidays and I had a couple of hours in between projects, so it's no problem.' He was a personable young man, tall, with cropped black hair and brown eyes that seemed to take in everything around him.

'I see you've found yourself a useful van,' she said, looking it over. 'I heard you'd passed your driving test.'

'Yeah.' His mouth curved. 'I was well pleased. The van used to belong to my stepdad, but he wanted something newer for himself and passed this on to me. I can get a lot of timber in the back, along with my tools and so on, so it's great. I'm happy.'

'That's good. I expect you'll need it in your line of work.'

He nodded. 'You said on the phone you wanted me to look at some hutches?'

'That's right. I'll take you over there. There's a low fence around the rabbits' and guinea pigs' enclosure that could do with some attention as well.'

'Okay.' Daniel took time to look at each of the hutches, jotting down some measurements in a notebook, and said, 'It should be easy enough to do. I'll have to cut off the rotten parts and fit new timbers. I do have quite a bit of wood back home that would suit the purpose, so I could make a start pretty much this week if you decide to go ahead. I'd just charge you for the time it takes, plus something for the materials.'

'Uh... how much would that be, roughly?'

He named a price that seemed reasonable to Sarah, and she gave a small sigh of relief. 'That seems fair enough,' she said.

'Good.' He nodded. 'I'll get on to it as soon as I can.'

'That would be great,' she agreed.

He walked back with her to the yard, glancing around at the outbuildings. 'Did you know there are some slates missing from your barn roof?'

'Are there?' She looked up in dismay to where he was pointing. How had she not noticed that before? But then, she'd been so busy of late, with one thing and another, and she'd had so much on her mind. 'Oh, no... oh dear. That might explain the leak.'

'Could be just the roofing felt that's been damaged. Once it was exposed the birds might have had a go at it for their nesting.' He turned to her. 'Do you have a ladder? Do you want me to have a look? There's a lad at College on a roofing course - he might be able to fix some slates for you.'

'Would you? Yes, please, Daniel.'

She showed him where the ladder was kept and waited apprehensively while he inspected the damage both inside and out.

He looked serious when he came back down to the ground and she pressed her lips together in anticipation of the verdict. 'How bad is it?'

'I don't know how long the leak has been going on - it may have gone unnoticed for some time - but some of the timbers have started to rot. They don't look very safe to me - I'd say you need to get them replaced as soon as possible.'

She closed her eyes briefly. That was all she needed. Pulling in a deep breath, she said, 'Can you give me a quote?'

He nodded. 'I'll talk to my mate, Josh, and we'll see what we can work out between us.'

'Thanks. I really appreciate you coming over here today, Daniel.'

'You're welcome... but I'm sorry to have given you bad news. I'll give you a ring when I'm coming over to start on the hutches and get back to you on that quote.'

'That's good.' Feeling heavy at heart, she watched him drive away. Was she taking on too much with this farm? At this rate, anything she might make on produce would soon be eaten up in staffing and maintenance costs. How could she afford to have the roof repaired? No wonder her Gran had struggled to keep up with things.

Still, she wasn't going to sit about and mope, was she? She was made of far sterner stuff than that, and there were things she needed to do. When Sarah had rung Natalie Griffiths earlier, she had indicated she would be at home this afternoon, and Sarah was keen to go and visit her to see what she could find out about the Griffiths' dealings with Jenny.

After lunch she changed from her work clothes into skinny blue jeans and a top, adding boots and a light jacket to finish the ensemble and then she set off to drive the three or four miles to the Griffiths' house.

It was a large, detached property, screened from the road by a luxuriant mass of shrubbery and mature trees, and approached along a winding path skirted by velvet lawns on either side. The flower borders were bright with bushy azaleas, giant pansies and pretty blue forget-me-nots. Keen eyed, Sarah noted that dotted among them were lupin plants, foxgloves and delphiniums, though these were not yet in flower.

She rang the ornate doorbell and after only a few seconds Natalie Griffiths answered the door.

'Hello,' Sarah said with a smile. 'I'm Sarah Marshall - I phoned earlier. I think we've met before once or twice, haven't we, at the village fête, or in the bank from time to time?'

'Of course. And, obviously, I know your mother from her catering business - she's produced some splendid dinners for me over the last few years.'

'She's very talented,' Sarah agreed cheerfully. 'As I mentioned on the phone, she told me that she would be preparing a dinner for you soon - and she also said that you were looking for table decorations.'

'Oh, yes, that's right,' Natalie murmured, leading the way into the rectangular dining room at the back of the house.

The room was furnished in shabby chic French chateau style, with a long, carefully aged ivory coloured table as its focal point. The sides and sturdy legs of the table were ornately carved and there were several matching chairs ranged along either side of it. Along one wall there was also a sideboard with the same pleasing patina as the table.

'I was hoping I might find something unusual, something with a kind of country feel, if you know what I mean,' Natalie said.

She was a woman in her fifties, well turned out as befitted a woman with her own hairdressing salon. She had an image to project, and she did it with flair. Her hair was dark and glossy, styled in a mid-length bob that swirled as she moved her head. Her appearance was immaculate. She wore a black sheath dress that fitted perfectly, and black stiletto heels that emphasised the shapeliness of her legs.

'Yes, I think I do,' Sarah said. She had brought with her an assortment of craft work that she'd found stored away in her grandmother's old oak chest up in the attic, and now she carefully placed the large cardboard box down on the dining table.

'I'm hoping there might be something here that you like. My grandmother had exquisite taste and was a skilled craftswoman. She had an interest in making things from natural products - I thought if you like any of these you might want to use them for your dinner party.'

She opened the box and took out several items, gently releasing them from their tissue paper wrappings. There were some beautiful hand-crafted centrepieces made from corn husks and twine, fashioned into large flowers arranged on filigree mats, or circular candle holders and amazing garlands and corn sheaves for wall decorations.

'I wasn't sure whether to bring these wall decorations with me,' she said, but looking around as Natalie examined the things she'd brought, Sarah noticed the walls in here were a little bare. There were no paintings or pieces of artwork, and there was no other furniture in the room to add interest. That seemed to her a little odd, considering the Griffiths were hoping to sell the house because, surely, they would want to present it at its best?

'Oh, these are lovely,' Natalie exclaimed. 'They're exquisite. Your grandmother was so clever to have made all these. I wanted something out of the ordinary and these are perfect, exactly what I'm looking for.' She sent Sarah a quick, beseeching glance. 'Do you think I might borrow them - all of them? I could put up some of the corn sheaves to give the room a countrified feel. It will make such a good impression on our guests.'

'Of course, I'm glad to help. My Gran would have been pleased to know her work was appreciated.' She hesitated a moment and then added, 'It sounds as though this dinner party is really important to you.'

A flush of pink stole across Natalie's cheeks. 'Well, yes. It's for my husband's business really. He's invited some influential Company directors and their wives, with a view to building up trade. He's an engineer, and he supplies machine shop products made to order, as well as sports equipment for gymnasiums and the leisure industry. We have an online outlet, but it's always important to drum up business in any way we can. I do my bit at the salon - if anyone mentions they need a gadget or something unusual made to order, I put in a word for our business. But business can be seasonal... it goes in fits and starts.'

Sarah nodded agreement. 'I suppose there's often a lull in trade after Christmas and New Year, until it starts to pick up again. Perhaps things will be better for you in the next month or so when people want to start getting fit again in time for their summer break.' She was assuming the business was going through a bad patch, and wondered if Natalie would pick up on what she said.

'Well, yes... we hope so.'

She didn't say any more, but looked uneasy, and Sarah murmured, 'It must be difficult for you, running your own hairdressing salon and trying to support your husband's business by giving a dinner party when you're trying to sell your house. You probably have a lot on your mind, a lot of things to deal with.'

Natalie seemed startled. 'Oh... you know about that? We don't have the *For Sale* sign up yet.' She looked puzzled for a moment, her brow furrowed, and then said, 'Oh, I expect your mother mentioned it to you.'

'That's right. She said Jenny Carter was making the arrangements. It's so sad, what happened to her.'

'Yes... yes, it is.' Natalie was clearly uncomfortable. 'She came and viewed the house and talked about putting it on the market for us, though there was a bit of an unfortunate delay in that. Mr Hollins will be dealing with it now, I suppose, so things might start to move a bit quicker for us.'

Sarah frowned, wondering if the delay was at the foot of the Griffiths' difficulties with Jenny and what could have caused it. 'Delays can be so frustrating,' she sympathized. 'Perhaps Jenny had a lot of work on at that time?'

'No, no, it was nothing like that.'

'Really?' Sarah gave Natalie an encouraging look, hoping she might expand on that, but to no avail. Natalie didn't appear to want to say any more on the subject.

'You have a lovely house,' Sarah commented. 'Anyone can see it's a substantial property, so I can't see that you'll have any problems making a sale. But then, Jenny must have told you that.'

'Well, yes...' Again, Natalie shifted restlessly, as though disturbed by something she wasn't inclined to talk about, and Sarah decided to try a new tack.

'Do you have another house in mind, somewhere in particular you're thinking of moving to?'

'We're still looking.' Natalie seemed relieved to be on firmer ground. 'This place is too big for us now, with both of our children finishing university soon and looking to find their independence. John's studying architecture and Molly wants to be a nurse,' she added proudly.

'They're both excellent career choices,' Sarah remarked. 'Most young people want to branch out on their own eventually, don't they? I certainly did.' Although, Sarah thought, if Natalie's son and daughter had only just finished their further education it might be a little early for their parents to start looking for a smaller place. 'I expect they'll want to come home from time to time, though. Most children do.'

'Oh yes... yes, of course. We'll just have to find the right place.'

Sarah was more convinced than ever that the Griffiths wanted to downsize because the business was going through a difficult patch. That could happen to anyone, but it still didn't explain why they had fallen out with Jenny.

'I'm sure Jenny would have helped you with that. She was very good at her job.'

'Hmm... yes, I expect so.' Natalie studied the table centrepieces once more and smiled. 'I must do something to thank you for lending me these,' she said.

'Oh no, really, that's not necessary,' Sarah protested. 'I'm happy to do it. They were just sitting in the attic.'

'No, no... I must.' Natalie studied Sarah's long, honey coloured hair. 'You have lovely hair, so silky and golden - but I'm sure I could make it look spectacular with a bit of layering at the sides and a fraction off the length. What do you think? We'll finish off with a blow dry. You must come into the salon and let me do that for you.' Without waiting for an answer, she went over to her handbag, which was on the sideboard, and rummaged inside. Producing a notebook and flicking through the pages, she said, 'Yes, here we have it - I have a cancellation tomorrow, or I could fit you in on Saturday afternoon.' Sending Sarah an expectant look, she said, 'What do you say?'

Sarah thought about it. Going to the salon would give her another chance to talk to Natalie, and perhaps find out a bit more. Maybe the hairdresser would be more inclined to let slip whatever it was she was holding back when she was busy at work and her mind was on other things. 'Oh, well... that's an offer I can't refuse,' Sarah accepted, her mouth curving. 'I'd appreciate that... I think Saturday would be best for me.'

'That's official, then,' Natalie said, making a note in her book. 'I'll look forward to seeing you then. You won't regret it.' She studied Sarah fleetingly. 'You have a perfect figure, definitely a photogenic face, and with your hair restyled you'll look fantastic.'

'Thank you,' Sarah laughed. 'It's very kind of you to say so.'

Natalie showed her out and said goodbye, closing the door behind her as Sarah walked through the long front garden and out to her car. She'd parked in the country lane in front of the house, and now, as she clicked the key to unlock it she saw another car pull up in front of hers. She recognized the sleek black Mazda. It belonged to Nick Holt.

'We'll have to stop meeting this way,' he said, sliding out from behind the wheel and coming to meet her. He gave her a lopsided grin that lightened his handsome features.

'Yes, how is it that it keeps happening? Are you following me, by any chance?' She said it in tongue in cheek fashion, but there was no doubt about it, she was running into the detective quite a lot, lately.

'I wondered that about you,' he countered. 'You're not by any chance checking up on anyone who had any connection with Jenny Carter, are you? After all, you admitted you'd been to the Estate Agency.'

She sidestepped that. He was too canny by far. 'I brought Natalie some table centrepieces. As to Geoff Hollins and the Agency, I do have a farm to put on the market, you know?'

He lifted a dark brow. 'Are you selling?'

'I don't know,' she answered. 'Jenny was advising me on the best course of action to take. The way things are going, I'll probably have to sell... if things start to disintegrate any more than they have already.'

'That's an ominous statement,' he said, frowning. 'It sounds as though you might be having a bit of bad luck?'

'Yeah, tell me about it! Every day, I'm finding more repairs that need doing.' She braced her shoulders to shrug it off and said in what she hoped was a nonchalant tone, 'So, are you here to see the Griffiths? Are they under investigation because of Jenny?'

He wagged a chiding finger at her. 'Now, you know I'm not supposed to be working on that case.'

'Ah, so it is a case, then?'

His mouth quirked. 'No, now don't start getting your hopes up. But we have had the results of the post mortem – Jenny died from cardiac arrest brought on by digitalis toxicity.'

She nodded. 'That's what we expected, isn't it?'

'That's right. But I'm here for something else entirely. I'm looking into those burglaries that have been taking place over the last few weeks. The Superintendent is getting twitchy about it.'

'Surely the Griffiths aren't suspects?'

'No, they're not. It seems they're victims.'

'They've been burgled?' Sarah was shocked.

'That's what I'm here to find out about,' he said.

She was thoughtful for a moment or two. 'I read about some of the burglaries in the local paper - the thieves seem to be going for bulky items like TVs and antique furniture, as well as jewellery and such like.' No wonder the Griffiths' home seemed a bit bare in places. 'It must be upsetting for the Griffiths. What an awful thing to happen when they're in the process of selling.'

'It's upsetting for everyone - actually, three of them have occurred in houses on Jenny's books.'

She sucked in a breath. 'You're not suggesting Jenny had anything to do with it?'

He shook his head. 'No, but someone may have had inside knowledge. I'll need to find out who made appointments to look around, and tie in with times when the owners were out. It may not have been a single-handed job, of course. Whoever's responsible had to be able to load up and move out quickly.'

'I hope you find them before anyone else gets burgled.'

He nodded. 'Yes, so do I. We've put warning notices up around the village so that people will be on their guard.'

Sarah pulled open her car door. 'Well, best of luck,' she said. 'I'll leave you to it. I have a date with some hens and half a dozen puppies.'

'That sounds interesting!' He gave her a quizzical look. 'Though if you're ever looking for a more conventional date, I'm more than happy to oblige.'

She smiled in amusement. He was teasing her of course. 'Really? You and me? Oh, I'll have to give that some serious thought!' Not that it was going to happen. She hardly had time to turn around, these days, let alone go out on dates. And as for spending time with Nick, would that be wise, given the number of times they'd clashed in the workplace?

'Drive carefully,' he said, watching her go.

She drove back to the farm and tried to put him out of her mind. She filled the feed troughs for the sheep and then made sure the rabbits were bedded down, before going into the house to get on with some chores.

Lexie needed some exercise away from the puppies, so once she had steered the hens into the run for the night, Sarah let her out into the cobbled yard and let her roam about the farm for a while. Darkness was falling and there was an eerie silence out here as the animals settled down to sleep. It took some getting used to. The barn door creaked, and Sarah jumped, and then scolded herself for being so nervy.

Usually, when she stayed at her flat, she was surrounded by neighbours, and there was often the sound of music coming through an open window from someone's radio or the lively chatter of village folk as they headed for the fish and chip shop down the road.

Here at the farmhouse it was very different. There were some houses nearby, but the farm was set back from the main thoroughfare and Sarah found it a bit unnerving when she was alone here.

Lexie took herself back into the kitchen, anxious to check on her puppies. Sarah fetched a torch from the store shed and went to inspect the barn, trying to see if she could make out the damage to the roof that Daniel had pointed out.

The moon's silver light filtered through the cracks in the roofing felt, and the torch beam threw dark shadows over the rafters.

She turned as she heard a rustling sound coming from outside the barn. Gravel crunched underfoot as though someone was heading away from here towards the cobbled yard.

'Who's there?' She hurriedly left the barn and shone the torch around in the darkness, but there were only black shadows thrown up by the outbuildings. 'Is anybody there?' she called again.

Lexie barked, at something she heard, or perhaps because Sarah had called out. It was impossible to know. Sarah had left the kitchen door ajar, and now she hurried back to the house, on the alert for danger. Alarm bells were ringing in her head and her pulse quickened.

She glanced swiftly around the kitchen. There was nothing out of place. Everything was exactly as she'd left it. Had there been an intruder or had she imagined things? Perhaps the darkness and the silence had been getting to her. There might be a simple explanation for the noises she'd heard. Maybe a stray cat had been trapped in the barn and rushed out, unseen when Sarah opened the door.

Taking a quick look around to satisfy herself that all was well in the house, she went back outside and securely padlocked the barn door. There was a lot of produce in there, potatoes ready to be taken to market along with carrots and onions from the fields. Another barn housed farm machinery. She would have to think seriously about putting up some security lights.

CHAPTER SIX

'**I FINISHED** one of my College projects ahead of time,' Daniel Richmond said, opening the doors of his Transit van to reveal neatly stacked timbers held in place by racking along the sides, 'so my time's my own for the rest of the Easter holidays. Will it be okay if I make a start on the hutches now? I tried ringing you to let you know I was on my way, but your phone was engaged.'

'Of course, that's fine,' Sarah answered. 'I was phoning around to see if I can get someone to come and shear the sheep in a couple of weeks. It'll bring in some money, which I could really do with right now. The bills seem to be mounting up lately.'

'Yeah, Mrs Marshall used to say this place was like a money trough with a hole in it.' He made a crooked smile. 'As fast as she put cash in, it drained out.'

Sarah smiled. 'You must have known my grandmother really well.'

'Oh yes. Me and my mates used to come to the farm in the holidays. She never minded if we hung about here, so long as we didn't upset the animals. She was a nice lady.'

'She was.' Sarah nodded.

'She'd give us pop and cakes, and tell us to stay out of trouble.' His features softened, remembering.

'Ah... she probably thought while you were here you weren't getting up to anything you shouldn't.'

'Yeah.' His face straightened. 'I'm sorry she's gone. She was good to me. Tried to tell me to stop hanging around with Tom Marchant's gang. I guess I should have listened.'

'You came to your senses, though, didn't you, in the end... you got yourself into College.'

'Yes... but she wouldn't have known that - I stopped coming around these last couple of years... you know how it is... you're busy doing stuff... you think you'll go and see her next week, next month...' His voice tailed off, sadness settling on his features.

'My Gran was a very astute woman, right to the end. She asked about you every once in a while, wanting to know how you were doing, and I'd tell her what I knew. I think she understood youngsters. She always thought you'd come right. She had faith in you. That's why I gave you the work.'

He smiled at that. 'I'm glad. Not everyone thinks that way.'

'No?'

'Once you've mixed with the wrong crowd and been in trouble like I was - even though it was fairly minor stuff and I was a juvenile - you're marked down as no good. Detective Sergeant Holt has me in his sights now for those burglaries in the village.'

Her brows lifted. That was a surprise to her. 'Has he said so?'

'Not as such - but he's asked me where I was on the nights they were done. For one reason or another, he's worked out they all took place at night when it was dark.' He winced. 'Trouble is, I can't remember what I was doing. Most nights I'm down the pub with my mates, or watching the footie on telly.'

Her mouth curved. 'Like most lads your age, I should think. I wouldn't worry too much about it, if I were you. If Sergeant Holt had anything specific on you he'd have said, wouldn't he?'

'Maybe.'

Sarah brought the conversation back to more pressing matters. 'Did you have a word with Josh about the barn roof?'

He nodded. 'It shouldn't be too big a job as long as we get on to it fairly soon. He can get hold of slates that match, and I'll supply the timbers.'

'That's brilliant, Daniel. Thanks.'

'You're welcome.' He started to unload wood from his van, but added thoughtfully, 'Have you thought what you're going to do with Lexie's pups when they're old enough to leave their Mum? They're pedigree from the looks of them, so you would most likely get a good price. That would help out with the bills, wouldn't it?'

'Hmm... that hadn't occurred to me. It'll be around eight weeks before that happens, and they'd have to go to good homes. I'd need to know who the puppies' father was, and get a proper pedigree drawn up, first. But I'm not sure I could profit from them myself - it wouldn't sit right with me, somehow. Not when Lexie wasn't mine originally.'

'You're not serious?' He sent her an incredulous look. 'What will you do, then?'

'Uh...' She thought about it. 'I'm not sure. I haven't had time to dwell on it... give the money to an animal charity, perhaps. That might salve my conscience.'

He made a soft whistling sound between his lips, and then chuckled. 'You'll never be rich, at that rate!' He shook his head. 'You know, I bet that's what your Gran would have done, too!'

'Yes, that's more than likely!'

He unloaded more timber and she stood to one side as he fetched his toolbox from inside the van. 'You know what you ought to do?' he said on a reflective note, as though inspiration had struck suddenly. 'You should set up a farm shop here, to sell produce. You could stand a large chalkboard outside the main gate, and post leaflets through doors. Then you'd have an income from people all around, and not just sell to shops.'

'That's a very good idea,' she told him, her eyes widening. 'I'll have to give it some thought, if I decide to stay.'

'Yeah... and grow herbs, too. Lots of them. They're the in-thing now, you know? Everybody wants to be like the chefs on TV. Leastways, my mate's Mum does!' He grinned. 'I could make little planters for you to sell - ones that fit on windowsills. I could carve the names of the herbs into the plant holders.'

She laughed. 'You're full of wonderful ideas today, aren't you? I promise, I'll think about it.'

Sarah left him to get on with his work, and busied herself with weeding between the rows of sprouting broccoli in the adjacent field. It was a peaceful pastime and gave her the space to think some more about Jenny and try to work out how she could find out who had reason to harm her. So far, she wasn't making much headway on that front.

She needed to talk to Natalie again and see what information she could prise from her, and then find out whether anyone had been seen acting suspiciously near Jenny's house on the day she was killed. That meant she needed to talk to the neighbours.

Lexie wandered across the field to see her on one of brief outings from the house. She came and sat alongside Sarah for a minute or two as she worked, then stood up, stretched her limbs and ambled towards where Daniel was working nearby. He gently stroked her, making a fuss of her for a while, but then she turned away and trotted back to the kitchen to nurse her offspring.

When she'd finished working in the field, Sarah collected eggs from the nest boxes inside the chicken house. There were also eggs hidden away in the hedges around the farmyard, so that by the time she'd finished she had more than a dozen in her basket. She put six in an egg box and gave them to Daniel to take home with him.

'Thanks for these... Mum will be really pleased to have them,' he said, accepting the box and placing it carefully in his large jacket pocket. He glanced around at his handiwork. 'I've repaired four of the hutches, and I'll be back to do some more tomorrow morning, all being well. I'll need to take a couple away to do some extra work on them, but I'll get them back to you as soon as I can.'

'Thanks, Daniel. I can see you've made a good job of the repairs.' She walked with him to his van. 'I'll see you tomorrow, then, hopefully.'

'Yeah.' He looked up at the sky, which was grey with cloud cover, getting darker by the minute. 'If it rains, I'll do the work in the barn -' he made a wry smile, '- at the far end, where it's dry!'

She returned the smile. 'That's a sensible idea. Thanks, Daniel. Bye.'

That evening, she spent some time working on her computer, checking emails, dealing with one or two queries that had come from the solicitors' office, even though she was officially on holiday, and then researching various topics to do with running a farm - preferably those that turned a profit.

A rumble of thunder sounded in the distance when she switched off the laptop around nine o'clock in the evening. A howling wind had built up outside, rattling the iron hinges on the gates and the old aluminium milk churns that stood by the door of the store shed. She heard the intermittent splatter of rain against the windows. Sarah put some more logs on the fire in the dining room and went to make herself a cup of tea.

On a night like this she was glad to be at home in the warmth of the farmhouse. If it weren't for the spooky noises going on all around, she might have been able to relax, curled up in the armchair with a book. Only these were sounds she wasn't used to... a scuffling, a clattering, and all at once a loud rapping on the kitchen door.

Startled by the intrusion, she went to find out who was there. She wasn't expecting any visitors. Pulling open the door, she took a step backwards in alarm when she saw Ben Reed standing there. He was a stocky figure, unkempt, his long brown hair straggly and wild, wet from the rain, his clothes rough. His grey eyes were bleary and he was swaying slightly, unsteady on his feet.

'You've got something here that belongs to me,' he growled. A cloud of beery breath wafted over her as he lurched forward, pushing her to one side so that she fell heavily against the doorjamb.

'Ben, you've no right to come barging in here like this,' she protested, straightening up and pushing the door shut against the wind. She went over to him.

He ignored her, heading for the secluded corner of the kitchen where Lexie and the puppies were snuggled sleepily in their bed. Sarah rushed to intercept him.

'Stay away from them,' she said tautly, planting herself firmly in front of him some two or three metres from the dog bed. She grabbed a chair from the table nearby and dragged it to the side of her as some sort of protective shield for the dog. He'd have to go through her and the chair to get to them. 'How did you know they were here?' she asked.

He snorted. 'Everybody knows. Word travels.'

She winced. The village grapevine was at work in prime condition. 'You shouldn't be here,' she said.

'She's mine,' he bit out, resentment etched into his features. 'You've no business with that dog. I own her, she's mine by rights, and those pups belong to me as well. They're worth a lot of money and they're coming home with me.' His voice was becoming louder with every statement.

'*Are* they? And how exactly are you planning to care for them? Are you going to look after Lexie the way you did before – half starve her to death and leave her out in the cold and rain? How is she going to look after her pups when she's weak and ailing?'

'I never starved her. She was fine with me. That poisonous bitch had no business taking her from me. No wonder she had ulcers... all that bile she had to swallow.'

'If you're talking about Jenny, she wasn't the one who took her, was she? It was the RSPCA who did that. And as to Lexie being fine with you, we have photos to show the state she was in when they found her – wet, bedraggled, covered in mud and shivering with cold. She lost a good deal of her fur through malnourishment, so how you could possibly believe you have any rights over her is beyond me to fathom.'

'I'm taking what's mine... her and her brood. She was given me, legitimate... payment for a job I done. I got it in writing. Ask Tony Ryedale. He'll tell ya.' He lunged forwards and Lexie barked suddenly in warning. Sarah stepped in front of him to block his way, pulling the chair with her.

'Keep away from them.'

'That bitch had no right to come interfering, poking her nose where it wasn't wanted.' He was lurching from side to side, befuddled with alcohol, his face contorted with rage.

Her mouth was dry. Her heart was thumping hard, the blood pounding through her veins. 'Is that why you killed her?' It certainly seemed as though he was capable of such an act.

His mouth twisted into an ugly, wrathful shape. 'Who said I done that?'

'No one. But you hated her, didn't you?'

'Get outta my way!' He tried to elbow her to one side, but she dragged the chair with her making him stumble.

'You're not taking them,' she said, pulling her phone from her jeans pocket. She started to video him as he glowered down at the dog. 'If you don't leave, I'm calling the police.'

'You wouldn't dare -' He aimed a swipe at her hand and sliced the air with his fist as she nimbly side-stepped him.

'Wouldn't I?' She was as angry as he was, by now. How dare he think he could come into her house and take Lexie?

'I'll stop you – I'll whack you good, you interfering busybody...' He charged at her like a bull in a red mist and she aimed a sharp kick at his shin. Luckily, she was wearing her leather boots with heels, and she must have hit home because he reeled back in pain, a stunned look on his face.

'You don't frighten me,' she said, lying through her teeth. 'I've met types like you before in my job and in Court. Right now, you're drunk, and probably incapable, so I wouldn't go throwing your weight around if I were you. In your state you're quite liable to fall over.'

He stared at her in fury and disbelief, his eyes glazed as they tried to home in on the phone in her hand.

'You should go,' she said. When he made no attempt to leave, she made a show of starting to dial the number. 'There's the first 9,' she murmured. 'And the second.' She ducked as he aimed a blow at her head. 'And the third. Police, please,' she said into the phone. 'Sweetbriar Farm. There's an intruder here in my kitchen. He's drunk and aggressive.'

'We'll send an officer to you,' the operator said, and Sarah thanked him, cutting the call.

'They're on their way,' she told Ben. Perhaps something of the reality of the situation began to seep through to him, because he stared at her wide eyed, listening to the sound of the operator on the phone. Then, without saying another word, he turned away from her and stumbled to the door, wrenching it open.

She followed him, making sure he left. 'Don't come back,' she warned him. 'You'll regret it if you do.'

She went out into the darkness of the yard and watched him weave his way back down the drive. She would definitely have to get security lights rigged up, as well as a safety chain for the door. How else was she going to feel safe? In the meantime, she needed to make another call to the police to tell them he'd gone.

Thunder rumbled in the air again, much closer this time, and she looked around, shivering. Everywhere was pitch black. Rain was falling in a tentative, slow stream, a forerunner to the main event. The sky was dark with oppressive, threatening clouds that chose that moment to open up and spill their load in a heavy, drenching downpour.

At least that would sober him up a bit. That was one consolation. She had barely registered the thought when a bolt of lightning cracked across the sky, and in the next second or two she heard the sickening sound of slates swooshing down from the barn roof. She stood in the pouring rain, soaked to the skin, and heard the ominous creak of timbers giving way.

Sarah went back inside the house, locking and bolting the door behind her. Then she phoned the police and told them the danger was over.

The operator took the news amiably. 'That's good. I'm glad you're okay.'

He rang off, and Sarah was suddenly conscious that her wet clothes were clinging to her, so she went upstairs and stripped off her jeans and shirt, changing into cropped leggings and a soft, loose top. Fleetingly, she hugged her arms around herself as though to keep warm - though it was really the shock of the last hour that she was trying to keep at bay. Ben Reed's visit had unnerved her, and after he'd gone she'd watched the storm batter the barn with a ferocity that made her hold her breath in stifled apprehension.

She went back downstairs to the warmth of the kitchen. It was too dark and wet outside to go and see what damage had been done. She would have to go and find that out in the morning. For now, she was in a kind of numb state, wondering what her next course of action should be. Was she foolish to hope that she might make a go of the farm? Why was she dithering?

And what should she do about Ben Reed? Was he Jenny's killer? How could she prove it?

Someone knocked on the kitchen door, and she froze. Had Ben come back? 'Who's there?' she called out. She glanced at her watch. It was ten o'clock at night. Who on earth would be calling on her at this hour?

'It's Nick, Sarah. I came to see if you're all right.'

Relieved, she unlocked the door and slid back the bolt. Nick's outer jacket was wet from the rain, and droplets were trickling down from his black hair. 'Come in and get dry,' she said, standing back to let him pass. 'Give me your raincoat and I'll hang it over the Aga rail to dry.' Beneath the coat he wore a smart suit, teamed with a dark mulberry coloured shirt and a tie. She went and fetched him a towel and he rubbed his hair vigorously until it stood up in wayward peaks.

'So, are you okay?' he asked, dropping the towel into her laundry basket by the washing machine. 'I was worried about you - you reported an intruder here.'

She nodded. 'Yes, I did, but I'm fine... just a bit shaken up, that's all.' She frowned. 'It's true I rang the emergency number, but a few minutes later, after he'd gone, I cancelled. The operator asked a few questions and agreed to stand down the response team.' She was puzzled. 'How did you get to hear about it?'

'I was working at the station when a colleague told me you'd called. He thought I would want to know.' He studied her. 'He was right. What happened? Who was it? Do you know who it was?'

'Yes, I know him well enough. It was Ben Reed, out of his head with drink. He wanted to take Lexie and the pups - I think he'd worked out they could be valuable, but obviously I wasn't going to let him go off with them.'

'Of course not.' His dark brows met. 'Why did you let him in?'

'I didn't - I mean, I didn't mean to, but he pushed past me. He's a scary man, Nick. So scary, it's made me wonder - do you think it's possible he could have killed Jenny?'

'Because she thwarted him?' His eyes narrowed momentarily as he thought about it. 'If we were to go along with your theory that she was murdered, then yes, I suppose it's definitely possible. He seems to be aggressive by nature... but killing someone by feeding them a poisonous substance takes some forethought, and I'm not sure that's his style. He's more likely to use violence as a means to an end.'

'Unless he went away and thought about it. He could have let it fester in his mind, and decided to act in such a way that suspicion wouldn't land on him. He's not drunk all the while or he wouldn't be able to work. There must be times when he stops to think things through.'

'Could be... it certainly can't be ruled out.'

'The only thing I can't figure out is how he would have had access to her house without her knowing.'

'There are several ways someone can get into a house - using copied keys, or sometimes through a garage if it's built on to the house. These days it's even possible to make a copy of a key using a photo and a 3D printer. You might only be able to use it once, but that would be enough.'

'That's a new one on me.'

He nodded. 'Look, I'll poke around and see what comes up - but in the meantime you should keep well away from him.' He sent her a steely eyed glance. 'I mean that. I don't want to hear of you getting involved with him in any way... you understand?'

She nodded. 'I do.' Her mouth curved. 'Thanks for coming to check on me. Would you like some coffee? I'll put the kettle on.'

'Yes, thanks.' He paused briefly. 'Do you want to press charges against him?'

She shook her head. 'Not at this time. I do have him on video, threatening me, so I suppose if he were to do it again I could use it as evidence. For the time being, though, I think I'll leave it. He'd had too much to drink, and when he sobers up and thinks about it, he might come to his senses.'

'Show me?' He held out his hand for her phone and she passed it to him.

'You did well,' he said, after studying the video for a while. 'And you're right, it is evidence of him threatening you. If you'll let me, I'll take a copy and keep it, just in case it gets lost.'

'Oh...' She shrugged lightly. 'Okay, if you think that's best.' She pushed a cup of coffee towards him and tipped some flapjacks from a container on to a plate. 'Help yourself.'

'Thanks.' He sent a copy of the video from her phone to his, and then handed her phone back to her. 'I noticed you'd locked and bolted the door before I arrived,' he said. 'That's good. But you need to get a chain fitted, and rig up some kind of security, so you know who's on your doorstep before you open the door.'

He looked across the room to where Lexie lay sleeping and asked, 'How did she react? Did she growl, or anything?'

'Not really. She barked, but I think she's too exhausted to do much more than that. She wasn't at her best before the pups were born, and now that they're feeding she needs all her strength for looking after them. I'm feeding her up and following the vet's advice, but she's not there yet, I'm afraid.'

'So, she's not going to be much good as a guard dog, then?'

Sarah laughed. 'Not yet, anyway!'

'Hmm. How about getting some geese?'

She chuckled. 'You're joking! Geese?'

'No, I'm serious. According to the people I've spoken to, they make excellent guardians. They can be loud and intimidating, they hiss, and they've been known to attack predators. In any event, they'll protect your chickens and keep away unwanted visitors.'

'I never knew that.' She looked at him in admiration. 'You're a mine of information!'

'Happy to be of service.' He grinned and bit into a flapjack. 'Actually though, I'm speaking from experience. I was working on a case once, at a house near a lake, and strayed too close to some goslings - the gander flew at me and tried to knock me over with the force of his wings. He was extremely fierce, I can tell you!'

'Wow, I'll have to think about that one... just as soon as I decide what I'm going to do with this place.'

'How soon do you have to make up your mind?'

'Well, I have another week's holiday left, and then I'm due back at work. I'm still trying to think of ways I can manage to keep my job and run this place. Otherwise, the bills are likely to cripple me. I need to know more about how to manage things properly.'

'Perhaps the bank will have a business advisor who can help you.'

'That's true. I'll have to ask.' She watched him finish off his coffee and flapjacks, and as he stood up to leave, she asked, 'I know you're busy with the burglaries, but have you been able to look into Jenny's death, at all? Have you managed to come up with anything yet?'

He pulled a face. 'I've made a few discreet enquiries, but it turns out there are a few people who might have had reasons to want her out of the way. And so far, they all have alibis for the time frame when it happened.'

She frowned at that snippet of information. Jenny had always seemed a likeable person to her. Why would anyone want to hurt her? 'At least you've been giving it some thought,' she murmured as she handed him his raincoat. 'That's good to know.'

He smiled. 'I'll see you around, Sarah. Keep safe.' He peered out into the darkness. 'Looks as though the storm's subsiding,' he added, on a note of satisfaction. He lifted a hand in a backward wave as he stepped into the yard. 'Bye.'

'See you,' she said, then locked and bolted the door once more.

She went up to bed, wrapping the duvet around her for comfort. It had been a difficult day, to say the least, and she was glad to lay her head down on the pillow, but she couldn't rest. Her mind seethed with questions that demanded answers. There had to be a way she could find Jenny's killer. It wasn't right that they could walk away scot free. A few people had reason to want Jenny out of the way, Nick had said, and for Jenny's sake she would do her best to find out who they were.

That wasn't her only worry, though. She slept fitfully that night, disturbed by dreams of demons chasing her and dark, swirling shadows tearing at the fabric of the farm.

CHAPTER SEVEN

IN THE morning, Sarah woke late and looked around blankly for a moment, confused, until she remembered where she was. She wasn't staying at her flat, instead she was in the room that had been hers whenever she stayed over at the farmhouse with her grandparents. They were such happy times, and remembering them brought a lump to her throat. This house had always been filled with warmth and love, the smell of freshly baked bread coming from the kitchen, and the laughter of her brother and sister rippling through the rooms. Thinking about it made her feel warm and cosy, and she tried to cling on to those memories. All too soon, though, the images faded and reality came flooding back.

Recalling the events of the previous night - the storm, in particular - she suddenly felt heavy at heart. How bad could it have been? She was suddenly desperate to hurry downstairs and find out exactly what damage the thunderstorm had wreaked. Pulling a lightweight robe over her pyjamas, she hurried outside to go and look at the barn.

Daniel was already out there in the yard. He had a ladder positioned up against the side of the barn, so she guessed he'd been up to take a closer look at the damage. 'It doesn't look too good, I'm afraid,' he said, turning to greet her. 'Some of the slates have fallen down and smashed, and it looks like a couple of the roof timbers have broken at their weak point. We'll have to get some plastic sheeting up there until it can be sorted out. I'm sorry, Sarah. It's going to be a bigger job than we first said.'

She swallowed hard, staring at the broken slates that littered the ground. Her glance travelled up to the roof of the barn and her heart did a quick flipover in her chest as she saw the wreckage that was left. Part of the mid-section of the roof had caved in. 'Yes,' she said quietly. 'I guessed it might be.'

'Do you have any insurance on the building?'

She shook her head. 'No, I checked. The house is insured, but not the outbuildings.' She sucked in a deep breath. 'How bad is it? Do you have any idea how much it will cost to repair?'

He studied the shattered timbers for a minute or two. 'I reckon it'll take me and Josh a couple of full days to fix it. Then there's the cost of scaffolding and materials - I can give you a written quote, but off the top of my head I'd say you were looking at five or six times the original price I gave you.'

She nodded. 'That's more or less what I was expecting. Yes, let me have the written quote, Daniel.' She studied him thoughtfully for a moment, as doubts began to creep up on her. 'Are you sure you and Josh are up to this? After all, you're both still at College, and your course isn't in roofing.'

'Ah, it'll be okay, no worries. It's not my field, but I've done roofing before - a couple of jobs my College tutor found for me as work experience. One of them was to repair a barn roof, and my tutor did the work with me. Old barns like this one have a special construction, so you need to know about the specific joints. And Josh is already a qualified roofer. His course ends next month - like me, he'll just be spending time finishing off projects till then.'

She let out a soft, relieved sigh. 'All right, that sounds good.' A thought struck her. 'You'll be needing money up front, I expect?'

'For the scaffolding, and timber, yes... although my tutor might be able to loan me some scaffolding at a reasonable rate. I'll ask him. He's usually pretty good that way. I'll have a word with him and with Josh and try and get back to you with a quote by tonight. That way, if you want, we can try to make a start this weekend.' He glanced back at the barn. 'Is it all right with you if I get Rob and Jason to help me fix the covers in place up there to keep the weather out? I'll finish off the hutches as soon as we've done that.'

'Yes... yes, that's fine. Thank you for offering. They're out with the truck, delivering produce to the market at the moment, but they should be back soon.'

'I'll start making repairs to the rabbit enclosure, then, while I'm waiting. It's only a small job.'

'Go ahead. Thanks.'

He looked around at the clear blue sky. 'The one consolation is that it looks like it's going to be a beautiful day today.'

She smiled weakly. He was right. The sun lent an iridescent hue to the dew on the grass, and gave the farm a clean, freshly washed appearance. 'It does,' she said. 'I'll leave you to it, while I go and get myself sorted.'

'Okay.'

She went back into the house to shower and dress. One thing was for sure... she needed to go and talk to the Bank manager, and that wasn't a chat she relished. She already had a mortgage on her flat, and a bank loan would simply add to the load. Should she do what Jenny had suggested as an option and sell the farm in its dilapidated condition? She winced. Trouble was, that went against the grain. She was a fighter, wasn't she, not someone who would give up at the first hurdle?

As soon as she had eaten breakfast, she phoned the Bank to make an appointment for later that same afternoon. Looking out of the window as she tidied up the kitchen, she saw a small group of children had congregated in the yard, watching the lads at work putting the plastic sheeting on the barn roof. She smiled, seeing their eager faces. They loved everything about the farm, the space, the animals, even the crops in the field had them pointing and wondering about the power of nature to make things grow.

'Come on, Lexie,' she said, 'you have visitors. Let's get you and your brood outside in the fresh air. It'll do you good.'

She settled the Boxer and her puppies outside in the shelter of a spreading oak tree and went to help clear the debris from the floor of the barn. 'You need to stay outside,' she told the children when they would have followed her inside. 'I'm afraid the roof isn't safe. But you can go and feed the hens, if you like?' A chorus of approval greeted this suggestion, so she said, 'I'll get you some buckets and fill them with food pellets. And after that, there are eggs to be collected.'

The children stayed for most of the morning, helping out with little tasks she gave them. Rob and Jason took grain out to the sheep feed troughs and then tended the crops in the fields. Sarah looked around in satisfaction. For all her problems, things seemed to be running smoothly once more.

In the middle of the afternoon, she set off for her appointment with the Bank manager, parking her Fiat in a space alongside the village common. The pub across the way, the Blacksmith's Arms, had its windows and double doors open to let in the warm spring air, and the smell of freshly cooked food, savoury pies, pizza and chips wafted on the air.

'Hi, Sarah.' A friend called to her and waved as she locked the car. She was with another young woman that Sarah knew from around the village.

'Hi Abby, Becca.' She crossed the road towards them, heading in the direction of the Bank. 'Are you both on a half day today?'

'Yeah, the boss closed the place early for stocktaking, so we're headed for the pub,' Abby said, her glossy black curls quivering. 'Do you want to come and join us?'

Sarah nodded. 'Yes, okay, I'd like that... just as soon as I've finished at the Bank.' She checked her watch. 'I have an appointment there at four fifteen.' She made a face. 'Wish me luck.'

Abby grinned. 'Ooh, it's that kind of appointment, is it? Good luck!'

As things turned out, her meeting with the manager wasn't what she would have called a resounding success. Maybe he'd seen her at the end of a long day, a long week, perhaps, when he wasn't at his most receptive, but she'd put her case forward in the most positive way she could, and was met with at best a lukewarm response.

She left the Bank some half an hour later, heading for the Blacksmith's Arms, feeling wrung out, drained dry after being forced to give a wealth of assurances she wasn't altogether sure she could keep.

'Hello there.' She came out of her reverie to see that Raj Sayed had come up alongside her.

'Oh, hello, Raj.' She managed a smile. 'I thought I saw you in the Bank as I was leaving.'

'That is right. I had to bank some cash. I just made it to the cashier's desk before closing time.'

'That's good.' Even though she didn't feel much like it, she made an effort to be sociable. 'How are you settling in at the Manor House? Have you managed to unpack all the crates?'

'Oh yes. We are settling in very well, thank you. My wife, Jyoti, is keen to start work on revamping the garden. We have not been married for very long — just under two years, and I am happy to indulge her. She has given me strict instructions that there is to be a corner for a kitchen garden - she wants to grow cumin and coriander and chillies, as well as garlic.'

She smiled. 'Oh, very nice... you'll have a selection of home-grown curry plants to choose from, then.'

'Yes, indeed.' He gave her a long careful look as they walked side by side along the street. 'Forgive me, but you seem despondent, Sarah. You did not look happy when you came from the Bank.' He hesitated. 'I heard about your problem with the barn. Is it troubling you?'

Her eyes widened. 'Good grief, that was quick! News travels fast around here, doesn't it?'

'Ah, I apologize. I do not mean to pry... it is just that this morning my wife spoke to the children who came from the farm. That is how we knew what had happened. I am so sorry for your misfortune.'

'Oh, that's all right. Don't worry about it. I'm fine, really.' She came to a halt outside the open pub doors. 'I... um, I'm supposed to be meeting some friends in here,' she told him apologetically, and he chuckled.

'Me, too,' he said. 'Perhaps I can buy you a drink?'

'Oh... okay, thanks. That would be lovely.'

They stepped inside the bar together, and Sarah looked around for her friends, but didn't see them. Perhaps they were outside in the beer garden.

'What will you have?'

'An apple and watermelon spritz, please.' Right now, she felt she needed something stronger, something with a bit of a kick, but she was driving.

'Coming up.' Raj lifted a hand to greet a man who walked into the pub at that moment, and she saw that it was Geoffrey Hollins, the Estate Agent. 'Geoffrey helped me to buy the Manor House,' Raj confided. 'He moved a lot of obstacles that were in my way and smoothed my path. I am very grateful to him. I had been looking for the right property for some time – I had set my heart on owning a Manor House, though they do not seem to come on sale very often. When I was living in London I scoured the agencies - and as soon as I saw this one advertised I got on the phone to the Meadows Agency right away. I had to have it. There were other people who wanted to buy it, but Geoffrey made it easy for me. It is like a new beginning for me – I want to invest in property and land.'

'Hello there, Raj...' Geoffrey came over to them, glancing at Sarah and inclining his head in acknowledgment. 'It's good to see you, Miss Marshall. Are things going well for you at the farm?'

'Umm...' Unsure how to phrase the thoughts that were going through her mind just then, Sarah opened her mouth to answer, only to have Raj intercept her comment. She took a sip of her drink instead. Perhaps he had taken pity on her.

'Sadly, Sarah lost part of her barn roof in last night's storm,' Raj said. He ordered a drink for Geoffrey. 'So, things are perhaps not going quite as well as she would like.'

'Ouch! That sounds expensive. Is that going to be a problem for you?'

'Possibly.' She swallowed some more of her ice-cold drink and placed the schooner glass down on the bar. 'I've just come from seeing the Bank manager. I was hoping to get the money to do repairs and a little bit more.'

'Did it not go well?' Geoffrey Hollins appeared concerned.

She gave a hollow laugh. 'It depends how you view things, I suppose. He gave me the strong impression that the money in the vault belonged to him, personally, and he begrudged handing any of it over to the likes of me. I had to practically lever his hands off the safe just to get a fraction of what I wanted - that and promise him my firstborn child.'

Geoffrey chuckled at her woeful description. 'I'm sorry for laughing... I know it isn't at all funny. Believe me, I do know how difficult these financial bods can be.'

'Oh definitely.'

Raj interjected. 'You know, my offer to buy the farm still stands. You do not need to do anything with the barn. I will be glad to take it as it is.'

She frowned. 'But you would have to go to the expense of fixing it, wouldn't you?'

'Not necessarily. I am not particularly interested in keeping the whole property as a working farm. Buildings can be pulled down... or maybe a barn conversion would be in order.'

'As a dwelling, you mean?' Sarah was startled by what he was saying. Was he thinking of obtaining planning permission to use the land for some other purpose? A small housing development, for instance? Her grandmother would never have agreed to something like that. Would the local authority allow it?

'It is possible,' he answered. 'The farm covers a good acreage and there are several options to be considered.'

'Yes, I suppose so.' She was silent for a moment, turning it over in her head. The way things were, could she afford to be picky? 'I'll bear it in mind.'

'Please do.' Raj was smiling. 'You would not need to take on a bank loan – that is one thing worth thinking about, is it not?'

She smiled. 'You're right. Yes, it is.'

'And I could help you with the transaction,' Geoffrey said. 'I could make sure everything goes through without a hitch.'

'Thank you, I'll certainly call on you if I decide to sell.' Sarah sent him a quick glance. No matter how amiable he appeared to be, she couldn't put aside the niggling suspicion that he might have been involved in Jenny's death. 'How are things going for you at the Agency? Are you coping without Jenny?'

'I'm not doing too badly. She was certainly the mainstay of the business,' he said, 'but I think I'm holding my own. At least I don't need to confer with anyone over my decisions, any longer, so in some ways things are a lot easier and quicker. I shall have to bring in an assistant, of course, because of the sheer amount of work, but in essence I'm at the helm now.'

He sounded positively jaunty, and Sarah had a feeling Geoffrey Hollins took pride in being in charge. Perhaps he had never liked playing second fiddle to Jenny. Did that give him even more reason to want to be rid of her? Certainly, he would have had the opportunity to act on his wishes. He could have gone to her house while she was at the office or conducting a viewing - it would have been easy enough for him to leave the Agency on the pretext of going to meet a client, wouldn't it? And as Nick had pointed out, there were ways for anyone to get into a house without leaving a trace if they were determined enough.

Working in the same office meant he might have found an opportunity at some point to take her key and have a copy made without her knowing about it. She would only have to leave her bag lying around in the staff room, while she was with a client, to give him his chance. He could have taken her door key to a locksmith and been back within the hour. If Jenny missed her keys in the meantime he could have suggested she'd mislaid them somewhere, or dropped them, and then he would miraculously produce them for her.

'So, there you are, Sarah. Excuse me, gentlemen.' Becca came up to the bar and greeted Sarah with a smile, jolting her back to the present moment. She was a pretty girl, with long chestnut coloured hair tied back in a ponytail. 'We've been wondering where you got to. I'm just about to order food for everyone - are you going to come and join us outside?'

'Oh, yes... I'm coming now.' Sarah glanced at the specials menu written up in careful handwriting in chalk on a board above the bar. 'Do you want to order me a chicken fajita with a side salad?'

Becca nodded and Sarah handed over the money to pay for her meal. Turning to Raj and Geoffrey, she said quietly, 'It was good seeing you, but I must go and join my friends in the beer garden. I promise I'll think over what you've both said. And thanks for the drink, Raj. I'll buy one for you next time.'

She left Becca to place the orders and went outside to where her friends had commandeered a table on the terrace next to a group of women who belonged to the Village Fellowship group. They were eating cakes and pastries, and drinking wine or coffee whilst talking animatedly with one another. She knew several of the women, who were good friends of her mother, and it occurred to her that this was an opportunity for her to find out a bit more about Jenny's relationship with the villagers. Nick had said she wasn't universally liked, so probably someone in the Fellowship group would have something to say about her.

She sat down next to Abby and chatted for a while about her friends' employment at the craft workshop. Their boss bought in items from other companies but the firm also made goods that were sold in the small boutique in the village.

When Becca came back to the table and began to talk to Abby about someone she'd run into at the bar, Sarah took the opportunity to speak to the lady seated close to her at a nearby table. She'd met the woman when she attended course in local history earlier in the year and she was someone her mother had pointed out as the chairperson of the Fellowship group.

'Pauline, isn't it? Pauline Dwight?' Sarah introduced herself. 'I'm Sarah Marshall. We met on the local history course a few months back.'

'Of course, I remember you.' Pauline gave her a beaming smile. She was a large woman, probably in her mid-sixties, with neat silver-grey hair and keen hazel eyes. She was wearing a blue panel dress with lace inserts in the upper bodice and sleeves. 'We both have an interest in the village and its origins, don't we? Being a librarian, I suppose I'm in the right place to gather together all the information I need.' She pushed her fork into her gateau and took a bite, savouring the taste on her tongue. 'Is it right,' she said after a while, 'I heard you'd taken over ownership of Sweetbriar Farm?'

'I inherited it recently, yes.'

'Ah... it wasn't mentioned on the course, but there's a bit of history attached to the farm, you know? Back in the 1700s the Reverend Thomas of the parish used to live at the Manor House, but stabled some of his horses at the farm. We have access to copies of original documents from the period at the library - they used to be on microfilm but now they've been digitized along with most family history records - they're to do with the farm and the Manor House and, if I remember right, they show payments for alterations to the property, bills for goods that were purchased and so on. You might want to take a look, sometime. These old documents can be quite interesting.'

'I'll do that,' Sarah agreed. 'I'd love to know more about the farm.'

Pauline nodded. 'You'll be keeping it on, I take it? I knew your grandfather - he loved the farm and put all his energy into it so that he could pass it on to his son - your father, of course.'

'I would be loath to part with it,' Sarah admitted. 'As you say, it's been in my family for three generations, and I feel it would be wrong to let it go. But I have a job in town and I don't know how I can do that and run a farm. There's the expense, too. I'm finding there are all kinds of bills that need to be paid.'

'Nothing much has changed there, then!' Pauline said, and then became serious. 'But I do know what you mean. It's a difficult decision to have to make. Is there anyone who could advise you?'

'Actually, I spoke to Jenny Carter, the Estate Agent, about it. She was very helpful.'

'Hmm... yes, I heard she was good at her job.' She said it in a matter of fact, almost grudging, way that put Sarah instantly on alert for what lay in her thoughts.

Sarah nodded. 'It was tragic the way she died... it was such a shock.'

'Yes... yes it was. Of course, I never thought it was a good idea to use herbal remedies the way she did. But she was always trying to convert people to her way of thinking.'

Sarah detected a note of dissension. 'Did you and Jenny not get on?'

'Well -' Pauline shifted uneasily in her seat. 'She and I never saw eye to eye - she could be quite overbearing at times, you know. Jenny was full of suggestions about what we should do with the Fellowship group and how we might change things. I told people she hadn't thought her ideas through properly and they would lead to problems, but the members didn't listen - and I was proved right in the end. You can't take something that's worked fine for years and turn it on its head. It's a recipe for disaster.'

'You've been the Chairperson for the group for a number of years, haven't you?'

'Yes... we always have elections and people vote for who they want. But they always seemed happy to have me running things. I organize the meetings, arrange afternoon teas and charity events, and bring in speakers... I've worked tremendously hard for the group.'

Sarah gave her a thoughtful glance. 'But I guess everything changed when Jenny came along - she was fairly new to the group, wasn't she?'

'She was. She joined just over a year ago, a few months after she came to the village. But being new didn't hold her back.' Her lips tightened. 'She was straight in there with plans for trips to here and there, without a thought for the appropriateness of her ideas - the time of year, the weather conditions, or the problems for members who weren't able to walk very far.'

'I suppose that must have made life difficult for you when you had already planned the year's activities.'

'Oh, that wasn't the half of it!' Pauline was animated, warming to her subject. 'There was the gardening club - I had made up a schedule for our sessions. We were going to work on planting seeds and bulbs and taking cuttings at various times in season - I'd organized sessions for flowers, vegetables and herbs, but no, she had this whiz bang idea that got everyone fired up into buying plug plants and potting them on for hanging baskets and tubs to be placed around the village. A very expensive way of going on, when we could have grown our own from seed.'

Pauline was breathing fast by now, obviously still aggravated by even the thought of what had gone on. Her nose had clearly been well and truly put out of joint. Perhaps she had even been worried in case Jenny was voted in as Chairperson when the next elections were held.

'It sounds as though all your plans were being pushed to one side.'

'Oh yes!' She frowned, her mouth tightening. 'It was intolerable!'

'And now? What will the members do now that she's no longer here?'

'We'll have to pull together a programme of activities.' She sniffed. 'I'll offer my services, of course, if anyone wants to listen.'

'I'm so sorry. I hope things work out for you.' Sarah glanced about her as a waitress brought a tray laden with chicken fajitas, lasagne and a pasta dish. 'Our food's arrived,' she told Pauline. 'Excuse me, please. It was good to talk to you.'

'Me too. Don't forget to call in at the library. I'll point you in the direction of those documents on the computer.'

'I won't, thank you.'

Pauline nodded, then lifted her coffee cup and took a swallow, before turning back to join in the conversation with the ladies at her table.

Sarah went back to chatting with her friends as she carefully ate her fajita, but Pauline had given her food for thought. There were, as Nick had said, several people who might have wanted Jenny out of the way. But which one had been prepared to kill to achieve that goal?

CHAPTER EIGHT

'**YOU SAID** on the phone that you were worried about one of the goats.' Matt wiped his shoes on the doormat and came into the kitchen.

'That's right. It's Clover I'm concerned about. She's begun to limp and her foot looks swollen.' Sarah waved him to a chair by the table. 'Thanks for coming over so quickly. I wasn't expecting you much before twelve. I thought you might have a surgery to deal with first thing.'

He shook his head. 'Not today - I'm on call all day, so one of the partners is standing in for me. I have to go out to the Westfield Stables to see to one of their horses - some sort of respiratory problem from the sound of it. Not too urgent, I think, from the description of the symptoms. Anyway, Sweetbriar Farm is on my way, so I thought I'd pop in here first.'

'That's good. I bet you guessed I was just about to cook up some eggs for a late breakfast - do you have time to stay for an omelette?'

His mouth widened in a smile. 'That sounds great to me – I'm absolutely famished. I've been out and about since six this morning and I'm afraid I didn't stop to get anything to eat.'

'That won't do, will it?' Sarah busied herself cracking eggs into a bowl while the omelette pan heated up on the Aga. She put bread into the toaster and then poured the egg mix into the pan, adding diced ham and chopped tomato, with a sprinkling of pepper and salt.

While she was busy, Matt took himself off to say hello to Lexie and the pups, stroking the dog's head and tickling her ears. 'They're coming along really well, aren't they?' he said. 'And Lexie's coat is almost back to normal. You're obviously doing the right things.'

'Thanks, I hope so. She loves the puppy food I've been giving her.' She spread butter on the toast and took warm plates from the grill. 'This is about ready.'

'Okay. I'll wash my hands at the sink, if I may?'

She nodded, and served up the meal, sliding the plates on to the table and setting out cups and saucers alongside the teapot.

'Tuck in,' she said, when he came back to the table. Sitting down opposite him, she poured tea into the cups.

He studied her thoughtfully as he picked up his fork and scooped up the buttery egg. 'You're quieter than usual, today. Is everything okay? Is it the farm, or are you still worrying about Jenny?'

'A mixture of both, I'd say.' She bit into her toast. 'It's frustrating, because I'm still in the dark about what happened to Jenny. I'm learning quite a bit more about her, though. She was a forceful character by all accounts, not afraid to take control and push her own ideas to the fore, but that obviously didn't go down well with some people who felt she was interfering or taking over.'

Matt bit into a slice of toast. 'I only know about her dealings with Ben Reed. I got the impression she had a conscience and wasn't afraid to do what she thought was right.'

'Yes, and I admired her for that. But it wasn't just Ben she had trouble with – she rubbed other people up the wrong way, too. From what I've heard, the members of the Village Fellowship were looking to vote her in as their next Chairperson... but that didn't sit at all well with the woman in charge. Pauline was miffed, to say the least. She'd had prime position at the Fellowship for a number of years before Jenny came along and had everyone wanting to follow her lead. And on top of that, Jenny had some kind of falling out with the Griffiths. I still have to find out what that was all about, but I'm going to Natalie's salon this afternoon, so I might learn a bit more then.'

'It's a tricky one. Perhaps Nick Holt will come up with something.'

She ate a mouthful of omelette. 'Let's hope so, but I think he's still concentrating on these burglaries. He has to keep the Chief Superintendent happy.'

'Well, he can't upset the boss, can he?' He grinned, and then asked, 'And what about the farm? How are things going for you here?'

She made a face. 'Not too well at the moment. You must have seen the barn roof when you came into the yard?'

He nodded. 'I guess it was the storm did that.'

'It certainly didn't help!'

'Your Gran was troubled by the state of some of the outbuildings. She told me she couldn't afford to maintain them properly... there were always other priorities. I can't help wondering if she passed the farm on to you because her instincts told her you'd stick with it as long as possible - you can be resourceful when you're up against it.'

She was pleased he thought that of her. 'I try... and that's all well and good, I suppose, but even I'm finding things difficult just now.'

'Are you going to be able to get it fixed?'

'I'm hoping so. I can't afford to go with big firms that will charge the earth, but Daniel Richmond and his friend have agreed to do the work for me.'

'Ah yes, I know him. He comes into the surgery from time to time with the family dog, or his sister's hamster. Drives a Ford Transit.'

'That's the one.' Her brow creased. 'He was supposed to be coming by this morning - he sent me a quote for the work last night, so I transferred some money to his account for materials. He told me he was planning on going to the timber yard first thing this morning, as soon as they opened at eight, and he said he would call me to let me know when he was on his way here. I haven't heard from him, though, not even a text message, and it's already getting on for eleven.'

'Perhaps he's been held up with something or other - his van might have broken down.'

'Maybe. But the timber merchant closes at twelve today, and he said he wanted to make an early start here. He's keen to get the work done before he has to be back at College next week for the last few weeks of his course. It's odd he hasn't rung me. He's been very reliable up to now.' She frowned. 'The only consolation is that at least we have the sheeting in place, to keep the weather out.'

'You must be feeling this place is something of a poisoned chalice.'

She winced at his choice of words. It reminded her all too sharply of what had happened to Jenny. 'That's more or less what Jenny said when she looked around. It's old and historic, with great character, but it's also a money pit. I'm not sure how my grandmother managed to keep going... though she did have a sunny, laid back nature that probably helped her to ignore any negatives.'

'That must be why she named the goats Clover and Shamrock, and gave the hens names like Gobble, Clucky and Egghead.'

Sarah laughed. 'Oh yes! And some of them even come when they're called!'

They finished their meal and then Sarah took Matt over to the goat pen where she had isolated Clover. 'She's a bit touchy at the moment,' she warned him.

'I'm not surprised,' he said, pulling on a pair of surgical gloves and bending down to examine the animal. 'She has an abscess - she probably scraped her foot on a stone, and the wound has become infected. I'll need to drain it and then clean it.'

She pulled a face. 'That sounds as if it's going to be painful.'

'Yes - I'll give her a painkilling injection first, and then an antibiotic.'

'Do you need me to help or shall I leave you to it? Have you everything you need?'

'I'll be fine with her. I know you're busy. I'll come up to the house to get some warm water.'

'Okay. I'm sorry to leave you to it, but I'm expecting my mother to arrive at any moment - she's catering a dinner party for the Griffiths later today, so I need to go and get a box of supplies ready for her.'

'That's all right.' He walked with her to the house and she supplied him with a clean bucket filled with warm water, before heading off to the kitchen garden.

She filled a couple of trugs with freshly picked spring greens and asparagus, and then added onions from the barn. There was spinach in cloches, ready to harvest, along with a variety of herbs, including rosemary, mint, chives and parsley.

'Ah, there you are,' her mother said, coming into the garden. 'I thought I might find you out here.' Lexie had come along with her to see what Sarah was up to, her tail going ten to the dozen with excitement at being out in the fresh air.

'Hi,' Sarah answered. 'I've gathered together what I thought you might need. I'll put some fresh eggs in the box as well - then I just need to fetch you a sack of potatoes from the barn and you're all set, I think.'

'That's brilliant. Thanks, Sarah.' Her mother looked around. 'I was shocked to see the damage to the barn.'

'Yeah, me too. I'm hoping Daniel will come and fix it for me.' She glanced at her watch and frowned. 'I should have heard from him by now.' She lifted the trugs and turned back towards the farmhouse. 'Shall we go and get some coffee?'

'Good idea.'

Sarah placed the produce on the worktop by the fridge and set about making coffee while her mother went to admire Lexie's puppies. 'They're gorgeous,' she said. 'Little beauties.'

'They are. You can see she's a very proud mum.' Sarah smiled and slid a cup of coffee across the table towards her. Lexie clambered out of her bed and came to stand next to her, wagging her tail appreciatively when Sarah stroked her soft fur. 'Are you all prepared for this evening's dinner party?' she asked her mother. 'There are going to be quite a few guests, from what Natalie was saying.'

'Oh yes.' Hannah came to sit down opposite Sarah. 'It's not a problem. She has a well-equipped kitchen and she gives me free rein, so I've no worries on that score.'

'That's good. I don't know how Natalie's going to pull everything in - she's working at the salon all day today. She's giving me a cut and blow dry at four, and then she has to go home and host the dinner.'

'Oh, I don't think that will be a bother for her. She only has to go and make herself presentable.'

'I suppose so.' Lexie settled down at Sarah's feet. 'Perhaps she manages stress better than most... they were burgled recently. That must have been upsetting for them, especially coming at a time when her husband's business is possibly going through a difficult patch. She tried to gloss over that, but I'm sure things aren't going so well for them at the moment.'

'Yes, I heard about that on the grapevine. Jenny told me they lost quite a lot of valuable antique furniture, along with some distinctive pottery and oil paintings that had been handed down through the family.'

'It was quite a haul, then.'

Her mother nodded, sipping her coffee slowly and savouring the taste. 'Jenny told me she made a preliminary visit to the house when they first asked her to assess it with a view to putting it on the market for them. They had some beautiful furniture in there, but when she went back to the house a second time to make a note of which fixtures and fittings and so on they would be leaving behind, she saw that it was quite bare.'

She turned her head towards the kitchen door as Matt knocked and let himself in.

'Hi,' he said, acknowledging her, and then asked Sarah, 'Is it okay if I wash my hands here?'

'Of course. How did it go with Clover?'

'Well, she wasn't too happy to be poked and prodded, to say the least, but I've drained the abscess and put an antibiotic cream in the cavity. Her foot's in a sock now, and I've bandaged it. I'll come back tomorrow to have a look at her and give her another injection.' He rinsed the soap off his hands. 'It could take a week to ten days before she's completely better.'

'Oh, poor Clover... but at least she'll be feeling a bit better now. Thanks for everything you've done, Matt. I appreciate it.'

'You're welcome.' He dried his hands and then picked up his medical bag, ready to leave.

'Are you not going to have a coffee with us?'

He shook his head. 'No, thanks all the same. I have to go. They're expecting me at Westfield Stables.'

'Oh, okay.'

She saw him out, and her mother said, 'I must go, too. I have a few more provisions to buy -

meat... and fruit for a peach cobbler - and then I have to get set up in the kitchen.'

Sarah fetched a hessian sack of potatoes from the barn and loaded it into the boot of her mother's car alongside the vegetables and herbs. 'I hope it goes well,' she said. 'Good luck.'

They hugged briefly and Sarah watched as her mother drove off. Then she walked back to the kitchen and glanced at her watch once more. It was gone twelve o'clock by now and still there was no sign of Daniel. Where could he be? A feeling of dread crept over her... could he have been involved in an accident?

She rang his mobile, but although there was a ring tone, there was no answer. Concerned, she dialled his home phone.

'Hello, Ellie Richmond speaking.'

'Ah, Mrs Richmond, it's Sarah Marshall here. I'm sorry to trouble you... I was expecting to see Daniel this morning, but I've not heard anything from him. Is everything okay with him, do you know?'

Ellie Richmond pulled in a sharp breath, and when she answered her voice sounded strained, as though she was near to tears. 'No... no, it isn't,' she said. 'I'm sorry, I was supposed to ring you, but I've been so het up, trying to talk to people and sort things out.'

'What's happened? Is he hurt?'

'No, nothing like that. He's been arrested.'

Sarah stifled a gasp. 'When was this?'

'About nine o'clock this morning. He went out early with the van and then came back to pick up some tools.' She sniffed tearfully. 'They think he had something to do with the burglaries in the village. He was allowed one phone call and he rang me and asked me to get him a solicitor. I rang your firm - the receptionist said they'll send someone out to see him, but I'm not sure who's on call there today. The police won't let me talk to him. He's in custody and he isn't allowed any visitors, not even me.' Her voice broke on a sob. 'Is there anything you can do to help, Sarah?'

'I'll do what I can, Ellie. With any luck his solicitor will be able to arrange bail. I think Martin Tyler is on duty today... I'll talk to him.' Martin was a colleague she worked with closely and she knew she could depend on him.

'Thanks, Sarah. I'm so worried. They've confiscated his van, his phone, all his belongings. They're even searching the house and the shed in my back garden.'

'I know it's upsetting, but try to stay calm. I'll do what I can – I'll see if I can talk to Nick and Martin to find out the state of play, and I'll give you a call later.'

'Thanks.'

Sarah cut the call. Upset, and anxious to know why the police had decided to arrest Daniel, she rang her colleague, Martin Tyler, and asked him if he was the one dealing with Daniel's case.

'Hi Sarah - it's good to hear from you,' Martin answered cheerfully. 'I hope your holiday's going well. Yes, I'm in the car on my way to the police station right now. Do you have any idea what it's all about?'

'I think it's all to do with the burglaries that have taken place in the village,' she told him. 'Three of the properties involved were on Jenny Carter's Estate Agency books, up for sale, but I don't know how relevant that is.'

'Hmm. I don't know yet if the police have any evidence to charge him. They're probably just fishing, but certainly I'll do what I can to get him released on bail.'

'Will you let me know how you get on?'

'Of course. It's interesting to know about the properties being up for sale. That might have some bearing on why he's been arrested. I'll find out.'

'Thanks.'

'Bye, Sarah.'

She cut the call and paced the floor for a minute or two trying to work out what to do next. Nick was investigating the burglaries, so most likely he was the officer behind the arrest. She couldn't believe Daniel would have done anything wrong. He'd moved beyond his silly, juvenile behaviour and now he seemed to have a meaningful purpose in life, but that didn't count for anything with Nick. He had always been suspicious of Daniel. He had never believed he could turn his life around, had he?

She dialled Nick's number, and was relieved when he answered fairly quickly. 'Sarah,' he murmured. 'I wondered when I'd be hearing from you.'

'Of course... you knew I'd ring you - you've arrested Daniel Richmond, haven't you?' she said in a clipped tone.

'That's right. We think he had something to do with taking goods from houses while the owners were out, or while they were unoccupied. We'll be searching his home for evidence of stolen goods, as well as any other places connected with him.'

'Then you'd better come and search the farm, too, hadn't you,' she said crisply, 'because he's been spending most of his time here in the last few days? Perhaps he's hiding the goods in my barn, or in the pig pen. Why don't you come and look around?'

'You should know by now your sarcasm's wasted on me, Sarah,' he said in a droll tone. 'I understand you think he's on the straight and narrow, but I have to find out for sure. I'm just doing my job.'

'Oh, of course you are!' The words came out in an angry rush. 'He's been through College and he has a trade now. He's repaired my hutches and the enclosure, and he was about to fix my barn roof before you intervened. He's been more than helpful to me just lately. He was going to fetch the wood from the timber yard this morning so that he could get on with it, but I hear you've taken his van.'

'You're not telling me you gave him money upfront, are you?' He sounded appalled at the notion.

'Of course I did. How else is he going to do the job? I just hope you'll see sense and realize that it's high time you gave him a chance. You have to lose your prejudices. Not every young tearaway becomes a hardened villain.'

'Let's hope your faith in him is justified... but I have to question him. I'll do that just as soon as his lawyer gets here.'

'And then, when you realize you have nothing to hold him on, you can let him go, can't you?'

'Obviously, if we can't charge him, he'll go free. That goes without saying. Although we can keep him for several hours while we try to gather evidence.' He paused for a moment and then said, 'Ah... I shall have to go. I can see through the glass panel in the office that Martin Tyler's just walked in through the main doors. Very well-turned-out man, Martin. Definitely looks the part... suit, tie, briefcase, braced shoulders, ready for action. Always ready to steer his clients along the right road.'

'Good. That means you'll have to keep your wits about you, won't you?'

'Oh, you've a sharp tongue today, Miss Marshall.' She could hear the smile in his voice. 'Are things not going your way?'

She ignored his comment. 'Please try to put aside any bias you might have towards Daniel and treat what he says as though it might possibly be the truth. I'd be really grateful if you could do that.'

'O-oh...' He was smiling again, she could tell. 'You'd be grateful? Now that brings to mind all sorts of exciting possibilities.'

She made a choked laugh. The nerve of the man! 'Forget it! Not in this lifetime!' she retorted. 'I'm serious. I need you to understand just how important this is to me.'

'Yeah... I do.'

She ended the call and tried to work off her annoyance and frustration by finishing a few chores around the farm, taking Lexie with her so that she could get a bit of exercise. The dog was looking fitter every day and had taken to following Sarah about the place when she wasn't tending to her offspring.

'Men, Lexie!' Sarah said. 'Especially certain policemen! They can be so irritating.' Lexie panted happily, obviously willing to agree with anything she said.

The afternoon went by quickly and before too long it was time to tidy herself up and head off to the salon on the Main Street of the village.

'Hello, Sarah. I'm so looking forward to doing your hair,' Natalie greeted her. 'You're going to look beautiful when I've finished with it.'

'That's great. I can't wait!' Sarah went off with the apprentice to have her hair washed and conditioned at the basin, and a few minutes later she was back in the chair in front of the mirror.

'Natalie's just finishing with another client,' the apprentice said, after placing a fresh towel around Sarah's shoulders and carefully combing her wet hair. 'Would you like a drink while you're waiting for her?' she asked when she'd finished. 'Coffee, tea... or we have a selection of herbal teas. We have fennel, camomile, raspberry leaf and rose hip.'

'Oh, thanks, yes... I'll have coffee, please.' Before the girl turned away to go and fetch it, she said, 'It's unusual to be offered herbal teas - is this something you've always done at the salon?'

'We've had them for the last few months, I suppose. Mrs Carter brought them in for us. She liked the raspberry leaf infusion - she said it was relaxing and refreshing.'

'Was she a regular client here? Her hair always looked perfect.'

'Oh yes... she came in every few weeks for a trim and a colour rinse. She seemed a nice lady, always happy to chat. She told me all about the different kinds of medicinal herbs and what they were for. I was really interested in knowing all about them - I get headaches sometimes, and I'm not keen on taking paracetamol or ibuprofen too often, so she said why didn't I try feverfew? And next time she came in, she brought me some different herbal teas to try.'

'It sounds as though you got on really well with her.'

'Oh, I did. She was very friendly - to me, anyway.' She paused, lowering her voice significantly. 'Though I think there was a bit of friction between her and our boss last time she was here.' She glanced furtively at Natalie. 'I'm not exactly sure what was said - something to do with her taking the boss's house off the market, I think - but there was definitely a frosty atmosphere. She didn't make a follow-up appointment. It was very strange.'

'When was this?'

'Last week, sometime.'

'Oh dear. It sounds as though something went wrong, somewhere.'

The girl nodded. 'I'll go and get your coffee.'

That short conversation had given Sarah something to think about. Natalie and her husband would have been upset and frustrated if Jenny threatened to take their house off the market. Why would she do that? Geoffrey Hollins wouldn't have gone against Jenny to reinstate the sale, so the Griffiths would have had to look further afield for another agency. She could imagine that would have been enormously frustrating.

Natalie finished working with her client and came over to Sarah. 'So, shall we layer the sides just a bit, like this, to give the hair more movement?' She lifted the strands of Sarah's hair with her fingers and looked in the mirror as she debated how to style it. 'And what about the length at the back? Do you want me to take some off – shall we say a couple of centimetres? More?'

'That'll be fine, thanks.'

'Okay, then.' She set to work with the scissors, creating the style they'd discussed. As Natalie snipped, and strands of honey gold locks fell to the floor, Sarah could see the shape beginning to form, framing her face.

Making conversation as Natalie began to blow dry her hair a few minutes later, Sarah asked, 'Have you had any joy with the sale of your house? You said Mr Hollins would be handling things now, didn't you?'

'Yes, that's right. We're hoping things will get moving now.'

'They were stalled for a while, for some reason, weren't they? I expect the burglary must have sent things off track - perhaps that's why Jenny Carter was slow to act.'

'We thought it strange that some of Jenny's properties were burgled. I mean, was she giving out keys to prospective buyers so they could look around while the owners were away? We took a few days out to go and see our son and daughter in London where they're training, and we stopped over with relatives. Someone could have come into our house then. How could they have got in without breaking and entering - they must have had a key.'

'What did Jenny say when you confronted her?'

Natalie gave a sharp shrug. 'She denied it, of course. She said she always accompanied clients when they viewed a property, but she could have been making that up. She was always nipping home at lunchtime, or going off to her Fellowship meetings.'

'So, your relationship with her must have pretty much broken down after that?'

'Yes, it did.' Natalie deftly wielded the brush and hairdryer as she spoke, bringing about a magical transformation as she worked. 'Let me get the hand mirror and show you the back view,' she said, putting down her equipment a few minutes later.

Sarah viewed her image in the mirror with surprise. 'Wow, you've done a wonderful job,' she said with a smile. Her hair looked golden and silky, swishing lightly with gentle waves that outlined her face in a way that softened her features. 'Thank you, I love it.'

'My pleasure,' Natalie said, adding a touch of spray mist. 'If you keep it trimmed every six or eight weeks it will stay in perfect condition.'

'I will.'

Natalie was clearly distracted by the need to see to her other clients - perhaps that was why she'd been so open with Sarah. She and her husband obviously had an axe to grind with Jenny, but would that have been enough to want her out of the way? Surely not?

Sarah left the salon and walked over to her car, deep in thought. She didn't feel she was any nearer to finding Jenny's killer - the number of suspects was mounting up, and to add to her problems she still had the worry of wondering what was going to happen to Daniel.

CHAPTER NINE

SARAH WASN'T sure what woke her on Sunday morning. The sun filtered through her bedroom curtains, playing on her eyelids and causing her to squint until her eyes became accustomed to the light. The window was slightly ajar to let in some fresh air, and the curtain wafted a little on the faint breeze. It was pleasant, just lying here in bed, doing nothing, but then the creak of van doors being opened had her sitting bolt upright and paying attention.

Lexie barked. Through the open window Sarah heard the sound of male voices coming from the yard. Blinking to wake herself up properly, she glanced at the clock on her bedside table. It was seven o'clock.

Pulling on her robe, she went to the window and looked out, her eyes widening as she saw Daniel and his friend unloading wood from the back of the Ford Transit van. Relief washed over her - late last night when she'd rung to enquire, Daniel was still being held at the station, but it seemed Martin had worked his magic and managed to get him out on bail after all. When he'd called her yesterday, Martin had said Daniel wouldn't be released until the police finished searching his home and his van and any other property that might be considered relevant. Presumably they'd done that.

She hurried to get washed and dressed and went downstairs, anxious to find out what had been going on. Switching on the kettle, she made tea and then took two mugs of the piping hot brew out to the lads.

'How are you doing?' she asked, going over to the barn and looking up to where they were already beginning to work on the roof. 'I wasn't expecting you - it's so good to see you here.'

They stopped what they were doing and came down the ladder, accepting the teas gratefully. 'Cheers, thanks for this,' Daniel said. Josh acknowledged her with a lift of his mug before taking a sip. 'And thanks,' Daniel added, 'for putting a word in for me with Nick Holt.'

Her brows lifted in surprise. 'He told you I'd done that?'

'Yeah.' His mouth twisted. 'He still thinks I'm guilty, though, but he didn't have any evidence to charge me, so he let me out on bail while they go on with their enquiries.'

Sarah frowned. 'What made him suspect you in the first place, did he say?'

He shrugged awkwardly. 'I'm not exactly sure. He just kept asking about some work I'd done at people's houses - I've been getting work here and there at weekends or sometimes in the evenings after College. Word of mouth, really. One woman wanted a kitchen cupboard repaired and some other bits and pieces, so that she could get the house up to scratch before it went on the market... and after he saw what I'd done her neighbour asked me if I could build in a wardrobe for him - he wasn't selling his house, though.'

'Did you do work for anyone else?'

He nodded. 'Yeah, me and Josh laid some decking at a big house a couple of miles out of the village, and then someone else wanted a door replacing in his conservatory.'

'Ah - from what I've heard, I think the big house belongs to the Chief Superintendent. So, does Sergeant Holt think you went back later and burgled the houses?'

'I guess so.' He drank some tea. 'I didn't do anything wrong, but no matter what I say he still seems to think I'm behind it, somehow. I've got to keep reporting back to the station for the next month.'

'Do you know if the police have questioned anyone else?'

'They brought Tom Marchant in, and Ben Reed, and one or two others, but they haven't found the stuff that was stolen. From what I've seen Ben and Tom both have vans large enough to carry the goods, but whoever did the burglaries has probably spirited the stuff out of town by now.'

'I suppose so.' She looked at the wood they'd unloaded from his van. It seemed to her that there was plenty there to keep them going for a couple of days working on the roof. 'I'm glad they let you go, anyway, and especially glad that they let you have your van back. Do they know exactly when the thefts took place - if you could find out where you were at that time, it would put an end to all the questioning? You need to establish an alibi.'

He wrinkled his nose as he thought about it. 'Sergeant Holt mentioned a couple of nights in particular, but I can't remember what I was doing on either of them. Like I said, I was probably at the pub. My Mum can't remember, either. And Josh is my best mate and he hasn't a clue!'

He sounded accusing in a light-hearted way and Josh laughed. 'Too steamed to know, mate, more than likely!'

Sarah smiled. 'Well, I'm glad you're both here now, and making a start on my roof. I appreciate it. Give me half an hour or so and I'll have some breakfast on the table for you - bacon and eggs and hash browns. Is that okay for both of you?'

'Okay?' Daniel echoed. 'I think you're my favourite person as of now!'

'Sounds great,' Josh agreed.

Sarah made breakfast and spent the rest of the day doing chores around the farm, helped by children who came to see Lexie's puppies and who then wanted to go and collect eggs. She showed them the ducks on the pond and let them play on the hay bales in the open sided hay barn.

Daniel and Josh made headway with the repairs to the roof of the storage barn through the course of the day. By evening, when dusk was falling, the timbers were all in place on top of fresh roofing felt.

'You've done really well,' she said as they were putting sheeting in place that evening. 'I didn't think you'd manage to get so much done.'

'We just need to come and fix the slates,' Josh said. 'We'll be back tomorrow after College to make a start on that.'

'Thanks. I'm really pleased - you've done some good work today.'

She took Lexie for a walk in the late evening after the lads had gone, and then locked up for the night. She was taking no chances that Ben Reed would come back and find his way into the house. One confrontation with him had been more than enough.

On Monday afternoon, she left Rob and Jason to look after the animals and see to the crops while she went to pay a visit to the local library where Pauline Dwight was in charge. She wanted to know more about the history of her grandmother's farm, but she also wanted to know if Pauline could be considered a viable suspect in Jenny's murder.

'I'm afraid she's out at the moment,' the library assistant told her, 'but I'm expecting her back any time now.'

'Okay, I'll wait, then,' Sarah said. 'Is this a one-off, or does she often have to go out during the day?'

'Oh, she has to liaise with other libraries in the region - they exchange stock with each other every so often, or they get together to talk about admin. Sometimes she fills in for the mobile library service if someone's off sick... I think she enjoys doing it for a change of scene... and of course she takes books around and about to people who are housebound. Mostly she does that on a Saturday. She'll usually pop in here first, to get together a selection of books to show her regulars.'

'It sounds as though she's a very busy lady, one way or another,' Sarah commented with a smile.

The girl's mouth curved. 'She certainly is. She likes to keep on the move, sorting things out wherever she can. I think she gets a buzz out of being involved. Me - I don't have the energy!'

'I know the feeling,' Sarah answered. 'I'm discovering a day on the farm is enough for me!'

She went off to browse the non-fiction shelves for anything to do with running a farm or managing a small business, and as she was leafing through a book on the joys and pitfalls of owning a smallholding she noticed Pauline coming into the library through the side door. She left her alone for a while, giving her time to take off her jacket and settle in, and then went to speak to her.

'Hi, Pauline. I wondered if you could you spare a few minutes to show me the local history documents you mentioned the other day?'

'Oh, hello dear.' Pauline placed a stack of books on a nearby trolley for re-shelving and gave Sarah her full attention. Her silver-grey hair was neatly styled and her face was carefully made up with a light dusting of cosmetics. She wore a flower-patterned dress with generous gathers to encompass her ample frame. 'Of course. How are things at the farm? Is everything going smoothly?'

Sarah made a wry face. 'I wouldn't say so, not exactly. But they're getting better, I think. The storm the other night caused a major problem with my barn roof, but that's being repaired, so it's all in hand. I'll be happy when the job's done, though.'

'Roofing - oh my goodness, that can be an expensive business,' Pauline murmured. 'Have you chosen a local firm to do the job? We do have one or two builders in the village.'

'Daniel Richmond is fixing it for me, along with his friend. They're doing a good job, so far.'

Pauline nodded. 'Yes, I know Daniel - I used to see him around the village from time to time. Not so much lately. He did some work for me a while ago... made me a cupboard under the stairs. Lovely craftsmanship. I was very pleased with the work. And he was polite, too. I do feel that's important - youngsters need to show respect. Too many of them hang about getting drunk and behaving abominably these days.'

'I guess that's true of some young people,' Sarah agreed. 'They like to let off steam.'

'Hmm. Although, some time after he'd done the work for me, I did come across Daniel one evening, having an argument with a girl in the pub - something about her going off with some other man. I was there having a meeting with the Fellowship group at the far end of the lounge bar. It was quite disturbing for a while, and I was just about to get up and ask them to go outside when they left.'

'I wonder what night that would have been? Daniel's trying to remember what he was doing on a particular night, and it might help him to pinpoint things.'

'I'm not sure exactly, but it would have been on a Tuesday – that's when our group meets.'

'Do you often have your meetings at the pub? I thought my Mum said you met up at the village hall.'

'We go to the Blacksmith's Arms about once a month, nowadays, for a change of venue, and occasionally on a Saturday for a get together - something else Jenny Carter instigated.' She sniffed. 'I suppose it's all right as long as you don't have to struggle to make yourself heard.' She straightened, wriggling her shoulders as though shaking off an irritating memory. 'Anyway, let's go and find these documents you're interested in.'

She led the way to the bank of computers that were arranged on tables at one side of the room. 'We need to log on to the site first.' She sat down in front of a computer and Sarah took the seat next to her. 'Here we are -' Pauline mused, tapping the keyboard, '- now, where will we find information on Sweetbriar Farm? Let's see - it's a long while since I've accessed these records. Ah - here we have it. You have the census records going back to 1841... then the birth, marriage and death records for the people in your family.

Oh, and here's Reverend Thomas and the Manor House... there are several items collected together here, if you want to look through them. You can print out any that take your interest... there's a small charge if you do that.'

'Thank you, I will.' Sarah took Pauline's seat when she stood up to go and attend to her duties.

'I'll pop back in a bit to see how you're getting on,' Pauline said '- but you can call me over any time you need any help. You have an hour for free on the computer.'

'Okay, that sounds good.' Sarah turned her attention to the screen in front of her, but it was hard to concentrate. Her mind was partly on Pauline and the way she had clashed with Jenny at various times. Pauline liked to be in charge, at the forefront of things. Was she the sort of person who would do anything to retain her leadership role? She seemed like a pleasant, helpful woman, but Sarah had seen a completely different side to her when she started to talk about Jenny.

True to her word, Pauline came back some half an hour later to see if she needed any help. 'How are you getting on?' she asked. 'Are you finding your way about the local history site without too many problems?'

'I'm doing fine,' Sarah answered. 'It's really interesting.' She pointed to the screen. 'Look, there's an old recipe here, written by the Reverend Thomas's wife. It's for a savoury herb pudding - it had to be wrapped up in a muslin cloth and then boiled for a couple of hours. It says here it's made from flour, oatmeal and breadcrumbs mixed with lard, and she adds parsley, sage and leeks, as well onions and beets.'

Pauline looked at the document that was displayed on screen. 'Look at that beautiful copperplate handwriting.' She gave a contented sigh. 'Isn't it lovely?' Her gaze skimmed the recipe. 'I imagine people would eat that kind of pie as an accompaniment to meat in the days before we started adding potatoes to our diet on a regular basis.'

'Yes, probably. I wonder if the Reverend's wife ever brought a pie over to the farm as a thank you for being able to stable the horses there?'

'I'm sure they paid their way for the stabling, but yes, I imagine she would have come over with some sort of gift - and probably went away with produce from the farm, too.'

'More than likely. From what I gather, looking at these records, we've grown crops at the farm for three centuries.' Sarah sat back in her seat and glanced at Pauline. 'You enjoy growing things too, don't you? Have you managed to sort out a plan of action for the gardening club? Your plans were put on hold when Jenny came up with some alternative ideas, weren't they?'

Pauline appeared to bristle at the memory. '*I* shall go ahead with planting seeds and bringing them on in the greenhouse ready for the plant stall at the annual fête, as I've always done in the past. The other members are insisting on going ahead and buying plug plants for their project.' She drew in an aggrieved breath. 'Jenny's idea was that they would enter a best kept village competition and put up baskets and display tubs anywhere there was a free space. The members are all enthusiastic and ready to go for it - they even want to install them in the communal gardens in the sheltered housing block.'

Sarah's brows drew together. 'Can they do that? I mean, won't the management of the sheltered housing have to agree to it - and the residents - they own those properties, after all - they may have their own ideas of what they want, and not like having someone else decide for them?'

'Exactly! That's precisely what I said.' She bristled some more. 'I pointed out to them that you can't put these things wherever you like. Apart from anything else there are health and safety issues to consider. You can't have tubs and urns blocking the terraces in case ambulances and the fire service need access.

And as for baskets, they have to be at the right height, and they must not obstruct the pathway - I don't believe anyone has thought this through properly, let alone spoken to the Parish Council about it. I said as much, but no, Jenny pooh-poohed my objections. Of course, she's on very good terms with a couple of the councillors, wouldn't you know? *Everything* I've done over the last few years, she pulled apart as if it was of no consequence. "You have to move on," she said, "be open to new ideas," as if I had no idea how to organize group activities.'

Her voice was quivering with emotion by now, so much so that Sarah almost felt sorry for her. Jenny's actions had obviously cut deep into Pauline's heart, and left a festering wound.

'I'm sure the members appreciate all that you've done to keep the group lively and interesting over the years,' Sarah said, trying to be tactful. Her mother had said Pauline worked hard to arrange activities and outings, but privately she admitted to Sarah that maybe it was time for a change. Jenny was new blood and had some great ideas. 'I don't think anyone wants you to feel bad about their plans - they're all taken up with a new idea at the moment, but I feel certain they respect you for your organizing capabilities.'

Pauline sniffed unhappily. 'Well, I hope so, but I doubt it.' The assistant caught her attention just then and she said quietly, 'Excuse me, but it looks as though I'm needed over there... things are getting rather busy.'

'Of course, don't let me keep you.'

Pauline went away to attend to people who were beginning to form a queue by the library counter.

Sarah finished her research on the computer and then printed out a few papers that she wanted to file away at home. She paid the assistant for the copies she'd made and then left, heading back to the farm.

Rob and Jason were busy filling up the feed troughs and putting out fresh water when she returned. Lexie was sniffing around, following them wherever they went, tail aloft, wagging happily. 'Are you managing, lads?' she asked. 'Has everything been all right while I've been away?'

'Yeah, no problems,' Rob answered. 'Matt Beresford came and looked at Clover's foot. He put a fresh dressing on it and said it was healing nicely.'

'Ben Reed came while he was here,' Jason said. 'He looked shifty, but when he saw Mr Beresford he kind of backed off. He said he was here to ask about doing repairs to the property - I think he was making it up as he went along, but anyway, Rob told him it was all in hand.'

Sarah was alarmed. 'Did he go anywhere near the house? He didn't get into the kitchen, did he?'

Rob shook his head. 'No, we locked up for you once Lexie was out and we knew we'd be away from the yard. He didn't get the chance. Anyway, Mr Beresford told him he wasn't to come around here without calling you first. He said the police would want to know why he was hanging about.'

'I don't suppose Ben reacted very well to that,' Sarah said. She was worried that he might have tried to intimidate the boys if they'd been here on their own, though they were strong lads, and probably able to stand up for themselves.

'He swore at us,' Rob said, 'and moaned that we'd no right to tell him what he could or couldn't do, but there were three of us, so he backed off eventually.'

'Do you think he's going to be a problem?' Jason asked.

'Possibly. You did right to lock up. Thank you for that. If he comes round here again while I'm away from the farm, give me a call.'

'We will.' Rob nodded and put the sack of feedstuff he was holding back in the store shed.

Sarah went inside the house, deep in thought. If Ben came around again and appeared threatening, she would have to get some sort of restraining order against him. She still had the video from his last visit. If he'd treated Jenny the same way, it was no wonder she'd been feeling stressed.

She was still thinking about Ben and how she needed to get someone to install a reasonably priced security system as she looked over the papers she'd brought back from the library later that afternoon. Anyone could climb over the farm gate if it was locked and gain access if they wanted. Perhaps, years ago, there were more farm hands employed here, and security was less of a problem.

She laid the photocopied documents she'd brought with her from the library out on the kitchen table. There were drawings of planned extensions to the main farmhouse building, along with eighteenth century invoices from local tradesmen for the work that was done. There were maps, too, of the area and of the type of land use and how it had changed over the years.

She looked up as someone knocked on the kitchen door. She'd left it slightly ajar so that Lexie could come and go as she pleased.

'Hi Sarah,' Nick said. 'Is it all right if I come in?'

'Yes, of course, you're welcome...' She frowned. 'Unless you've come with a warrant to search the place.'

He laughed. 'No... no warrant. Though I am looking for Daniel. He's not here by any chance, is he?'

She shook her head. 'He'll be at College, I imagine.' She waved him to a chair and flicked the switch on the coffee machine.

'No, I've already tried there.' He sat down at the table. 'They say he was in classes until three thirty pm and then he left. He's not been home, either. I assumed he might have come straight here if he's going to work on your barn. I take it he'll start doing the repairs - he did use the money you gave him to buy timber?'

'Yes, he did, and he gave me a receipt for it. Actually, he made a start on the barn yesterday.' She frowned. 'He would have started on Saturday if you hadn't decided to lock him up.'

His mouth twitched. 'Sorry, but I didn't really have a choice. He's a prime suspect, after all. Anyway, do you have any idea where he might be right now?'

'No, sorry, I can't help you. Perhaps he's doing a job for someone - a woodworking kind of job, I mean,' she added hurriedly when his brow lifted in a cynical arch. 'Or maybe he's gone to pick up the slates for my roof.'

'Yeah, maybe.'

'Why do you need to see him, anyway?' she asked. 'You're not planning on arresting him again, are you?'

'Not right now... but somebody came forward this morning - said they saw his van around the village one evening in the vicinity of one of the houses that was burgled. I need to look into it.'

She sighed as she poured coffee into two mugs. 'I'm sure he'll have a legitimate reason for being out and about. You've checked him out, searched his van and his house and not found any evidence. Perhaps that should tell you something.'

He smiled. 'You make a staunch ally. Anyone ought to be glad to have you ready and willing to fight their corner.'

'Innocent people, certainly.' She gathered up the papers from the table and laid them down in a pile on the worktop. Then she put home-made scones on a plate and slid them towards Nick, setting out plates and cutlery, a butter dish and a jar of home-made strawberry jam on the table. 'Help yourself,' she said. 'I suppose you at least deserve one of these for letting him out on bail.'

He chuckled, and sliced his scone in half, carefully spreading butter on each slice and adding a spoonful of the rich, fruity preserve. 'I knew there was something about you I couldn't resist,' he said, biting into it with relish.

She made a dismissive gesture. 'Yeah, sure.'

He studied her thoughtfully as he ate. 'There's something different about you,' he said. 'Have you done something with your hair?'

'There speaks the detective!' she said with a laugh. 'Yes, I had it cut.'

'Mm.' He inclined his head. 'Looks good. You look good.'

'Thanks.'

'So, what are the papers you were looking at?' he flicked a glance towards the worktop. 'Anything interesting?'

'To me, yes. I don't know if they would be to anyone else. They're old documents concerning the farm. It's intriguing to me, to know the history of the place.'

'Does it make you feel more attached to it?'

'I suppose so, yes, in a way. It's such a dilemma, wanting to respect my Gran's wishes, and not knowing what to do.'

'Sometimes you just have to follow your instincts.'

'Yes, but they might turn out to be much more than I can afford. I'm half tempted to sell up. I don't know how I can keep it all together, not with things going on the way they are at the moment.'

'Then you need to come up with a plan... work out how you're going to make it pay, and if that's not an option, make the decision to sell, and walk away.'

She pulled a face. 'Maybe. I know you're right, but the thought of turning my back on it gives me a kind of guilt feeling, and anyway, I have other things on my mind right now. I can't think straight while I'm in the dark about why Jenny died. I have to know who killed her. I hate the thought that whoever did it is walking about, mixing with people, as free as air.' She sent him a penetrating glance. 'Are you getting anywhere in your investigations into it, or are you taken up solely with the burglaries?'

'Not just burglaries... there are other crimes being committed, maybe not around here in the village, but further afield in my district. But where Jenny Carter's concerned, among other things, I'm checking CCTV footage around the time of her death to see if I can find out where people were at certain times, or who was coming or going in the area where she lived. It's not easy, because the cameras are only situated in the main part of the village, so you can only get a general sense of where people were.'

'It must be difficult to be certain. But while we're on the subject, you should check CCTV footage to establish where Daniel was at the time of the burglaries. That could clear his name once and for all.'

He made a wry smile. 'Wow, I'd never have thought of that!'

'Okay, enough of the sarcasm. I'm just wondering if you've actually looked.'

'It's ongoing. There's a lot of footage to sift through. So far nothing's turned up, but it occurred to me that we might find something regarding Jenny Carter's killing.'

'Hmm. Do we know what time period we're looking at? I mean, the leaves could have been put in the basket several hours before she went home for lunch.'

'Well, they were fresh, so that suggests they were gathered some time on Saturday morning... any longer than that and they would have been dry and brittle. She must have gone home after visiting the pharmacy, so that gives us a time frame from when she left the house at eight in the morning to pay a brief visit to the Estate Agency, and around twelve thirty in the afternoon when she arrived home.'

'So, we need to establish alibis - but the other day you said everyone you suspected could account for their whereabouts.'

'They can, but there's always the chance they found an opportunity to slip away for half an hour or so.'

'Yes, that's true.' She thought about that for a moment or two. 'Pauline Dwight could have taken a break from delivering books to the housebound, and Geoffrey Hollins might have left the Agency for a while that morning. Ben Reed could have been anywhere on his travels between jobs.' So far, she didn't know the whereabouts of Lewis and Natalie Griffiths.

'You've been busy!'

'Yes. Do you have a prime suspect?'

He shook his head. 'Not yet... we have several people in our sights, and they each have a different motive. It's hard to tell which is the strongest. Money is always a strong incentive for murder, but so are resentment, hatred and revenge... and the grasp of power, of course. People have all sorts of reasons for wanting to kill others.'

'So, we need to find the motive and work out whether the alibis stand up to scrutiny.'

'No, Sarah. *You* need to concentrate on running the farm and working out what you're going to do with it. *I* need to find out who our murderer is.'

There was absolutely no way she was going to give up on her search for the killer, but she wasn't about to argue the point with him. Instead, she gave him a sweet smile, murmuring, 'In that case, you'll need lots of energy to keep you going, won't you? You'd better have another scone.'

CHAPTER TEN

'**HI, MUM.**' Sarah walked into her mother's kitchen and sniffed the air appreciatively. 'Mmm... home-made bread... scrumptious... it smells delicious!'

'I know, I love it, too,' Hannah answered, checking the contents of the coffee percolator. 'Makes the place feel warm and homely, doesn't it? Don't worry, I've saved a loaf for you!' She placed a couple of mugs on the worktop by the coffee pot and glanced searchingly at her daughter. 'You've had your hair layered at the sides - it suits you. It looks perfect.'

'Thanks... and for the loaf. Natalie did my hair for me on Saturday afternoon.' Sarah sat down at the table and offloaded a basket of fresh vegetables. 'I brought you some more supplies,' she said.

'Oh, that's great, thanks. Just what I needed.' Her mother looked around. 'No Lexie today?'

Sarah shook her head. 'No, I'm afraid not. She doesn't like to be away from the puppies for too long. They're still tiny and very needy - I suppose they'll be that way for two or three weeks until they begin to see and hear properly.'

'I think they're gorgeous.'

Sarah smiled. 'Yes, me too.' She stretched her jeans clad legs out under the table. 'So, how did the dinner party go at the Griffiths on Saturday?'

'I thought it went off really well. Everyone seemed to like my food, anyway. One woman asked for one of the recipes!'

'Well, that was a compliment!'

'Yes, it was.' She poured coffee and passed a mug to Sarah. 'I'm always pleased when people make favourable comments.'

'I imagine you get a lot of those.' Sarah added sugar to her cup. 'How were Lewis and Natalie? Did they seem pleased with the way the evening went?'

Her mother's mouth twisted a little. 'I'm not sure about that, actually. Oh, they were happy with the food, definitely, and their guests were all relaxed and quite merry - not surprising, really, after the amount of wine they drank... but I thought Natalie and Lewis were a bit tense. I doubt their guests would have noticed, but I was aware of it whenever either of them came into the kitchen.' She was thoughtful for a moment or two. 'I'm not certain why that was, exactly -

though I think Nick Holt had been to see Lewis earlier. That might have troubled him a bit. I was in the kitchen, preparing the food, so I only heard snatches of conversation... it was to do with the burglary, I think. He said they'd arrested someone, but he wanted to know more about what they thought Jenny's part was in it. I didn't hear any more.'

'They thought Jenny had allowed somebody access to their property while they were away for a few days, but that doesn't seem very likely to me.'

'No, nor me. She was a stickler for doing things right. To be honest, the Griffiths seem a bit cagey to me, just lately. It could be business worries, or perhaps they might be unhappy about downsizing - though from what I gathered on the night, Lewis did get some offers of work.'

'That's good. I suppose the burglary must have shaken them up. It must be really upsetting to know that your home has been invaded and ransacked, that strangers have been through your belongings. It must make them feel very unsettled.'

Her mother nodded. 'I know they were very put out when Jenny said she would take their property off the Agency's books. They were worried they would have to go further afield to find an agent to act for them.'

Sarah frowned. 'Well, I don't see how that would have been too big a problem for them.'

Hannah looked uncertain about that. 'I think it might make people anxious if they've built up their hopes, gone through with all the photography for advertising and had the surveys done and so on, and then find they have to start all over again. I've a feeling Lewis was quite disturbed at the prospect.'

'Still, Geoffrey Hollins will be dealing with the sale now, won't he?'

'Yes, he is. He's found them a smaller property about three miles away from here. It's a three-bedroom house, so it'll suit their needs, albeit it's much smaller than their present place – that's what Natalie told me.'

Sarah swallowed her coffee. 'I think I might go and talk to Mr Hollins again, and see if I can find out more about this business with Jenny and the Griffiths. I can't help feeling there's something they're not telling us.'

Her mother tilted her head to one side, looking at her with a mixture of anxiety and understanding. 'You're determined to find out what happened to her, aren't you? Are you sure that's wise? Perhaps you should leave it to the police - I don't want you to get hurt, and I think, if you start delving too deep, you might stir up something you can't control.'

Sarah shook her head. 'I can't leave it to the police - except for Nick, they think it was suicide or an accident, and they won't put any resources into an investigation. I'll be fine. Believe me, Mum, I can look after myself.'

'I hope you're right.' She looked worried. 'Be very careful, Sarah.'

'Of course, I will.' Sarah patted her mother's hand in a comforting gesture, and a few minutes later she stood up to leave. She took with her the loaf her mother gave her, wrapped in tissue paper, and throughout the journey to town the wonderful smell of newly baked bread wafted around her in the car.

She found a parking space in a bay some way down the street from where the Estate Agency was situated. It was a busy area close to the centre of town, and she walked past a number of businesses, which included a hardware store, a locksmith and a pub. There was a greengrocer, too, displaying fruit and vegetables on stalls covered with green grass matting outside the shop front.

Geoffrey Hollins was dealing with a client when she walked into his office a few minutes later. He acknowledged her, mouthing silently, 'Be with you shortly,' and she nodded, using the time to wander around the room and study the photographs of properties for sale or to rent.

Her glance skimmed over pictures of flats for sale similar to the one she owned in the centre of the village. It seemed that prices had risen in the few years since she'd bought it. Houses like her mother's, on the other hand, were very much sought after, and were at the upper end of the market. She moved on to look at the commercial property boards, and discovered there were a couple of smallholdings being offered for sale. She noted the details of the kinds of prices they were selling for.

'Ah,' Geoffrey said, coming to stand beside her after his client had left. 'I see you're looking at the farms on our list. Does that mean you're considering Mr Sayed's offer?'

'I'm certainly thinking about it,' she told him. 'I'm finding it quite difficult to manage at the moment - there are so many bills to pay... staff wages, food supplies for the animals, vets' bills... and that's without all the repair and maintenance costs for the buildings.'

He gave a soft, sympathetic sigh. 'It always sounds like an idyllic dream, doesn't it - the good life in the countryside, with a few grazing animals and some crops in the field? Unfortunately, as you're discovering, there's a little more to it than being a so-called 'gentleman farmer'. It isn't such an easy life.'

'You're right. It's turning out to be a lot more involved than I thought, and very expensive. I keep going over and over it in my head. I need to keep my job at the solicitor's office just to pay off the bank loan. Even if I hire more staff, I don't see how I can do both jobs properly. Perhaps I need to think things through a bit more carefully.'

'Do you want me to look into Raj's offer?'

She pulled in a deep breath. 'Well, at least you might find out what he's willing to pay for the farm if it's in good condition. After all, the barn roof's been repaired, the hutches and enclosure are almost all fixed, and there's only the fencing along the perimeter of the sheep field to be mended. I know the kind of money I'm looking for - it all depends if he's prepared to meet it.'

Geoffrey smiled. 'I think you'll find he's more than happy to give you what you want... he's so keen to own the property.'

She wasn't quite as convinced as he was. 'Won't he be overextending himself? I don't know his circumstances, but he's just bought the Manor House, and that must have left a big dent in his finances.'

'Oh, I don't believe that's going to be a problem. I said as much to Jenny when she said much the same thing as you've just done. Of course, she didn't know him the way I did. She hadn't even met him. I was the one who carried out all the negotiations on his behalf - a lot of it on the phone, because he was in the middle of doing a business deal in London. As it was he practically bought the Manor outright, and when the proceeds from this latest deal come through he'll be able to buy the farm with only a small mortgage.'

'He's a wealthy man, then... which means he shouldn't have too much trouble coming up with the right price for the farm.' She frowned. 'Even so, I'm not making a definite commitment. I haven't quite made up my mind what I want to do.'

'Don't worry about it - it's a woman's prerogative to change her mind, or so they say. I'll make it clear to him that you're just exploring alternatives at the moment.'

She smiled. 'Thank you.' She decided to change the subject. 'And how are things going for you here at the Agency? Have you managed to hire an assistant, yet?'

'Not yet, unfortunately. I'm still looking. I've been interviewing people, but I haven't found the right candidate yet. I need someone who has some knowledge of the area, and who can be organized and pay attention to detail. And someone who can be trusted to deal with clients while I'm away from the office.'

'Yes, of course - it must be difficult for you at the moment, having to stay in the office all the time to see prospective clients who come in off the street.'

'Oh, there are times when I have to go out - to view properties, and show people around. It was a lot easier when Jenny was here, in that respect, anyway, because we could work things between us. Now, if I need to go out, I have to shut up shop and put a notice on the door.'

In that case, he could have done the same thing on Saturday morning while Jenny was away from the Agency, talking to Sarah at the farm. And on the same principle, he could have perhaps taken the house key from Jenny's bag while she was busy with a client in the ante-room and slipped out with it to the local locksmith's shop to have a copy made. That would only have taken a few minutes. It was all conjecture, of course, but it was possible.

'It sounds as though you and Jenny didn't always see eye to eye,' she said, picking up on his comment about it being "easier in that respect, anyway." 'You seemed to imply that being here with her was maybe not easy sometimes.'

'Well, I mean her no disrespect, but she could be difficult at times. She was a very forceful woman, who knew what she wanted, and she generally tended to get her own way. We disagreed over a few things.'

'Really?' She lifted a brow in query. 'May I ask what kind of things?'

'Oh, I suppose the last one was the Richmond lad.'

'Daniel?' She was surprised to hear his name mentioned.

'That's the one. He came in one day, not too long ago, actually, and wanted to leave some business cards and leaflets with us. His stepfather had arranged for a bundle of the cards to be printed and Daniel was keen to put them about and try to find work before he left College. Enterprising of him, I thought. He said he wondered if any of our clients needed repairs doing, if they were selling up, or if they wanted bespoke furniture fitting in properties they were buying, perhaps we would hand them one of his business cards and maybe put in a word for him.'

'Wow, that sounds as though he was keen to get ahead.'

'Yes, I thought so, too. I said I was happy to recommend him to our clients, but Jenny wouldn't hear of it.'

'She wouldn't?' Sarah was surprised. 'That must have been a setback for the lad.' Even though this had happened in the past, she was disappointed for him.

'Oh yes, you could see he was taken aback. But she said she lived in the same village as him and he'd been a hooligan in his younger days and couldn't be trusted.'

Sarah frowned. 'He must have tried to tell her that he'd changed, surely?'

Geoffrey nodded. 'He did, but she wasn't ready to listen. She was curt and almost rude to him. I could tell he was upset. After all, it was a snub, like a slap in the face. All the colour drained out of him.'

'But he did actually find work with some people who were on Jenny's client list, didn't he? How did that come about, do you know?'

He shrugged. 'Word of mouth, I think. And he put cards in the local newsagent's window, and anywhere else that would take them. Dropped leaflets through letterboxes, too.'

'Jenny must have thought she was doing the right thing, protecting her clients. I imagine in business you can't afford to take risks. Your reputation is everything if you want to keep bringing in customers.' She shook her head. 'That's why I can't imagine her giving the Griffiths' house key to people so that they could look around while they were away. Would she have done that?'

'It's unlikely, I'd say, but possible if she really trusted someone.'

Sarah stayed to chat for a little longer, but then as a customer came into the office and Geoffrey went to deal with him she took her leave. She drove back to the farm, her mind busy turning over everything she'd learned.

Daniel arrived late in the afternoon as she was coming back from collecting duck eggs from the grassy area around the pond. Lexie trotted alongside her, enjoying the walk.

'Hi,' Daniel said, jumping down from the cab of his van and going around the back to open up the doors. 'I've brought the last two hutches with me. They're all finished now - I've strengthened the doors and renewed the wire mesh and the safety catches.'

He lifted them down to show her and she inspected his work. 'That's brilliant, Daniel. They're perfect. Thank you.'

'I'll carry them over to the enclosure, for you,' he said, and she quickly called Rob and Jason over to help. 'They're too big and cumbersome to manage on your own.' Her grandmother's rabbits had the best in luxury accommodation, weatherproofed two storey homes with double doors and a covered run.

'That's probably about it, as far as repairs are concerned,' Daniel said, when the hutches were in place in the enclosure and Rob and Jason had gone back to work, planting out potatoes in the lower field.

'Actually, there is one more job that needs doing,' Sarah commented. 'The fence in the field where the sheep graze is falling apart. I made a temporary repair last week, but it looks as though it's not holding, and there are other parts that are breaking down. I wondered if you would have a look at it for me?'

'Sure. Shall we go over there now?'

'Good idea.' Lexie bounded along beside them, happy to have a few extra minutes of freedom away from her demanding brood. As they walked, Sarah remembered her conversation with Pauline Dwight. 'I was talking to someone the other day,' she said, 'who says she saw you in the pub one evening with a girlfriend. I wondered if that might jog your memory at all - could it have been one of the days the sergeant was asking you about? You were having an argument with the girl.'

'That would be Charlotte,' Daniel said, nodding. 'We're not together any more. I found out she was two-timing me, so I finished it.' His brow creased. 'Can't remember what night that was. We'd had a drink, and we were going to get an Indian takeaway, but then while I was at the bar, I saw her talking to this fair-haired guy from the gym. She was all over him, wide eyes, lapping him up, so I lost it a bit. He was all muscle, you know, tee shirt showing off the dragon tats on his arms, and a big grin on his stupid face.'

He was silent for a while, thinking. 'We had a row and she went off with him, and I went and

201

found Josh at the chippie. He'd had his preliminary results from College, so he'd bought a pack of lager and celebrated by having a few too many.' His mouth made a faint grimace. 'I don't know if it was one of the days Sergeant Holt was asking about.'

She sympathized with him. 'Well, the publican will probably remember you, if you and Charlotte were being loud. And they might remember you and Josh at the chippie.'

'Probably... Josh spilled a can of lager all over the floor.'

She laughed. 'Oh dear.'

They arrived at the field where the sheep were grazing and Sarah showed Daniel the fence posts that had rotted after years of being battered by the elements. 'Is it going to be a big job?' she asked.

He walked along the length of the field, studying the damage. 'No, not too big. About half a day should do it.'

'Will you have time to fit it in, with your College work?'

He thought about it. 'I need to work on my final project so my tutor can grade it within the next couple of weeks, but I could probably come and fix the posts early Sunday morning if that's okay with you.'

She nodded. 'That's fine. Do you need money in advance for the wood - do you have to go to the timber yard?'

'No, that's okay. I should have what I need in the lock-up.'

'I didn't know you had a lock-up. What is it - a garage or store of some sort?'

'It's a garage... in a block of garages that are for rent... belongs to my stepdad, but he lets me store stuff in there.'

'Oh, I see. That's handy for you. Is it close by?'

'It's at Barton Wick, a couple of miles from here.'

'Barton Wick,' she mused, 'isn't that near Brackley Close? I seem to remember the name from when I went over to Jenny Carter's house.'

A muscle twitched faintly in his face at the mention of Jenny's name, but he said, 'Yes, that's right. The Griffiths have a lock-up there, too. Theirs is on the corner, a couple of doors down from mine.'

'Do they? I didn't know that. I'd have thought they would have preferred something closer to the business premises.'

'Maybe they bought it before they got the business, so that they could store odd bits and pieces.'

'Yes, perhaps.'

'I didn't get a good look,' Daniel added, 'but I did see some stuff in there, recently. It didn't look like anything to do with engineering. I was loading some timber on the van, and Lewis was just coming out of his lock-up. I don't think he took too much notice of me, because Jenny Carter was going by just then, taking Lexie for a walk. I sort of nodded to her, but she didn't acknowledge me. She probably wouldn't anyway, but she did seem a bit distracted at the time.'

He frowned. 'It was a bit odd, really, come to think of it, the way she reacted. She was looking at the lock-up and trying to keep Lexie from going in there and sniffing around, but she seemed to go a bit strange all at once. I thought she was embarrassed at seeing me and was being awkward or something because we'd had a bit of a run in earlier, but I'm not so sure now.'

'Did Lewis speak to her?'

He shook his head. 'No, he just quickly shut the door and padlocked it and then got in his car and drove away.'

'It might have been nothing at all, but it does seem a bit strange.'

'Yes, it does.' He glanced around. 'So, do you want me to go ahead and repair the fence?'

'Yes please,' she told him. 'I'd be glad if you could fix it for me.'

She walked with him back to his van and waved him off, but all the time she was deep in thought. 'Go back into the house, Lexie,' she told the dog as she opened the kitchen door. 'I think your puppies will be wanting you.'

She flicked the switch on the coffee machine. Had Jenny seen something that night that led to her murder? Somehow, she had to go and find out what was in that lock-up. Most garages had a window somewhere, didn't they, so with any luck she might be able to take a look inside.

Taking her coffee over to the table, she sat down and tried to work out a plan of action. Perhaps if she wrote down everything she had learned so far about Jenny and the people who had dealings with her, she would be able to see her way through the facts she had assembled and pin down the person responsible. It was how she worked as a paralegal, gathering together information, keeping records, sifting through statements, ready to present them in Court.

Working late into the night, she wrote names on cards, names of people who were connected in some way with Jenny, along with any statements they'd made, and anything she'd learned about their whereabouts on that crucial Saturday morning.

Darkness fell, and she got up to stretch her legs and put another log into the wood burning stove. She poured herself a second cup of coffee and ran her fingers through her hair in frustration. There were a number of people who might have had grievances against Jenny, but would they have been driven to commit such a terrible act?

Lexie barked suddenly, making her jump. The dog was alert, ears pricked, anxious and on edge. Sarah went over to her and stroked her head, murmuring softly and trying to calm her.

'What's wrong, Lexie? Did you have a bad dream?'

Lexie barked again, and this time Sarah heard a faint scraping coming from outside in the yard, followed a few seconds later by the sound of breaking glass. As she listened, stunned, another cracking, shattering explosion of noise rent the air. And another. And another.

Scrambling her wits together, she hurried to unlock and unbolt the kitchen door with fingers that were shaking with foreboding. Who was out there? What was going on?

Snatching up a torch from the kitchen cupboard, she ran outside and looked around.

'Who's there? Come and show yourself. Face up to me.'

There was no one to be seen, only the light of the moon throwing long shadows from the buildings out over the cobbled yard. A vehicle started up, somewhere out beyond the farm gate. She heard the burst of acceleration and the crunch and spatter of gravel as it moved away at speed.

She'd heard glass being broken, somewhere in the distance, but whereabouts had the damage been done? Shining the torch over the outbuildings, she could see that all the windows were intact. She frowned. So where else should she look?

Then it came to her... there was glass in the kitchen garden, in the old cold frames where she was nurturing her spinach and herbs and salad vegetables... had they been the target of the unknown vandal? They were coming along so nicely and she would be devastated if she discovered all their hard work had been destroyed.

She made her way over there in the darkness, and aimed the torch beam over the garden. It was too dark to see much, but the rays of light danced off the glittering shards of glass that lay all around.

'Wretch!' she muttered. Whoever had done this was a vengeful, hateful person. And who was the likely candidate who would want to make her pay for what she had done to him?

There could only be one answer, surely. This was the work of Ben Reed. It had to be. But how could she prove it?

Basically, she couldn't... that was the exasperating truth of the matter. Just as with Jenny's murder, she was no nearer to pinning down the culprit.

CHAPTER ELEVEN

'**THANKS FOR** letting me know, Sarah.' Martin Tyler, Sarah's work colleague, paused for a moment on the other end of the phone line, and Sarah guessed he was jotting the information down on a notepad. 'I'll check with the publican and the proprietor of the chip shop and see if we can come up with dates and times. The same applies to the exam results Daniel's friend received. It shouldn't be too difficult to find out when they were given out.'

'That's great, Martin. I appreciate it. It would be good to know if Daniel has an alibi that stands up to scrutiny.'

'Yes, I'll look into it and then if I manage to come up with something, I'll let you and Nick know.'

'That sounds good. I don't know anything about the man from the gym that Daniel mentioned - I go to the fitness centre myself once a week, but I've never come across him. I guess I could make enquiries. He would be another witness to say where Daniel was on that particular night.'

'Oh yes... it all helps... the more information we have at our fingertips when we're working a case, the better.'

Sarah knew that, of course. As a paralegal she was used to checking into these sorts of things in the course of her work.

She heard a slight clicking sound as Martin set his pen down on his desk. 'So how is the holiday on the farm going? Is it all working out for you?'

She gave a soft laugh. 'Holiday? You're joking! I don't think holiday is quite the right word... and as to whether it's working out, I'm not at all sure. I've already had to pay out for repairs to the barn and the animal housing, and just when I thought I was getting on top of things someone came to the farm in the early hours of this morning and vandalized the kitchen garden and smashed the glass in the cold frames.'

Martin sucked in his breath. 'I'm so sorry to hear that, Sarah. Did you see them? Is there any reasonable chance of getting the person who did it?'

'No, I don't think so. All I saw were shadows. It hasn't rained, so there are no footprints to be seen, and I don't think he's left any other evidence behind. It's probably one of those things I'm going to have to chalk up to experience. I've rung the police and they've given me a crime number, but I doubt they'll send anyone out to see the damage any time soon... lack of resources is the usual response.'

'So, what will you do, about the farm, I mean? Have all these setbacks put you off?'

'Maybe. It was a bit disheartening having to deal with yet another problem - all that work the boys have put in on the kitchen garden has been destroyed.' She sighed. 'Part of me would love to be able to carry on here, to make a go of things, keep them in a job and work out a way of making it pay, but so far I'm not coming up with any answers. Even with Rob and Jason doing the heavy stuff around the place, the farm is time-consuming, and I'm beginning to realize I won't be able to do it justice while I'm carrying on with my job at the office. It's just not feasible.'

'Hmm...' His voice was full of sympathy. 'I admit, I was quite apprehensive when you said you'd inherited the farm. I knew at some point you'd have to make a choice between taking it on or staying with us... but I must tell you, it's not been the same without you this last week. I hope you know we would hate to lose you, Sarah - this firm needs you. The boss was just saying the other day how smoothly the office runs when you're around, and the clients love your calm and organized approach. One or two have been asking for you while you've been away.'

'Oh, it's nice to hear that.' She smiled. 'It's reassuring to know that people value what you do.'

'They certainly do. They know that you care - that it isn't just a job to you. You've helped a lot of people through difficult times with your practical, efficient way of going on. I can't help hoping that you'll decide this is the life for you, and that you'll keep working with us.'

'Thanks, Martin. It's good to know you feel that way. I promise, I'll let you know as soon as I've come to a decision.'

Sarah spent the rest of the day doing jobs around the farm, first of all photographing the destruction from the night before. Then she cleared up the broken shards of glass from in and around the cold frames and tried to work out what she could do to protect the plants from the elements. It was only when she moved some of the lettuce leaves to one side in one of the cold frames that she noticed a half brick lying on the soil, and realized it must be one of the missiles that the intruder had thrown. Inspecting it closely without touching it, she saw that there were some red specks on the surface of the buff coloured clay.

'Have you found something?' Rob asked, and she nodded.

'Perhaps. I'm going to take a photo of that brick in situ and then I'll put it in a bag to show Sergeant Holt when I next see him.'

'There were some in the other cold frames,' Rob said. 'Sorry, I threw them in the skip with the old wood and rubbish.'

'That's okay, don't worry about it.' She went to fetch a polythene bag from the kitchen and carefully, without touching the brick with her fingers, put it into the bag and sealed it. 'The lab won't be able to get fingerprints from it, but there may be DNA evidence on there,' she said. 'I'll stow it away for safe-keeping.'

Rob nodded. 'Good idea. I'll wrap up the glass for you and put it in the skip. At least the crops in there have survived, for the most part. Shall I cover the cold frames with polythene sheeting until you can get the glass replaced?'

'Yes, please, Rob. That's a good idea.' She sighed. 'I'll have to get my tape so that I can measure up and get some replacements cut.'

He glanced at her. 'Are you okay? We were wondering, me and Jason, if you'd been upset by all this. You seemed a bit low, first thing. We thought perhaps it might have left you feeling down and make you want to give up.'

She thought about it. 'I suppose it might have, and I *was* out of sorts this morning when I saw all the broccoli and spring greens trampled and broken - all your hard work ruined - but strangely enough, I think this latest setback is beginning to have the opposite effect on me. While I've been clearing up I've been feeling more and more annoyed that someone should have the nerve to come here and try to wreck the place. I'm determined that I'm not going to let these things get me down.'

'Good for you!' He grinned, and went off to the barn to fetch some old newspapers to wrap up the glass.

Sarah tackled the rest of her jobs with gusto, a fire in her belly, and a new burst of vigour urging her on. She went back into the house and cleaned the Aga, getting rid of all her pent-up feelings of aggravation and then, late in the afternoon, she went to the hardware store in town to get the replacement glass cut.

In the evening, when everything was quiet on the farm, she took time out to study the notes she'd made on Jenny's murder the previous night, and tried to make sense of them. Only one thing became clear. She had to go out and find out more... and she would start by taking a look at Lewis Griffiths' lock-up. If there was a window in the garage it might well be high up where she couldn't reach, so she would need to make provision for that. With that in mind, she brought the foldaway steps from her kitchen and stowed them in the boot of her car. The biggest problem was making sure she wasn't seen. How would she explain her actions if anyone challenged her?

Sarah waited until it was dark outside, and then she pulled a black hoodie over her black jeans and shirt and drove the couple of miles to Barton Wick. The sky was overcast, the moon masked by a dark cloud formation. She felt a pang of sorrow cramp her stomach as she went by Brackley Close, where Jenny used to live, remembering how she'd found her slumped unconscious on the floor of her kitchen. A feeling of helplessness washed over her and she began to feel nauseous. She was used to dealing with criminals and criminal behaviour in her line of work, but she'd never been involved with murder before. It was a shocking, dreadful act.

She parked her Fiat some distance from the lock-ups, in a shadowy part of the street where overhanging trees provided a sombre backdrop. She pulled the hood of her jacket over her long blond hair in the hope that no one would recognize her and debated whether to get the steps out of the boot. In the end, she decided to leave them where they were and weigh up the situation before she acted.

Then, carrying a torch that she'd had the forethought to bring with her, she walked through the dark night to the corner where Daniel had said the Griffiths' lock-up was situated. Seeing the padlock on the door, and no window in sight, her spirits sank. She didn't see how she could get in to manage even a glimpse of what was in there.

Maybe she would fare better around the back. There was nobody about, and the place was eerily quiet, but at least it meant no one could see what she was up to. She went round to the other side of the buildings and found herself on a piece of common ground, part grass, part gravel. There was a street lamp here, making her uncomfortably aware that she would no longer be hidden from prying eyes. About a dozen garages made up the block, with a corresponding dozen facing opposite. Each one had a narrow rectangular window at the top, near to the edge of the flat roof.

She studied the corner lock-up carefully for a while. How was she to get up there, to see what was inside? Did she need to go back to the car to fetch the steps? Looking around, a solution presented itself. She saw several wheelie bins that had been left out at intervals in the adjoining street, ready for the bin men to empty in the morning. Being as quiet as she could, she dragged the nearest one over to the Griffiths' lock-up and clambered up on top.

From this height, she could easily reach the window and peer inside. She shone the torch into the darkened interior, waiting for her eyes to grow accustomed to the shadowy shapes.

'Oh, wow!' It was no wonder Jenny had been shocked.

What she saw made her eyes widen. There was a large collection of antique furniture in there, carefully stacked to make the most of what space was available. She saw what looked like a regency bookcase, a rosewood and brass inlaid desk, a secretaire bookcase... there were what must have been paintings as far as she could discern from the shape, covered with hessian type cloths, and in a display cabinet on the shelf close by the window she saw a glimpse of what looked like distinctive Clarice Cliff pottery.

'Oh, wow...' she said again, under her breath. There must be thousands of pounds worth of stuff in here. She shone the torch around the storage unit once more, but stopped suddenly when she heard the sound of men talking on the other side of the garage.

'It's all in here,' a man said. It was hard to tell, but there was something familiar about his voice. In the next moment the door's operating mechanism made a grinding noise in complaint as someone started to open it, and in a panic, worried that she would be caught out, Sarah shut off the torch beam. Light flooded the storage space as Lewis Griffiths flicked the switch on the wall, and Sarah pulled in a shaky, anxious breath. Swiftly, she ducked down so that she wouldn't be seen, and then, a moment later, risked a careful peep above the window frame.

'You said you were interested in certain paintings,' Lewis was saying to the man who was with him. 'I can show you a couple of David Weston oil paintings, both of locomotives, and three Frank Egginton landscapes. They're over here, protected by tissue paper and bubble wrap.' He lifted the hessian cover and started to take down one of the paintings.

Sarah was nervous, but at the same time intrigued, wanting to see what was revealed when he removed the wrapping from around the artwork. She saw an ornate frame and then, to her dismay, just as the painting came into view, a dog started barking fiercely nearby, startling her and almost making her lose her balance. The sound was getting closer, and in the next moment a sandy haired terrier was snapping and growling at the foot of the wheelie bin.

'Freddie! Come back here!' A man's voice called out sharply and Sarah looked around in alarm. He would be around the corner and on to her at any second and she would be discovered, clearly up to no good, on top of the bin. She had to get away.

'Quiet!' she hissed at the dog. 'Sit! Stay!' She said it in a forceful, authoritative undertone, hoping that the dog had been taught enough commands to know which ones he had to obey.

She jumped down onto the ground, and the dog seemed to be momentarily taken aback and stunned into silence by her actions. It didn't take long for him to gather his wits, though, and he after a second or two he started to snap at her heels.

Sarah didn't hang around. Thankful that her hood stayed in place, she took off at a run, heading out along the street and away from the garages, with no idea where she was going. Guilt washed over her as she raced away. Maybe someone would drag the bin back in place before the refuse collectors came around in the morning, otherwise at least one of the local householders was going to be frustrated and annoyed to find it still full of rubbish at the end of the day.

By now, the dog had got up a head of steam and was chasing after her, kicking up a fuss, barking and growling in equal measure.

'Freddie!' his owner shouted, perplexed. 'Get back here! Now!'

Freddie was gaining on her by now, and from the way she felt his hot breath around her ankle he seemed very interested in catching hold of her leg, so she concentrated all her efforts on getting away. Just as she felt at tug on the hem of her jeans, something in the sharpness of his master's voice must have finally caught his attention and made him hesitate. Sarah took full advantage of the dog's distraction and kept going without looking back, running as fast as she was able.

'What's the matter with you, Freddie? Enough of that. Come on, let's go.' It sounded as though the dog's owner finally had him under control, and Sarah slowed down, turning a corner and coming to a halt by a hawthorn hedge, out of sight, her breath coming in short bursts.

She didn't know how long she stood there, but after a while, when she had recovered, she looked around and tried to get her bearings. She frowned, tipping back her hood and sliding her fingers through her hair. Wasn't that Ben Reed's house just a few yards away? In her determined attempt to find out what the Griffiths were hiding, she'd forgotten that Ben lived nearby. A streetlamp highlighted the street. The front and side of his house were still an eyesore, with junk from his plumbing work and elsewhere littering the ground. There was an old wash-basin, the drum from a washing machine, a satellite dish and a couple of mottled plastic chairs among grass and weeds that were several inches high.

'What are you doing around here? Are you spying on me?' The words came at her with guttural ferocity.

Sarah recoiled in shock as Ben Reed appeared alongside her. He must have come from a nearby street, one that housed a pub, most likely, from the whiff of alcohol on his breath. 'Of course not,' she retorted. 'Why would I do that?'

He was in his work clothes, dirt spattered over-trousers and a scruffy sweatshirt. Perhaps he'd just finished a long shift working on someone's plumbing, judging from the streaks of plumber's paste all over his trousers.

'You've got a nerve - coming here, to my house. I know your game. You're not happy with taking my dog and her brood - you want to get me thrown out of here, like she did - like that bitch wanted.'

He raised his fist in anger as though he would strike an imaginary foe, and Sarah took a step backwards, at the same time noting the grazes on his hand.

'Interesting scratches you have there,' she pointed out with a reckless lack of caution. 'I wonder how you came by them? Could it have been from catching your hand on my wall last night when you were searching for something to throw at my cold frames?'

'Clear off!' he snarled. 'You ain't got nothin' on me.'

'Don't you believe it,' she retorted. 'I know it was you who came to my farm last night, and if I see you round there again, I'll slap an injunction on you. And if you break that, you'll go to prison. Don't say I didn't warn you.'

'I'll do as I please,' he growled. 'You know what you can do with your fancy injunctions.'

'Yeah, right.' He was all talk and nothing much else, and they both knew it. Pulling her hood over her hair once more, she turned away from him and started to walk briskly back towards her car. She'd had enough for one day. Supper and bed were the only things on her agenda right now.

Which was perhaps why she found herself standing in line in the village chip shop a few minutes later, waiting to place an order. Or it might have been the fact that she fleetingly spotted someone who matched the description of Daniel's 'fair haired guy from the gym' standing outside with a friend as she drove by. Working on instinct, she parked up, and a short time later she was a couple of places behind him in the queue.

'Good night last night,' his friend was saying. 'Played snooker down the club with Harry. Thrashed him! You should have been there.'

'Nah, too busy, mate. Had to help my sister move into her flat.'

The line diminished as people were served and melted away into the night. The tattooed man flicked her a glance and his eyes lit up.

'What'll it be, guys?' the man behind the counter asked. 'The usual, Jamie? Pie and chips?'

The friend, Jamie, nodded. 'Yeah, thanks.'

'And what about you, Rhys?'

Rhys, the one with the dragon tattoos snaking along his muscled arms, glanced at what was on offer in the glass cabinet. 'Give me a couple of chicken drumsticks, sausage and chips, mate.'

'Coming up.'

Sarah would have loved to ask him what had happened the night Daniel had fallen out with his girlfriend, but she couldn't quite pluck up the courage to bombard a stranger with questions. Then again... she was never one to miss an opportunity, was she...?

'Hey there,' she began tentatively, as his order was being put together, 'sorry for intruding, but aren't you a friend of Charlotte? I recognize your tattoos from something someone said.'

Rhys's eyes sparked with interest as he slid a glance over her, taking in her shining blond hair and her neat figure in the slim fitting black jeans and the almost black hoodie that she'd unzipped to show her broderie anglaise white shirt beneath. 'Hello there, gorgeous. Why haven't I met you before? I think you and I need to make up for lost time.'

Her mouth curved in a sweet smile that had him leaning in towards her even more. 'Well, yes, maybe it is strange we haven't met - unless you don't live locally?'

'True, I'm from Colstow, down the road.' He named a nearby village. 'I'd move here in a flash, babe, if I thought I'd see more of you.'

She laughed softly. 'And what would become of poor Charlotte, then?' she queried gently. 'She adores you, or so I've heard. She was Danny's girl, but you went off with her, didn't you?'

'Ah, but that was before you came into my life.'

'Oh yes, let me see, it must have been all of what - three weeks ago?' She chuckled. 'Let me think... it was a Tuesday when you took up with her, wasn't it? What would that be... the 4th... no that's too soon... let me get this right...'

'28th March,' he said with a wry smile, 'if we're getting into specifics. I remember because it was my sister's birthday and she'd just signed the agreement to rent her flat.'

'Really? There you are, you see.' She lifted her hands in an expression of "I told you so." 'Three weeks and here you are, ready to give up on poor Charlotte.'

He shrugged, his biceps rippling. 'We were never that into one another. But you... now, you're definitely the one to light my fire.'

Her cheeks dimpled. 'I'm flattered, really I am... but maybe I'm not quite ready to start any fires just yet.' She glanced at the counter and the man who was serving. 'And I think your chicken and chips are ready.'

'Yeah, come on, Rhys,' Jamie said with a hint of impatience. 'Let's go. I'm starving and my food's getting cold.'

She moved up to the counter. 'I'll have cod, chips and add a carton of mushy peas, please,' she said. Somehow, she'd worked up an appetite. She only hoped Rhys and Jamie would grow tired of waiting and move on before she stepped outside again. Tuesday, March 28th. That was all she'd needed to know.

'Be seeing you around,' Rhys said, leaning in close again before he left the shop. 'That's a promise.'

She gave him a smile. We'll see about that, she thought.

She took the chip supper home and devoured it in the warm kitchen. Lexie was extremely interested in the contents of the paper and polystyrene bundle, and so Sarah saved her half a dozen chips and some of the batter.

'Here you go, Lexie,' she murmured, tipping the food into the dog bowl on the worktop. 'Let's keep this a secret from Matt, mind you. He wouldn't approve.' She made the dog sit and stay as she placed the bowl on the floor. 'Okay. Eat that, and then you can have a run outside before bedtime.'

Lexie didn't need a second bidding. She demolished the lot in less than fifteen seconds and then looked around in hopeful anticipation of more.

In the morning, Sarah was up early to make a start on feeding the animals. It had rained in the night, but now the sun was shining, lending a bright glow to the colours of nature all around her. The leaves on the trees seemed greener, the meadow grass more lush, and closer to home the flowers in the cottage garden were a medley of pastels with splashes of vibrant blue iris, and glorious scarlet petals of the Japanese quince.

Her spirits lifted as she looked around her, drinking it all in. If she ignored what had happened to her kitchen garden, the rest of the farm was beautiful, and seeing it made her glad to be alive.

She finished the feeds and went indoors to phone Nick. She wanted to update him on everything she'd found out.

'I'll come over to the farm,' he said, 'and we can talk then. I have to come to the village to talk to a couple of pensioners who say someone tried to break into their house last night in the early evening. Some items were stolen from their garden shed before they were discovered and the thieves managed to make a getaway. I'll go and see them first and after that I'll come over to your place. I should be with you in a couple of hours or thereabouts.'

'Okay. That will put us at about lunchtime, won't it? I'll make us a lasagne.'

'Sounds great!'

Sarah put together the ingredients to make a quick ragu - minced beef, olive oil, onions, tomatoes and tomato purée, and added a generous amount of herbs. When this was cooked, she assembled alternate layers of ragu, grated cheese and white sauce in a dish, covering each layer with easy cook sheets of lasagne. Then all she had to do was slide the oven proof dish into the Aga and leave it to bake. She made enough for four people, so that Rob and Jason could have some, too. It would keep warm in the oven until they finished their morning's work.

'Hey there, so what's new?' Nick asked when he came into the kitchen around lunchtime. He greeted Lexie, tickling her silky ears and patting her flanks and then he bent down to stroke the puppies. He sniffed the air. 'Mmm, that smells good.'

'Let's hope it is.' She filled a carafe with sparkling water and then placed a bowl of fresh salad on the table along with a basket of crusty bread that her mother had made. 'Sit down at the table,' she said. 'I'll serve up.'

'You said on the phone that you'd found out something more about Daniel's whereabouts when one of the robberies was taking place,' he prompted her as he helped himself to the steaming hot lasagne.

'That's right. I came across the man Daniel mentioned - the one from the gym. He said they'd been in the pub on 28th March - which is one of the days when a burglary took place, isn't it? So, if Daniel's story checks out with the chippie, that he was there with his friend, Jason, then he's in the clear, isn't he?'

'He could be, yes. I'll have to check up on the facts. It all depends on the timing – what part of the evening the burglary took place.' He paused, a fork full of lasagne hovering close to his mouth. 'How exactly did you find this out?' He looked at her with suspicion, his blue eyes narrowing.

'I bumped into the man from the gym last night in the chip shop, and I sort of quizzed him a little.'

He raised a brow. 'Sort of?'

She ignored that. 'His name's Rhys, by the way. He went off with Daniel's girlfriend that night.' She ate some of the food, enjoying the flavours of the meat and the sauce and the silkiness of the pasta. 'I'd already guessed it must have been a Tuesday night, because the ladies from the Fellowship group were in the pub having one of their meetings. They usually take place on a Tuesday.'

'Hmm. "*Sort of quizzed him a little*," you said. Why does that not surprise me?' He ate some more of the lasagne and added a side serving of salad to his plate. 'This is good,' he murmured approvingly. 'Very good. You must have inherited your mother's talent for cooking.'

'Well, thank you.' She smiled at him. 'I've always enjoyed cooking, when I have the time.'

He nodded. 'You said on the phone there were a couple of other things you wanted to tell me. Is one of them to do with the vandalism the other night? One of my colleagues at the station told me about it.'

'Oh... yes, it was. I found half a brick in one of the cold frames. It had some red specks on it, and I think, if you were to have it tested, that you'd find it's blood. And, oddly enough, would you know it, Ben Reed has a fresh set of scratches on his hand? So, if you were to put two and two together...'

'I take it you have this piece of brick?'

'I do... and photos.' She added salad to her plate, digging her fork into slivers of red onion and lettuce and savouring the taste of the dressing she'd made, a combination of red wine vinegar, oil and mustard. 'I'm not sure, though, if I want to prosecute him... I'd rather just keep my powder dry until he tries something else.'

He was thoughtful for a while. 'I think we need to frighten him. We could send the evidence to the lab for testing - we do have his DNA on file from his previous run-ins with the law. If it is blood on the brick, and if it matches, I could bring him in for an interview - I have to talk to him again in connection with the burglaries anyway - so it might be enough simply to caution him.'

She nodded. 'Okay.' Now it was her turn to be pensive, and Nick picked up on it straightaway.

'Out with it. What's on your mind?'

'It's about the burglaries - or at least, one of them.' She hesitated. 'I don't believe the Griffiths were burgled. I think they might have made it up as some sort of insurance scam.'

His brows rose. 'And you know this, how?'

'Um...' Now that was the difficult part, the bit that she didn't really want to get into.

But Nick was waiting, his piercing blue gaze fixed intently on her. '*Um*...? What did you do?'

'I heard about this lock-up garage that they have out at Barton Wick. So...'

His eyes narrowed. 'So...?'

'So, I went along to take a look last night. And it's full of antique stuff - and paintings. Though I doubt some of it will still be there, the paintings, I mean, because while I was looking through the window at the back, Lewis came, and he was trying to sell them to a man - only then someone's dog found me and started barking, so I had to make a run for it.'

'Someone's dog found you?' Nick raised his eyes heavenwards. 'How many times have I told you to leave it to the police and to stop going off and prying into things on your own? It must be umpteen times already.'

'Well, yes, you did tell me.' She lifted her shoulders in a dismissive gesture. 'But you know, Nick, there is a saying...' He lifted his brows in query and she continued, 'Don't they say the definition of insanity is to keep doing the same thing over and over, expecting a different result?'

He spluttered on his sparkling water. 'You're incorrigible! You could have got yourself into a lot of trouble, with the dog, and more especially with Lewis, if he'd found out what you were doing. Let alone the fact that he might have a perfectly good reason for storing those things in his lock-up.'

'He might. But you and I both know that's unlikely. They have to be the stuff he says was taken from his house, and you can check that. You have a list of property that was said to be missing from each of the burgled houses, don't you? And I'll bet it includes David Weston paintings and Clarice Cliff pottery.'

She speared a forkful of lasagne and let her fork hover over her plate for a while. 'And the point of it is, Daniel was there the other day when Jenny walked by with the dog and saw what was in the garage. He told me about it... that's why I needed to find out what was in there. I think Jenny knew about the scam they were trying to pull, and that's probably the reason they fell out and she threatened to take their property off her books. Worse still, she probably told them she would report what she'd seen to the police - she might have done it straightaway, except the business with Ben Reed intruded and she found herself with other problems on her hands temporarily. They couldn't afford to let her do that.'

She looked at him intently. 'Don't you think it's possible that Lewis killed her to stop her from exposing the scam?'

He nodded thoughtfully. 'It's definitely a possibility. Money is a strong motive for murder, and from what I've seen, the insurance claim would amount to a huge pay-out.'

'Yes, and we know they're strapped for cash.' She ate the lasagne and waved her fork in the air to emphasize the point she was making. 'That's why they're downsizing. That would give them every reason to want to make a false claim.'

Nick pondered the situation for a moment. 'He could have been panicked into taking action and did what he could to make it look like natural causes. Obviously, I'll look into it... although we're already investigating their claims as a matter of course. With several burglaries to look into, it's taking a while.'

'Hmm... at least it's ongoing.' She frowned. 'The only thing is, I don't know how he would have managed to get into her house. He doesn't have a key, presumably, and they don't have any connection outside of the Agency.'

He shook his head. 'You're jumping to conclusions. This is all hypothetical. Just because she was about to expose them it doesn't necessarily follow that they killed her. Like I said, there were a number of people who had problems with Jenny. And as to how the killer got into the house, who's to say she didn't invite him in? Or Natalie may have visited her, for that matter?'

Sarah's mouth flattened. 'They could have taken the digitalis with them. They do have some foxgloves in their garden.' She put down her fork and studied him, a frown creasing her brow. 'We're not getting very far with this, are we? Every day brings more questions than answers.'

'That's the way it goes, sometimes.' He stood up. 'Shall I make coffee, or do you want tea?'

CHAPTER TWELVE

NICK WENT back to work after lunch, and after he'd gone Sarah invited Rob and Jason to come and finish off the rest of the lasagne that she'd kept warm for them in the oven.

'I have to go out for a while this afternoon,' she told them, 'so I want you to make sure you lock the door behind you when you leave the house, and keep an eye open in case Mr Reed decides to pay a visit.'

'Okay, we'll see to it,' Rob said. 'Do you think he was the one who smashed up all the crops in the kitchen garden?'

'Possibly. He's the only one I can think of who might bear a grudge against me, and I doubt it would have been mindless vandals in the early hours of the morning. I don't think he'll come back, but it's best to be on the safe side. Call me or Nick Holt if you feel concerned in any way.'

'We will,' Jason said, sitting down at the table at her bidding and beginning to tuck into the food. 'Thanks for this, I'm starving.'

'Me, too,' Rob agreed, taking a seat opposite his friend. 'Do you think it would help to put up some security lights - the kind that detect movement? If anyone tried to come on to the farm at night they would be caught in the beams from the lamps. I know alarm systems are expensive, but that's an alternative. Although, I suppose it's still a lot to pay out if you're not sure whether you're keeping the farm.'

'It is yet another expense,' she agreed, 'but I think we need to feel safe until everything's sorted out one way or the other.' She was still disturbed by the way Ben Reed had come into her kitchen the other night. 'Besides, everything I've done so far should mean that I'll get the best price for the farm.' She weighed things up in her mind for a second or two. 'I think you're right about the security lights. No one wants to be caught in the middle of a spotlight when they're thinking of committing a crime, do they? I'll pop into the hardware store today and see what I can find.'

'A motion activated camera would be a good idea, as well,' Rob said, adding with a frown, 'I don't know how much it would cost to buy one and have it installed.'

'Yes, I need to look into it. And of course, then I'll need an electrician to install the lights, and maybe the camera, too.' She pulled a face. 'I might have just about enough money left from the bank loan to cover everything.'

'My brother might do it for you,' Jason said. 'William's a qualified electrician. He works for a firm in town, but he sometimes does small jobs at the weekend or in the evening. I don't think he'll charge too much. He did ours at home, and it didn't take him long.'

'Oh, that would help me out a lot, Jason. Would you ask him if he could find the time to do the work for me? I might need to get half a dozen lights to cover the house, the yard and the outbuildings and maybe a camera to focus on the driveway.'

'Yeah. I'll do that.'

'Thanks.' She gave a relieved sigh and then glanced at her watch. 'I have to go out for a couple of hours, or so... I shouldn't be too much longer than that. Do you both have your work schedule for the afternoon?'

They nodded. 'Clear up the kitchen garden, save what we can and re-plant,' Rob said with a smile.

'And give Clover a bit of a walk around the yard and the duck pond to give her some exercise,' Jason added. 'Her foot seems to be a lot better, so she should be all right to do that.'

'Good. I'm glad to see you're both on top of things.' She looked at them with appreciation. 'I'm so glad I set you on here after my grandmother died and things were in disarray.' The other staff had left, not knowing what was going to happen to the farm, and found other jobs. 'She would have set you both on here, I'm sure, if you had wanted a job. You would have been an enormous help to her. And she always spoke very highly of you, Rob.'

'She was a great lady. I'm sorry she's gone.' Rob's features were sad. 'Mind you, she always said she could do with more farm hands around here.' His eyes widened as a thought occurred to him. 'If you do decide to stay on here, and keep us on, do you reckon we could have another couple of workers to help out? Girls, maybe?'

She laughed at his hopeful expression. 'I'll definitely think about it!' Then she sobered, sensing a seriousness underlying his train of thought. 'I know it's difficult for you both, now, not knowing what's going to happen, but I can tell you I don't want to have to sell up. If it does come to that, I'll make sure the agreement says that you two have employment here for as long as you want it.'

They were both relieved, she could tell, and she felt better for clearing that up. Whatever Raj planned to do with the farm, or anyone else who put in a better offer, she would make the boys' employment part of any legally binding document.

A short time later, she set off for the large hardware store on the outskirts of the nearby town, and spent nearly an hour looking at security light fittings and cameras and discussing them with a member of staff. Satisfied, eventually, that she'd made the right purchases, she stowed them in the boot of her car and drove back to the village, going by way of Brackley Close.

She parked her car outside Jenny's house, hoping that luck would be with her and that Jenny's neighbours would be at home, and that they would be agreeable to talking to her. She wanted to find out what they knew of the day the Estate Agent was poisoned. Perhaps they'd seen or heard something. Nick might already have questioned them, but she wanted to find out for herself if there were any clues as to what had gone in the neighbourhood that day.

The task was made a bit easier for her when she saw an elderly couple coming out of the house next door to Jenny's. They had a little dog with them, a small black and white Cavalier King Charles spaniel, full of beans and raring to go.

Sarah slid out of her car and locked up, nodding to the couple as they walked down their drive towards the gate. 'Hello,' she greeted them cheerfully, stopping to admire the excitable little dog. 'Isn't he adorable? He doesn't look very old – is he still a pup?'

'He's eight months old,' the woman said, smiling as she came through the gate. 'We called him Jonjo. You'd think he'd have calmed down by now, wouldn't you, but he's always been exuberant, like this.'

'I can see that,' Sarah said, laughing. 'He's full of it, isn't he? His tail's going ten to the dozen.' She bent down to stroke him and the little dog lapped it up, trying to jump up and lick her, wanting even more fuss.

'Were you planning on going next door?' the man asked as she finally untangled herself and stood up, 'only I'm afraid the lady isn't there any more.'

'I know.' Sarah nodded, her mouth turning down. 'I was hoping I could talk to someone about her.'

'Was she a friend of yours?' His manner sharpened as a thought struck him. 'You're not a reporter, are you? We've had a few of those around here, from the local paper.'

'No, I'm not a reporter. I'm Sarah Marshall - I live in the village and work in town in a solicitor's office. Jenny was a friend - she was helping me out with a property matter – and as things turned out I was the one who found her that day, when she was taken ill.'

'Oh, I'm sorry, my dear,' his wife said. 'That must have been a terrible shock for you.'

'Yes... yes, it was. The thing is, I'm still trying to find out what happened to her that day. I wondered if you saw or heard anything? Did she have any visitors? Were there any strangers in the area?'

'Well, now... there were a couple of things that morning that made us wonder what was going on.' The man waved a hand towards his companion. 'I'm Jack Watson, by the way... and this is my wife, Mary. We both heard the row that went on, first thing.'

'First thing?' Sarah echoed.

'That's right. It would have been about...' He looked at his wife for confirmation, 'about eight o'clock in the morning.'

Mary nodded. 'We were having our breakfast,' she said, 'and we could hear the barney going on, loud and clear.'

'It was that Ben Reed from over the road,' Jack put in. 'Having a right go at her, he was.'

'I can't think why she let him into the house,' Mary said, shaking her head. 'Except, perhaps she thought she might get him to see reason. She'd told him she would call in the environmental people if he didn't clear up the rubbish outside his house, and he didn't like it one bit. Then she said he could be fined if he carried on ignoring the authorities and that really got to him.'

'It was all true, what she said,' Jack added. 'His place is an eyesore, but he was ranting and raving like a madman. We thought about calling the police – and we were going to go round to see what we could do, but then all the noise stopped and he stormed off.'

'I went round to see her, to see if she was okay,' Mary said. 'She was upset, and she was struggling to get her breath a bit – her heart, you know?' Sarah nodded, and Mary went on, 'I sat her down, and made her some tea, and she took a tablet. Apparently, she'd told him she would call the police unless he left, and in the end he must have seen sense. I stayed with her for a bit, but then, after a while she said she had to go to work and call in at the office.'

'We thought that might have caused her to collapse later on... all the upset, and her heart problem, you know?' Jack frowned.

Sarah nodded again, unwilling to comment on the nature of Jenny's death. Jenny had told her she was stressed that morning, and it was no wonder, from the sound of things. 'You must have seen her on a regular basis, and got to know her – did it seem as though she struggled with her heart problem?'

'Well, no... not especially.' Once again, he looked to his wife for confirmation.

'It was something that had come on gradually, and the hospital was controlling it with medication. She did mention she might have to have an operation at some point, but she was coping, I think. We were so shocked when she died.'

'The whole business was upsetting,' Sarah agreed. Her brow creased. 'You mentioned there were two incidents that morning?'

'Ah... you'd be better off talking to Moira... Moira Linklater, at number 22,' Jack said. 'She heard what went on there. She's definitely at home... we're just off to the shops to fetch her a few bits and pieces – she's laid up with a chest infection right now, but she's up and about if you want to go and have a word with her.'

'Okay, thanks... I'll do that.' She looked down at Jonjo who was twirling round and round with boredom and getting his lead in a twist. She laughed. 'Thanks for your help,' she told the couple. 'I won't keep you any longer – I can see Jonjo's ready for the off.'

She watched them go, and then went to knock on the front door of number 22.

'Hello, Mrs Linklater?' she said with a friendly smile as a thin, grey haired woman opened the door a few inches.

'That's me. What do you want? I'm not buying anything.' The woman was wheezing, clearly finding some difficulty with her breathing, and Sarah felt guilty for disturbing her.

'No... no, it's nothing like that,' Sarah hurried to explain. 'It's just that I knew Jenny, next door, and I'm trying to find out a bit more about what happened that morning when she was taken ill. Your neighbours, Mary and Jack, told me you heard something going on next door. I wondered if you'd mind telling me what it was about.'

'I already told that policeman that came here,' Moira said through the crack in the doorway.

'Oh yes... the police are looking into the circumstances of her death, of course. This is more personal – I was acquainted with Jenny... I'm looking after her dog, and I feel I don't understand enough of what happened to her. I'd be very grateful if you could tell me what went on that morning.'

'Hmph... you'd better come in.'

'Thank you.' Sarah followed her along the hall to the sitting room where, despite the warmth of the day, a fire glowed in the hearth. A tortoiseshell cat was curled up on the arm of the sofa, enjoying the extra heat. It opened one eye as the women came into the room and gave Sarah a baleful stare as though she was intruding on its territory.

Mrs Linklater waved her to a seat. 'How do you know Jenny?'

'Through her work,' Sarah explained. 'She was advising me on a property matter, but we'd already met in the village from time to time and got to know each other. She and my mother were both members of the Fellowship group.'

'Hmph,' the woman said again. 'Jenny liked to be part of things. She tried to get me to join, but I can't be doing with going out and about, doing this and that. I've got Sylvester over there, and my knitting and the telly, and I'm happy.'

'That sounds cosy,' Sarah smiled. 'I know Jenny was one for getting involved in projects.'

'She liked to keep busy, and she liked to have her say. Of course, that didn't always go down too well with others.'

'Others?'

'Some folk at the sheltered housing were upset that she was trying to organize their communal gardens. Then there was the landlord at the Blacksmith's Arms - he was annoyed because she wanted to stop the late-night music at the pub. He has a licence for it but, between you and me, it was a lot louder than it should have been in my opinion, and sometimes he let it go on later than he should.'

'Were there any more people who had an axe to grind with her?'

'Well, there was Pauline, of course, our librarian. She was extremely put out by the way Jenny went on. She felt she was being pushed out. She told me she'd worked her socks off to make a success of the Fellowship group, organizing activities, and trips out in the summer, but whatever she did, Jenny came up with something different, or found a reason why her ideas weren't suitable. Like the day trips Pauline set up – some people weren't happy with being dropped off near the shops in town, when they wanted to go to the Promenade instead, or they felt there wasn't a lot to see or do in some places. So, Jenny decided it all needed a re-think – different seaside resorts, different ways of going on.'

'That must have upset Pauline,' Sarah commented.

'Upset! I'll say!' Moira wheezed and had a coughing bout that lasted for a minute or so before she recovered. 'She was absolutely livid! She had the programme for the summer all worked out, bookings made and everything. That's what the argument was about that day. She came round to Jenny's house around lunchtime and let rip. Told her exactly what she thought of her, called her an interfering, egotistical control freak, who wanted a finger in every pie going.'

'She didn't mince her words, then?' Sarah said with a faint smile.

'Well... it was a bit pot calling the kettle black, if you know what I mean?'

Sarah nodded. 'I think I do. They were both strong characters. How did Jenny react, do you know?'

'She gave as good as she got. A real humdinger of a row, it was. You could tell from the way her voice became louder and louder that Pauline was spitting bricks.'

'So how did it end?'

'I heard the door slam, and Sylvester jumped up on to the windowsill to see what the noise was all about. We both watched Pauline get into her car and drive away. I didn't hear anything after that.' She frowned. 'I rang Jenny to see if she was all right – I didn't feel well enough to go around there. She said she was going to lie down for an hour, but when she didn't get in her car and go back to work, I assumed she'd decided to take the afternoon off.' She coughed again, and seemed to be brooding on that for a while. 'It must all have been too much for her. She probably came downstairs again and, from what the police said, she had a drink of that herbal medicine of hers and then had some sort of heart attack.'

Sarah thought about what Moira had said. If Jenny had gone to lie down for an hour, anyone could have crept into the house and put the foxglove leaves in the basket without her knowing. Pauline could have come back to talk some more and then taken advantage of Jenny being out of the way, asleep upstairs. Presumably, the kitchen door would have been unlocked.

'Thanks for telling me all that,' Sarah said a short time later as she stood up to leave. 'You've been really helpful. I hope your cough clears up and you start to feel better soon.'

When Sarah arrived back at the farm in the mid-afternoon she said hello to Rob and Jason and then took Lexie for a walk over the field and out by the duck pond. Several children came to join them once they'd been home from school for tea and had permission from their parents to come and visit for a while. Sarah insisted on them getting that permission – although it wasn't very deep, she worried in case they came to any harm by getting too close to the pond, and she warned them not to get too near the edge. She made it a rule that young children always came with an older brother or sister to watch over them.

'Are there any fish in the pond?' one little girl asked, but Sarah shook her head.

'There may be a few tiddlers that come in from the stream, but I'm afraid they probably wouldn't last long with the ducks around.'

'There are some eggs in those rushes,' a young boy pointed out. 'Will they hatch into ducklings?'

'They might do, if the duck lays a clutch of eggs and sits on them and keeps them warm, but she'll have to do that for about a month, off and on with breaks to feed and so on.' She showed them eggs that had been laid singly and at random in the rushes. 'These won't hatch, so I usually collect any like these that have been abandoned.'

'Can you eat them?'

'Oh yes. They're bigger than chicken eggs, and you can fry them, poach them, scramble them, the same as the eggs we're used to.'

The children were fascinated with the pond and the ducks and all the wild life around them, and were full of questions that Sarah tried to answer.

'Will chicken's eggs hatch into chicks?' a little girl asked. She looked to be about seven years old, with bright, flaxen curls that danced as she moved her head. She didn't look too happy at the prospect. Perhaps she was thinking of her breakfast egg.

'Some of them will – only those that have been fertilized if there's a male bird around,' Sarah said. 'And again, they need to have the mother hen sit on the eggs to hatch them – or they could go in an incubator... that will do the same thing.'

The boy's eyes widened. 'What's an incu...wotsit?'

'It's a glass box with lamps to keep the eggs warm while the chicks inside develop.'

Sarah walked back with the children to the yard a short time later, and left them helping Rob and Jason with the animal feeds. She went into the house as she heard the landline ringing. It would be her mother phoning, she guessed. She always preferred to use the landline when she wanted to chat.

'Hi Mum,' she said, 'how are things with you?'

'Fine,' her mother answered. 'I'm just checking in to see if you're okay. You'll be back at work in the office next week, won't you - that only leaves a few days for you to get to grips with the farm. Have you had any more thoughts about what you're going to do?'

Sarah made a face, thinking about it. 'I don't think I have that many options,' she said, sitting down on an upholstered seat and getting comfortable. 'I don't want to leave the farm in the hands of a manager — if I'm going to stay I prefer to see to things myself. But like you say, they're expecting me back at work next week, and after experiencing what the day to day life is like on the farm I know I can't do justice to both.'

'You have your own client list at the office, don't you? Couldn't you suggest that you go part time? Would your boss let you do that? If not, surely there must be other firms that could use your talents.'

Sarah blinked. 'Part time? I hadn't thought of that. I'd need to think it through, and put it to my boss, to see if he would go for it. I suppose a job share would be another solution.' She said cautiously, 'You sound as though you're edging me in the direction of keeping the farm.'

'Yes, I think maybe I am,' her mother answered readily enough. 'It seems to me that you've spent quite a bit of money on the place in this last couple of weeks – and that makes me feel that deep down you don't want to let it go.'

'Hmm... you could be right. But that's another thing – how am I going to afford to keep the place going? I can pay off the loan by working at the office, but at the rate I'm going I'll need another one before the year's out.'

'There's always your flat... you haven't lived there for the past couple of weeks and you've been comfortable at the farm, haven't you? You could put it on the market.'

Sarah's eyes widened. 'You're full of ideas, today, Mum. You've obviously been thinking about this a lot.'

'I suppose I have. I ran into Geoffrey Hollins in the village the other day, and he was asking after you, wanting to know how you were managing at the farm. He told me how much your neighbour wanted to take it off your hands.

He said Mr Sayed was full of plans for renovating the barn and the outbuildings and perhaps adding to the herd of sheep.'

'It sounds as though Mr Sayed has been giving it a lot of thought.' Sarah was a bit sceptical about his true motives, though. 'I'm still not sure that he won't try to alter the land use in part. He talked about renovating the barn and making it into a dwelling, and I suspect he might want to add a few more. But Geoffrey Hollins is certainly anxious to make a sale, isn't he?'

'Oh, definitely. In fact, he's very keen to keep that Estate Agency business on the up and up. I think Jenny used to be a little bit concerned that he didn't look into things properly... it was all "push, push to close a deal and rake in the commission" at any cost with him, whereas she preferred to work closely with people to see what they wanted and then she would try to do her best for them. That's how it worked when she was in business with her husband at the agency back in Kings Langley. She told me she went into partnership with Geoffrey because she had no family to inherit her estate and it would all simply go into the government coffers if she died. She had everything drawn up by a solicitor.'

'So, not only did they have a partnership agreement, but she must have made a Will naming him as beneficiary?'

'That's right.'

Which would give him all the more reason to want Jenny out of the way. Sarah didn't say that out loud. Her mother would only worry if she thought she was investigating what had gone on. 'Do you think he'll try to push for a quick sale for the farm, to please Mr Sayed? After all, he did arrange for him to buy the Manor House. Perhaps he feels he owes him some loyalty?'

'He may do. They're golfing partners and they belong to the same fishing club. It's up to you, of course, to do the thing that's best for you. But I do believe that, after all the repairs you've done, you need to have a few more potential buyers in the mix, so that you can get the best price – if you decide to sell. I think that's what Jenny would have advised you to do if she'd been alive today. Most times she said she liked to urge people to make the best of a property.'

'Yes, I guess you're right. I just wish she could be here now – it's true she seemed to have upset a few people with her forthright way of going on, but I felt she was honest and had people's interests at heart.'

'Yes, she certainly didn't deserve to die.'

CHAPTER THIRTEEN

SARAH FINISHED inspecting the pea crop that was growing in the field beyond the kitchen garden and went back to the cobbled yard as she heard car tyres crunching along the gravel drive.

She'd spent most of the morning tending the crops, weeding and watering, and planting runner bean seeds in pots in the polytunnel, and now she was about ready to take a break. She had a lot to think about and she wasn't altogether sure she was in the right mood for visitors, but Matt had phoned to see if it was all right to come over and she could hardly turn him away.

Seconds later, he parked his dark green four by four to one side of the wide driveway and walked towards her, medical bag in hand.

'Hi there,' he called out to her. 'I've finished my rounds for the morning, so I just dropped by to take a look at Clover. I hope that's okay with you?'

'Hello, Matt,' she greeted him with a smile. 'Of course, that's fine.'

'Good. How's she doing? Has she been exercised, as I suggested?'

'Yes, the lads have been taking her out to get some fresh air. Come and see her – see what you think. To my mind she looks a lot happier.'

He walked with her over to the pen, stroked Clover's head and gave the goat a titbit before starting to examine her foot. 'She certainly looks better in herself. It's only been a few days since the abscess burst, but she seems to be picking up, which is a good thing – these ailments can sometimes take weeks to heal. Perhaps we caught it just in time.'

Sarah nodded. 'Plus, she's had the daily benefit of your expert care, of course,' she commented, and watched as he changed the dressing on Clover's foot. The goat nudged his chest with her head as he bent to tend to her, and Sarah chuckled. 'She likes you... that's a definite sign of approval!'

'Hmm...' He made a wry face. 'I'm not so sure about that. She tried to push me into a hay bale a couple of days ago.'

Sarah grinned. 'She can be a bit temperamental.'

When he'd finished bandaging the tender area, Matt straightened up and went back with Sarah to the house so that he could clean up. Sarah took a minute or two to remove her gardening apron and change out of her boots in the outhouse, putting on a pair of black trainers that blended well with her black jeans, and then she went into the kitchen to wash her hands, too.

'I'm hoping you have half an hour or so to spare,' Matt said as he finished drying his hands and replaced the towel over the rail. 'I brought something with me – it's in the car.'

She nodded, sending him a querying look. 'Okay. What is it you want to show me?' she asked.

He smiled. 'I thought, as it's lunchtime, we could maybe have a picnic? The sun's out, it's a glorious day, so I thought we might find a nice place to sit for a while. I brought some food with me, and a bottle of something to drink. I wanted to repay you for the omelette you made for me the other day.'

'Heavens, you didn't need to do that!' Her mouth curved. 'But I do like the sound of a picnic.'

They went out to his car where he retrieved a wicker basket from the boot. 'Shall we go down by the copse? There's a picnic table there, if I remember right, and the stream runs past it.'

'Okay, that sounds good to me.' She called Lexie to come with them and take a break from the puppies for a while, and the dog bounded happily along beside them.

Sarah was intrigued to know what was in the picnic basket. It had been several hours since she'd eaten breakfast and she was beginning to feel hungry again.

It took only a couple of minutes to reach the clearing. The sun was a brilliant orb high in the sky, spreading golden beams over the glade and sparkling on the gently flowing stream that ran alongside the copse.

'This used to be one of my favourite areas on the farm whenever I came to visit my grandmother,' she told him, as they sat down opposite each other on the wooden bench seat by the table. Lexie sat down beside her, gazed around and then lay down, enjoying the sunshine. 'It's so peaceful here,' Sarah murmured. 'I love the way the light filters through the trees, and the sound of the brook as it trickles over the stones.'

Matt smiled, nodding agreement as he began to open the wicker basket. Lexie immediately looked up, alert, nose twitching, eager to know if there was any food in the offing.

'How does it compare with being at the office?' Matt asked, taking out a dish of salad, along with a container filled with chicken drumsticks.

She gave that some serious thought. 'That's a difficult question to answer,' she told him. 'I love my job as a paralegal and I would hate to give it up. I enjoy meeting the clients and helping them with their problems. I get a buzz out of doing any research that's necessary, too.' She glanced around. 'But it is lovely to be able to take time out to come and sit here and enjoy the rural life, to see the greenery around me. I love to listen to the birds singing and watch the squirrels darting up and down the trees. I could certainly get used to it. It would be good to know that all this could be mine for always. I feel at one with nature here, even if it is hard work sometimes.'

'That's how I guessed it might be. You've been doing a lot of work around here, and that makes me think you'd be reluctant to let it go.'

'Maybe. That's what Mum said.' Her mouth watered as he added a tub of coleslaw to the items on the table, along with scotch eggs, mini pork pies and a plate of sandwiches. It must have been all too much for Lexie, because the dog started to gently push her head against Sarah's leg to get her attention. Not wanting to end up with a dog that was constantly making demands at mealtimes, Sarah absently stroked her head whilst steadfastly ignoring her pleas for food. 'Oh my!' she said, looking at Matt, 'you've brought enough food here to feed a small army!'

'Do you think so?' He wrinkled his nose. 'Maybe I did get a bit carried away. I was hungry when I put all this together.' He was still lifting things out of the basket... a sponge cream cake and a bottle of sparkling wine. He produced two glasses and poured the wine, handing her a glass. 'It's not very alcoholic,' he said in an apologetic tone. 'I have to drive home, so it's only a four percent variety, I'm afraid.'

'I love it,' she told him, taking a sip. 'It's very refreshing.'

'I'm glad.' He slid a plate towards her. 'Help yourself to the food.' He watched her for a moment as she added chicken and salad to her plate and began to eat. 'It's good to see you looking relaxed,' he said. 'Realistically, though, do you think there's any chance you might keep the farm?' Matt bit into a pork pie and waited for her to answer.

'I hope so.' She gave up trying to ignore the fact that Lexie was nudging her leg in the hope of getting a tasty snack. 'No, Lexie,' she said in a firm voice, turning to the dog. 'You have to wait until we've finished.'

Lexie gave a disgruntled sigh and flopped back down, resting her head on her paws in frustration.

Sarah turned her attention back to Matt, and they spent the next few minutes eating the food and drinking the wine and chatting about the farm, his work, and all manner of things.

He was intrigued to know that there had once been horses stabled on the farm, and said thoughtfully, 'That might be an idea for the future... if you choose to stay.'

'Oh yes, as long as they don't cost a small fortune!'

They ate and chatted about this and that, and when they had eaten all they wanted, they started to clear up the remains of the picnic and began to pack it away in the hamper.

Sarah finally gave in to Lexie's hypnotic stare and dropped some chicken pieces on to the grass, along with the remains of her pork pie and a ham sandwich. Matt might well have disapproved of the doggy diet she was feeding the Boxer, but he merely raised an eyebrow and looked pointedly at the food on the ground.

'It's too late to object,' she told him a moment later. 'She's already wolfed it down.'

'I give up,' he said, lifting his hands in a submissive gesture. 'Proper dog nutrition's out of the window, I guess.'

She laughed. 'Don't be such a stick in the mud!'

He grinned, and then stretched his long limbs. 'I have to go and take afternoon surgery,' Matt said reluctantly. 'I enjoyed having lunch with you.'

'Likewise,' she murmured.

It had been pleasant to spend a little while free from the everyday cares that had besieged her over these last few days, but as they walked back to the house a bit later on, Sarah knew that her problems were still there to harass her, and would be so until she made up her mind to do something about them. And she still had to grapple with the one puzzle that obstinately resisted a solution. Which one of the suspects she'd come up with would have had the motivation and the callousness to kill Jenny Carter?

That was still on her mind when she drove to the village centre an hour or so later and parked up alongside the parade of shops on the High Street. She wanted to pay a visit to the small hardware store to buy one or two things that she needed.

'Hello, there, Sarah,' the shop owner called out to her as she walked in through the door. 'Is there anything I can help you with?'

Sarah shook her head. 'No thanks, Tim. I'll just browse, if that's okay.'

'Sure, go ahead.'

She walked down the first aisle, moving past neatly stacked rows of crockery, and small electrical appliances, heading for the section where she might find a brush and dustpan to replace the worn out set that her grandmother had left in the kitchen cupboard. Turning the corner at the end of the row, she came across shelves filled with tins of paint and all the equipment that went along with it, like brushes, rollers and white spirit for cleaning.

'Hey there... I said we'd meet up again, didn't I? And here you are, still as beautiful as ever.'

Sarah's heart sank as Rhys, the man with the dragon tattoos rippling along his arms, confronted her. His smile widened as he looked her up and down, taking in the sight of her slender figure in black jeans and cashmere top that clung to her curves. 'Not that I expected to see you in here. This is a pleasant surprise.'

'Oh, hello,' she answered, trying to get her mind back on an even keel. 'I could say the same of you — I wasn't expecting to find you in here.'

'I'm just getting some paintbrushes — it's my trade, painter and decorator, as you might have guessed...' He indicated his paint-smeared overalls. 'I'm on a bit of a rush job and some of my brushes are the worse for wear — I'm doing up my sister's place. She's very particular - she wants it done in shades of teal and cream emulsion.'

Sarah recalled the evening in the chip shop when he'd told her about his sister signing the lease. 'That sounds like a good combination. How is she getting on in the flat? Has she settled in okay?'

'Yeah, she loves it. There were a few flats to let, but even so it took a while to find the place she wanted. She got there in the end, though.'

'That's good... it can be quite difficult searching for the right property – I know when I looked for my flat there were so many that just weren't suitable. You get to know the jargon after a while... *compact* means just about enough space for a hamster, and *in need of a little attention* means pull it down and start again.'

He laughed, and she went on, 'It does help to go through an agency, though, which is what I did in the end, because they can keep a lookout for suitable properties and notify you when something comes along.'

He pulled a face. 'Yeah, she tried that. She went with the Meadows Agency in Caulders Lea, but it didn't work out.'

Sarah's brows lifted in surprise. 'The Meadows Agency?' she echoed. That was Jenny Carter's firm.

He nodded, his expression souring. 'That's the one. I went with Katie to help her out, and we found a couple of properties she was keen on, but Mrs Carter turned her down. Said she didn't have the references the landlords wanted.' He scowled. 'Snooty cow. I was well wound up, I can tell you.'

Sarah frowned. 'I'm sorry to hear that. It must have been upsetting for your sister if she'd built her hopes up.'

'Yeah.' His features darkened, a complete contrast now to his earlier bright demeanour. 'I was mad as hell. I don't think it had anything to do with references – I think she done it out of spite. I done some work for Mrs Carter when she moved into her place but she was a pain to work for. She kept getting me back to do stuff – said the wall was patchy... I told her to wait a couple of days for it to dry out and it would be okay, but she wouldn't listen. She had me paint it again. Then she said I'd knelt on her draining board to paint above the window and that I'd stopped it draining properly. The woman was a menace.' His face was etched with anger at the memory, his fists clenched, and Sarah felt an involuntary shiver ripple down her spine. There was a lot of pent up violence in him.

'Obviously you didn't get along with her.' Clearly, he was a man you wouldn't want to cross.

He snorted, his face twisting with contempt. 'Nobody would get along with her. I'm not surprised she had to keep drinking that herbal stuff. That woman's stomach must have been made out of pure acid.'

Sarah briefly chewed on her lip as she digested that. It appeared he was a man of mercurial moods, flirtatious and full of cheer one minute, but engulfed with hatred the next. Just how deep had Rhys's dislike for Jenny gone? Was it enough to make him want to hurt her... maybe he wouldn't go as far as murder, but could he have tried to make her suffer for causing him and his sister grief? If he'd been working at her house it would have been easy enough to find an excuse to go back and slip some foxglove leaves in the basket on her worktop.

She felt cold with unease. Her list of suspects was growing but, so far, she had no evidence to pin the awful crime on any of them.

'So how did your sister manage to find her flat, after all that?' she asked, doing her best to keep a steady voice.

He seemed to calm down a bit. 'She got it through a friend. He's not using it at the minute – he's gone to live with his girlfriend – so he's letting her stay at his place.'

So, the flat was being sub-let, and probably wouldn't be too secure a tenancy as far as his sister was concerned. Sarah pushed that thought to the back of her mind. There were other, more relevant problems that she needed to ponder, without getting involved in other people's dilemmas.

'Well, I'm glad she's happy with what she has,' she murmured. She looked past him to where the buckets and kitchen equipment were displayed. 'If you'll excuse me, I need to make a few purchases. Time's running out and I should be getting a move on.' All at once she was keen to get away from him. He was giving off bad vibes and she was becoming increasingly unsettled.

'Sure. Maybe you and I could get to see each other again?' he suggested.

'Maybe,' she said, moving past him to reach the display stand. 'Sorry, I must rush.' She saw exactly what she needed on the shelves, and added a brush and dustpan and several small blue plastic buckets to her wire basket.

Rhys watched her go over to the counter to pay for her purchases. She could feel his gaze burning into her back, and hoped that he wouldn't pursue her.

'Well, what have we here?' the shop owner said with a smile. 'Are you planning on starting a bucket factory?'

She made an effort to return the smile. 'No, I need these to hold the food grains for the animals. The children who come over to the farm love to help out, and there just aren't enough to go around.'

'Ah, kids always like being around animals, don't they? My own kids love having pets – over the years we've had guinea pigs, rabbits and tortoises, among others. I must say, they're not so happy when it comes to cleaning out the cages, though. Half the time it's me or their mother who ends up with the job!'

'I can imagine!' she answered, paying for the purchases and taking the opportunity to make a quick getaway. Something about the tattooed man put her on edge, and she wanted to put as much distance between them as she could.

She reached her car without being followed, and drove off, a sense of nervous apprehension enveloping her as she headed back to the farm.

Nick was there, she discovered when she parked the Fiat and went over to the yard. He was talking to Rob and Jason, passing the time of day from what she gathered, and she brightened on seeing him, a sense of relief enveloping her. He was the solid arm of the law, and all at once she felt safer, somehow.

'Hi,' she said, acknowledging the lads with a nod, and then turning her attention to Nick. 'Is this visit for business or pleasure?'

'It's always a pleasure to see you, Sarah,' he answered with a roguish smile that lit up his already perfect good looks.

'Hmm. I bet you say that to all the girls.' She beckoned him over to the farmhouse. 'Come on into the house – I'll put the coffee on.'

Once they were in the kitchen, she set out coffee mugs and a plate of cookies, and waved Nick to a chair by the table. 'How's the investigation going?'

'Which one?' he countered. 'I'm running several cases at once. If you're asking me about Jenny Carter, all I can say is I'm still making enquiries. The neighbours came up with a couple of visitors to her house that morning – which I'm sure you already knew...' He gave her a reproving look, and she lifted her chin and did her best to maintain an air of innocence. 'Both Ben and Pauline had reason to be mad at her, and they might both have been vindictive enough to take measures to make her pay for what they felt she'd done to them.'

'And the Griffiths?' She poured coffee into the mugs and added brown sugar and milk to her own. 'Didn't they have a motive to get her out of the way?'

He nodded. 'It seems as though she knew about their fraud with the insurance – that might have been enough for them to decide to ensure she kept quiet. We checked it out and the garage was full of the stuff they said had been stolen, so the insurance company will be pursuing them about that. As it is, either of them could have gone to see her on the pretext of talking about the sale of their house – that would have given them the opportunity to slip the deadly leaves in with the comfrey. With each of them being their own boss, they would have been able to slip away from their place of work at some point.'

She nodded. 'And what about Geoffrey Hollins?' she put in. 'He has the biggest motive of all, doesn't he? He stood to inherit the business and her Estate. It wouldn't have taken much for him to have a key made and then slip into her house when she was at work.'

'That's true. But as with all the others, as yet we have nothing to prove that any one of them committed the crime. The pathologist's been working on various forensic items that I took from Jenny's house that day but, so far, we haven't come up with anything helpful. Ben Reed's and Pauline Dwight's fingerprints were on the doors and some surfaces, but we know they were there that morning. And up to now there's no DNA evidence to work with... except in connection with your vandalism report.'

'What did you find?' She looked at him expectantly.

'There was blood on the brick, as you guessed, and it belonged to Reed. Like I said, we have his DNA on file from previous misdemeanours... so it's up to you if you want to press charges.'

She thought about it. 'Maybe we could do as you suggested, and caution him. If he's presented with the facts, he might realize he can't slip up again or he'll have to go to Court.'

'Okay, if that's what you want, I'll go down that route.'

'So, going back to Jenny's death, we have nothing you can charge anyone with?' It grieved her to say it. 'Whoever did it will get away with it? They've committed the perfect crime?'

He shook his head. 'I'm not in the habit of giving up, Sarah. I'll keep at this until we find our killer. We'll get him or her sooner or later.'

She wondered whether she should tell him her thoughts about the man she'd met in the hardware store just a short time ago. Was she being over-sensitive in thinking Rhys might have been goaded into taking action against a woman who grated on his nerves and appeared to be instrumental in stopping his sister from getting a flat?

Nick started to speak just as she was about to voice her thoughts. 'You might not like this,' he said, 'but there's Daniel Richmond to be considered as a suspect, too. According to Geoffrey Hollins, the lad was extremely taken aback when Jenny wouldn't let him leave his business cards and leaflets with the agency. He thought she was being too hard on him and was stopping him from building up his own firm. Hollins thought he was upset and brooding on it when he left the Agency.'

'Oh, come off it, Nick!' she protested. 'That's hardly a reason to want to kill someone!'

'No, it isn't, I agree with you on that score... but perhaps he didn't mean to kill her. Maybe he wanted her to feel poorly for a while, to teach her a lesson.'

She shook her head. 'No, absolutely not. I won't hear of it. Daniel wouldn't do something like that. He's not a vindictive person.'

'And I suppose he wouldn't burgle houses, either, in your opinion? Think about it... he'd done carpentry work at some of the places that were hit, so it wouldn't have been difficult for him to go back and steal whatever took his fancy.'

'It's not possible. Don't even think it.' Her words were becoming more clipped with every sentence. 'You have completely the wrong idea about him.'

'Perhaps,' he conceded. 'But I'm a policeman, Sarah. I have to think of all the possibilities, whether it goes against the grain or not.'

'Well, I don't believe for one minute that he did any of those things.'

'And I hope, for your sake, that you're right.'

'Does this mean that Daniel's still your main suspect for the burglaries?' The notion that the young lad could be in the frame for both murder and burglary had completely knocked her out of kilter.

'Not necessarily. We're interviewing other suspects who might have had a prior connection to the houses, or the people in the neighbouring properties, or to Jenny's agency. It's ongoing.'

'Well, I'd appreciate it if you would stop thinking of Daniel as a criminal and do everything you can to try to clear his name.'

He gave her a wry smile. 'I promise, I'll do whatever I can. I just want to get at the truth.' He stood up, getting ready to go. 'I'm due back at the station – the pathologist has been checking boot prints in Jenny's garden and comparing them with Jenny's gardening boots, along with the soil samples I took. I'm expecting those results to be on my desk this afternoon.'

'You've been very thorough, considering your Chief Inspector wanted you to pass it off as an accidental death,' she said approvingly. 'But the results have been a long while coming, haven't they?'

'That's quite normal. We aren't the only ones who use the facilities of the laboratory. It serves a wide area, and the work is prioritised. You were lucky with the DNA on the brick. It must have slipped through the net.'

She smiled, wondering if he'd had something to do with that. 'Thanks for letting me know what's happening, anyway, Nick. I appreciate it. Perhaps the lab results will show us the way.'

'Let's hope so.'

Sarah saw Nick out to his car and waved him off, before walking slowly back to the house, deep in thought.

It was coming up to the weekend, and on Monday her holiday fortnight would be over and she was due back at work. It was high time she stopped shilly-shallying and made some positive decisions.

With that in mind, she went into the living room and sat down in the cosy armchair and picked up the phone.

'Hi Mum,' she said cheerfully, her spirits lifting when she heard her mother's voice.

'Sarah, sweetheart... how are things with you? Are you okay?'

'I'm fine, Mum. I've been thinking about what you said the other day, about keeping the farm, and after a lot of heart searching I've decided I need to give it another six months to see if I can make a go of it. After all, as you pointed out, I've invested money and time in it already, and I have this really strong feeling that it's what Gran would have wanted me to do. She would have wanted me to keep it in the family.'

'Ah, I'm glad, Sarah. I thought you might do that.' Her mother sounded pleased. 'If you want me to help in any way, let me know.'

'Thanks, Mum.'

'Any time.' She paused. 'What will you do about your job?'

'I spoke to Martin yesterday to sound him out about the work situation before I approach my boss, and he thought they'd be all right with me doing half time. He said they don't want to lose me. In fact, he suggested that I might be able to do some of the work from home.'

'Oh, that's a good idea. Would you be able to do that? I mean, is it feasible in your line of work?'

'It may be. I can do research on the computer, and deal with emails and documents. There must be a lot I can do away from the office.'

'That's brilliant. And if Martin thinks that way, I'm pretty sure your boss will agree to it.'

'Possibly. Either way, I've made up my mind. If I have to go on working full time for a while, I'll bring in more staff to cover, and oversee things in my free time. Failing that, I'll find another firm that will let me go part time.'

'That sounds as if you're determined.' Sarah could almost feel her mother's smile at the other end of the line. 'So, what's your next move?'

Sarah screwed up her face a fraction. 'I think I'd better go and see Raj and tell him that the farm isn't going to be up for sale. It doesn't seem fair to keep him hanging on. As Mr Hollins said, he's already been making plans as to how he can change things on the farm to suit his requirements. I dare say there will be other pieces of land he can buy if he's really interested in becoming a landowner, albeit they won't actually be right next door.'

'I'm sure he'll understand. He'll be disappointed, I expect, but he has the Manor, and that's quite a substantial property, albeit there's not a lot of land to go with it.'

'I'll go round there now and see if he's at home. There's no time like the present... I've made up my mind, and now I just want to get on with things.'

'That's my girl!' The smile was back in her mother's voice. 'You've always been like that, ever since you were little – once you get your teeth into something, you don't want to let go... you have to finish it.' She paused momentarily. 'It's the same with hunting for Jenny's killer, isn't it? You'll keep on going until you find who did it? Are you making any progress?'

'Not as much as I'd like, to be honest, but Nick's expecting some forensic reports back from the lab, so it's possible they may help. If not, I have to do some more digging to find the answers.'

'Be careful, Sarah,' her mother said in a worried tone. 'You don't know who, or what, you're dealing with.'

'I will.'

CHAPTER FOURTEEN

JYOTI SAYED came to the door of the Manor House when Sarah rang the bell a few minutes later. She was an attractive, slender woman, wearing a pale gold sari that was beautifully embroidered with tiny scarlet flowers.

'Oh, it is so good to see you, Sarah,' she said, giving her a bright smile. 'Come in, please.' She ushered her inside the house along the wide hallway and into a glass walled conservatory. As she led the way, Sarah saw that her shiny black hair was neatly held in place at the back of her head with a jewelled clasp.

'Please, sit down.' The conservatory was a light, tastefully decorated room, with a sandy coloured carpet and floor length pale green silk curtains at the windows. The furniture was traditional cane work, two settees with deeply upholstered seats and scatter cushions that added bright splashes of colour.

Sarah took a seat on one of the settees and Raj's wife sat down opposite her.

'Raj and I were so pleased that you took the trouble to come and welcome us to the Manor,' Jyoti said. 'And I have been hoping that you would call on us again. If not, I was going to come and see you with a gift of my chutney.'

'That would be lovely,' Sarah answered with a smile. 'I would love to have you visit the farm any time. I've been meaning to come over again before this, but I've been so busy just lately.'

Jyoti nodded. 'Raj told me that you had to have repairs done to the barn roof after the storm.'

Sarah pulled a face. 'That's right, along with several other things. Everything on the farm is quite old and it generally needed some work doing on it.' She glanced around. 'Is your husband not at home, today? I know he must be a busy man, but actually I was hoping that I might be able to see him and talk to him.'

Jyoti smiled. 'He is playing golf with his friend, Geoffrey, but he should be home very shortly.' She shook her head slightly. 'Those two have become great pals – you wouldn't think they had met only a few weeks ago.'

'Yes, I noticed they seemed to get on well when we saw each other in the Blacksmith's Arms. I suppose they're both businessmen at heart, so they have something in common.'

Sarah didn't know exactly what business Raj was involved in, but he'd mentioned having his fingers in a few pies, and she knew that property development was one of his interests nowadays.

'That is true. He says men discuss business while they are on the golf course, so it cannot be called relaxation, or purely a leisure interest! I am not sure that I believe him!'

Sarah chuckled with her, and Jyoti said, 'Would you care to take tea with me? I usually make a pot of tea at this hour of the afternoon, and have a bite to eat.'

'Thank you, but please don't go to any trouble on my behalf. I had quite a substantial lunch,' Sarah explained, although that was several hours ago.

'Just a few sandwiches,' Jyoti murmured. 'Please do share them with me. I am so pleased that you have come to visit.'

Sarah felt a slight wave of guilt wash over her, considering that she had come to advise her husband that she wouldn't be selling the farm to him, but Jyoti was set on playing the perfect hostess, so how could she let her down?

'Is there anything I can do to help in the kitchen?' Sarah asked, but Jyoti shook her head.

'I will only be five minutes,' she said, getting to her feet. 'Please, make yourself at home. Have a look through the magazines that are on the table, if you like.'

'Thank you, I will.' Jyoti left the room, and Sarah spent a minute or two leafing through the glossy home and garden magazines that had been carefully placed on the glass and cane work coffee table.

Her attention wandered after a while, and she looked around, noticing a small alcove where the conservatory joined the hallway. There was a glass fronted cabinet in there, holding a collection of wooden, gold embossed shields and silver trophies.

Jyoti came back in wheeling a gold edged trolley laden with teapot, cups, and a plate full of perfect triangular cut sandwiches. She set the plate down on the coffee table and began to pour tea into the cups.

'Help yourself to sandwiches,' she bade Sarah. 'There are cucumber and mayo, or salmon and cream cheese.'

'Thank you.' Sarah added a couple of triangles to her plate and bit into one of them. 'Mmm... these are delicious,' she said, savouring the taste of the salmon and the soft, fresh bread. Glancing around the room once more, she added, 'I noticed that there are a lot of trophies on display over there. Are they yours, or your husband's... or both?'

Jyoti laughed. 'Oh, they are my husband's, most definitely. He is very proud of his sporting prowess. He has trophies that he won in fishing competitions, and for golf, and even ones from his younger days when he played football.'

Sarah smiled with her. 'There's a plaque in there that is quite different to the others,' she pointed out. She couldn't make out any of the detail from where she was sitting, but it looked as though it was carved out of crystal or some kind of acrylic material, and there was a photograph next to it, showing a man holding up the plaque.

'Oh yes... that is an award that was given to Raj for his achievements in business. He ran a car dealership, and they won the best dealership and best website award five years ago.'

Sarah was impressed. 'So that must have been back in London, was it?'

'No, no... we were only in London for just over two years. That is where we met, and were married. Before that Raj lived with his family in Hertfordshire. His company was based there, in Hemel Hempstead.'

They drank the tea and ate, companionably chatting for a while, until a few minutes later they heard a key turn in the lock of the front door, and Raj came to join them in the conservatory. The sun was lower in the sky by now, but the room retained its light, airy appeal, catching the last of the rays.

'Hello, Sarah. It is good to see you.' Raj smiled, nodding to his wife and added, 'I am pleased to see that Jyoti is looking after you.'

'Yes, she is. I'm really enjoying these sandwiches. I hope we've left enough for you. I expect you're famished after your round of golf.'

He laughed. 'That is true.' He sat down next to his wife. 'I hope this is just a social visit?' he asked Sarah. 'Perhaps you have good news for me... about the farm? Or am I being too hasty?'

'I'm sorry, Raj.' Sarah swallowed and wondered how best to break it to him but, in the end, she came straight out with it. 'The fact is, I've decided to keep the farm and see if I can make a go of it. I do appreciate your offer to buy it from me, but I feel I haven't given things a fair chance, yet. The farm has been in my family for generations, and I can't help thinking I would be letting everyone down if I were to sell up without at least trying to make it work.'

His face fell and for a second or two she saw him struggle to master his disappointment. 'I understand,' he said after a while. 'I am sorry, of course. I had great hopes and ambitions for what I might do with the land... but it is not to be. I have no choice but to accept that.'

'Perhaps there will be another farm locally that will come on the market and suit your needs,' she suggested.

'Perhaps.'

They made small talk for a while, but eventually there was an awkward silence, and Sarah decided she might have outstayed her welcome. 'I should get back to the farm,' she excused herself. 'It's getting near to dusk and the hens need to be gathered into the coop for the night.'

'Oh, yes...' Raj said. 'I will see you out.'

'Thank you.' Sarah stood up and began walking along the length of the conservatory towards the hallway. As she passed by the display cabinet she glanced at the crystalline award and the photo that stood alongside it. *Lakuni Car Dealership, Kings Langley,* she read, engraved into the plaque, *Dealership of the Year Award.* The photo next to it showed a man that must have been Raj, although his hair was shorter and he was minus his goatee beard back then. He was wearing a smartly tailored dark suit, and he was standing next to an equally well-dressed man who was sitting in a wheelchair. There was a similarity between the two men... both had black hair and dark eyes, and their faces were strikingly angular.

Something about the photo and the award bothered her. Were they half-brothers? Perhaps that was why the name of the dealership was Lakuni and not Sayed. Or perhaps she was getting it all wrong.

'Oh... it says here the name's Lakuni – is that a trade name?'

'Lakuni... it is my uncle's name,' Raj said, sensing her puzzlement. 'He started the business and then, in time, it passed to me and my brother.'

'Oh, I see.' She didn't really, not fully, because something else was bothering her and she couldn't quite put her finger on it, but it seemed appropriate to agree just then. Perhaps it was simply that Raj had never mentioned a car dealership before this – as far as she knew, he didn't own one now and seemed to have diversified to other business interests. 'I didn't realize you were in Kings Langley – Jyoti mentioned Hemel Hempstead.'

'That is right. We moved to new business premises not too long after that photo was taken.'

'Of course, that would be it.' Still, though, something was niggling her. 'Jenny Carter had a large, well known agency in the centre of Kings Langley,' she said. 'She was Geoffrey Hollins' partner, as you're probably aware... I wonder if you might have come across her back then in your search for new premises? After all, Kings Langley's not that big a place, and I doubt there would be many agencies there.' Geoffrey had said they'd not met, but he could have been wrong.

'Ah... um... well, the thing is... you have to understand - I met a lot of people...' His voice trailed away.

'I suppose so.' He'd clearly been thrown off balance by her question, as though he didn't want to answer, and that was strange, she thought. Why would it bother him to tell her whether or not he'd known Jenny, or to say that he couldn't remember her? She only hesitated for a moment, thinking that through, but she was aware that Raj was watching her, frowning, and that all at once he was stiff and tense. She decided it was time to go, turning to Jyoti and saying warmly, 'Thanks for the tea and sandwiches, Jyoti. They were delicious.'

'You're very welcome.' Jyoti must have made a quick dash to the kitchen a few minutes ago while Sarah and Raj were talking, because she pressed a gingham-topped jar of home-made chutney into her hands. 'You must have this... I hope you like it.'

'Thanks,' Sarah said again, and walked with Raj to the door. 'Bye, Raj,' she murmured. 'I'm sorry to have let you down over the farm. I know how much you were counting on it.'

'Please, do not concern yourself,' he said. 'It is fine.' He didn't look fine, though. His features were strained, and he seemed to be preoccupied with his thoughts.

Sarah walked back to the farm, stopping at the store shed to fill a bucket with granular feed for the hens. Then she unlocked the coop and called them to come from the yard and the nearby grassed area to get it. It was one sure way to bring them all inside the run for the night.

Satisfied that they were all safely in the coop, she padlocked the gate to the run and went back to the farmhouse.

Lexie came to greet her, tail wagging, and she bent to stroke her silky fur and stopped to look at the puppies in the large oval dog bed. 'Hey, Lexie, aren't you proud of your little brood? They're gorgeous!'

Lexie's tail was working overtime as they both gazed down at the puppies. They were still clumsy in their movements and unable to see properly, but already they were developing their individual characters. Socks, the puppy that had been born first, was definitely going to be a leader – he was into everything and trying to explore, even if it meant climbing all over his siblings. Biscuit, one of the female pups, was a timid little thing, whilst Boss, one of her brothers, was an individual through and through, who wanted his own space and didn't much care to join in the general mayhem.

Sarah stroked them all in turn, before going to fill up Lexie's food bowl and give her fresh water.

'There you are, Lexie. Eat up.' Not that the Boxer needed to be told. She was sitting at Sarah's feet, alert and at the ready, waiting for the signal to dive in.

That done, Sarah set up her laptop computer on the kitchen table and sat down to try to answer some of the questions that had been troubling her ever since her visit to the Manor House. Over the years, she had learned it was best to follow her instincts, and alarm bells were starting to go off inside her head.

First of all, she wanted to know why there was a name change... the award was for the Lakuni dealership, and not Sayed. Raj had offered a simple explanation, but he was a proud man, a man who enjoyed his status as a landowner and businessman, who loved to show off his trophies and she couldn't help thinking he would have re-named the business when he took over. The business was based in Hertfordshire, near Hemel Hempstead, Jyoti had said, although it started off in Kings Langley, and that too caused a stirring of unease in her, but she wasn't sure why.

Research was a substantial part of her job as a paralegal, checking into facts to aid in the defence of a client when his or her case came to Court, and she used that skill now to chase up any information she could find on the Lakuni Car Dealership.

It appeared the business had been sold two and a half years ago, so she concentrated her efforts on finding out about the Lakuni name and the award they had received. That brought up a photo from the newspapers – the same photo that she had seen in Raj's display cabinet.

The five years old article that accompanied the photo talked about the two brothers who built up the business until it was a thriving enterprise. Raj and his brother, Jamil, had bought into the business with money they'd inherited from their father. Unfortunately, Jamil had very recently suffered a stroke and was confined to a wheelchair.

There was no mention of an uncle, so Sarah searched some more, looking for anything at all to do with the brothers and how they started up in business.

After a few minutes she was rewarded by the appearance of another Press photo, this time concerning the opening of new offices in Hemel Hempstead, Hertfordshire. The caption read *Lakuni Car Dealership celebrates Award win in new prestige headquarters.*

Sarah looked closely at the picture and then gasped as she recognized someone there. 'Surely not... it can't be...'

Raj was there, in the forefront, looking every bit the proud businessman, but it was the woman in the background that caught Sarah's attention. Jenny Carter was toasting the business partners, glass of wine in hand. Why would Jenny have been there? And why had Raj not admitted to knowing her? More than likely he was the one who would have finalized the arrangements for the celebration because his brother was clearly too ill.

Quickly, she scanned the accompanying article. *Raj Lakuni, of Kings Langley, and his brother, Jamil, held a party to celebrate the opening of their new premises in Hemel Hempstead. They invited clients, new and old, along with colleagues, and Jenny Carter, owner of Kings Langley's Carter Estate Agency, who helped Raj to find their new headquarters.*

Lakuni... not *Sayed...* Raj's surname was Lakuni, according to the newspaper article. Why was he calling himself Sayed? And Jenny and Raj obviously knew each other, something he'd tried to deny.

Sarah reached for the phone and called Nick, needing to talk to him about what she'd found out. Glancing at the clock on the wall, she saw that it was getting on for nine in the evening. He would probably be at home, or out enjoying himself in his free time, and she felt a few misgivings for disturbing him but quickly dismissed them.

'Hi Sarah, what's new?'

'Hi, am I calling at a bad time? Only, there's something I wanted to talk through with you.'

'Sure, fire away. I'm still at the station – we're interviewing a couple of suspects about the burglaries, but I'm just taking half an hour to grab a bite to eat... spagh-bol.'

'Ah... Sounds yummy. I don't like to interrupt your meal... but I've found out something that's giving me pause for thought. I'm not sure whether it's important or not.'

'Go on...'

She heard the clink of cutlery and guessed he was taking a forkful of food. 'It may be nothing,' she said, 'but I've just discovered that Raj Sayed used to be known as Raj Lakuni, and that Jenny knew him when she lived in Chesham, in Buckinghamshire. He ran a car dealership with his brother, and Jenny found premises for them. Her Estate Agency was called the Carter Agency then – it was in Kings Langley, where Raj used to live – when he called himself Lakuni. Chesham isn't too far from either Kings Langley or Hemel Hempstead.'

That must have been what had struck a chord with her... the proximity of the towns and the fact that Raj lived in the town where Jenny had her agency. 'It's not much, but it's peculiar, don't you think? I wouldn't normally give it much attention, but since Jenny died...' Her voice faded. 'Anything out of the ordinary needs to be investigated, don't you agree?'

'I do. That *is* interesting. She must have decided on a new name for the agency when she moved here. I've been going through the Meadows client list, looking for anyone who had dealings with Jenny that might fit into our scenario. The purchase of the Manor House came up, but it was Geoffrey who handled all the negotiations, wasn't it? And it was all done over the phone initially, because Raj was too busy to come to the Cotswolds at that time, so Jenny and Raj never communicated with one another.'

'That's right,' she agreed. 'As I understood it, Jenny hadn't seen anything of Raj when he bought the Manor House.' Her mind was ticking over. 'So, she wouldn't have known he was the man she knew back in Kings Langley. Why would she, when he told Geoffrey his name was Sayed?'

'As far as I'm aware,' Nick said thoughtfully, 'Geoffrey sent the paperwork by post to Raj for his signature. He was living in London at that time.'

'Yes, he was. Something must have happened to make Raj change his name... but what? Why would he do that?'

'Hmm...' He took another forkful of spaghetti. 'I'm guessing, from all this newly acquired knowledge, that you have your computer switched on?'

'Yes, I do.'

'Try making a search for anything to do with the sale of the business.'

'Okay.' She turned her attention back to the computer. 'That would have been two and a half years ago...' she murmured. 'About six months before Jenny moved house and came to live here in the village.'

Sarah tapped the keyboard once more. A horrible suspicion was growing inside her and it would gnaw at her until she found the truth.

'Uh-oh...' Her breath snagged in her throat.

'What have you found?'

'It's a Press report from around the time of the sale.' She quickly scanned the article while Nick continued to eat his spaghetti. 'There's a headline here: *Jamil Lakuni broken after brother's disappearance.*

'That would be Raj's brother, I take it?'

'Yes. According to this article, Jamil lost everything when his brother *fraudulently* sold the business and absconded with the money. He'd already suffered the effects of a stroke some years before, but his health took a sudden downturn when he realized his brother had taken everything. It says here he has a wife and two children to support.'

Nick put down his fork. 'This throws a whole new light on the investigation. If Raj committed fraud and then hoped to get away with it by leaving town and changing his name, he has a definite motive for killing Jenny. He'd only been in Woodvale a week and then Jenny died suddenly and unexpectedly. That certainly puts him in the frame.'

'I think so, too. If they had come face to face, she would have known he was Raj Lakuni, who'd cheated his brother out of the business and emptied the bank account.'

'Does Raj know you've been checking up on him?'

'No.' She let out a sharp breath. 'But he might realize that I suspect something. I was at the Manor House earlier, and he saw me looking at a photo of him and his brother. There was a banner saying *Lakuni Car Dealership*. He said it was his uncle's name. Then, when I mentioned Kings Langley and the fact that he might have known Jenny, he reacted badly and looked quite tense. I think he might guess that I'll look into it - he knows I've made the connection with Jenny and her agency, and with him looking for new premises, as well as the fact that he supposedly didn't know her... and I questioned his surname. I think before too long he'll want to know exactly what I've found out.'

'That's a strong possibility. Okay, I'm on it. I'll see if I can get a warrant to search his property. Forensics might be able to come up with something. But you could be in danger, Sarah. If he killed Jenny and believes you know who he really is and what he's done, he might try to silence you. I'll go and find him and bring him in for questioning. In the meantime, I think you should lock your doors as a precaution. I'll come over to you as soon as I can, just to check things out and make sure he's not hanging about near the farm.'

'I'll do that.' It occurred to her that the door was unlocked at the moment because Lexie needed to go out soon for her nightly wander around the yard. She would lock up as soon as she'd attended to that. Just then, though, Lexie started to bark. 'I have to go Nick...I think Lexie needs to go out.'

'All right. Be safe.'

Sarah cut the call and stood up, glancing at the dog.

Lexie left her puppies in the bed and came to stand by Sarah's side. She was staring at the door, still barking, tail straight out behind her, and Sarah knew a sudden shiver of apprehension as she realized she might have misread Lexie's warning bark. From the way the dog was standing, Sarah realized there might be someone outside.

There was a tap on the door and then, as she watched, the door was pushed open.

Raj walked into the kitchen. He was wearing the same casual trousers and shirt that he had on earlier, topped by a thin suede jacket that he had left undone. 'Ah, forgive me, I did not know if you would hear me knocking, with your dog barking so loudly.'

'Raj,' she said, 'is there something I can do for you? Was it something to do with the farm?'

'Uh - I wondered if we should talk a little more about that. Maybe I could make you a better offer?'

She shook her head. 'I'm sorry, but I don't think so, Raj. I've made up my mind.' She had the feeling he was making it up as he went along. He had needed an excuse to come over here. As he spoke, he looked beyond her to the computer on the table and the screen that showed the photograph and the newspaper headline about his brother. His mouth became a grim, straight line. He didn't like what he saw.

'You have been checking up on me, haven't you, Sarah?'

Sarah wondered if she should brazen this out and pretend that she knew nothing. 'Checking up?' she queried. 'I was interested in the award you won, that's all.'

She was clutching at straws, and from his taut, steel-eyed expression she guessed he knew it, too.

'Hmm… The trouble is, Sarah, you are an intelligent young woman, and you have already worked it out, haven't you? I knew, as soon as I saw you looking at that photo that you would figure out what was going on. Anyone else accepts without question that Lakuni was my uncle's name, but I knew, deep down, that you would not be so easily convinced.'

She followed the direction of his gaze, and saw the picture of Jamil in a wheelchair, looking pale and haggard. 'How could you do that to your own brother, Raj? You left him penniless.'

He shrugged. 'Jamil was sickly. I was the one doing all of the hard work, while he did the accounts and dealt with the shipments of vehicles. Anyway, he is my half-brother. We were never close.' He spat the words out as if he despised him. 'My father married again shortly after my mother died. It was disrespectful to my mother's memory. Jamil should never have been born.'

She was deeply shocked by his cold, dismissive attitude. 'So, your brother had to pay for your father's actions? You took his money and left him to pick up the pieces?'

'What would he have done with the money? He had a stroke that left him paralysed down

293

one side. He struggled to walk and needed help to feed himself.'

'From what I've read, he was receiving physiotherapy. He might have made a decent recovery.'

'Perhaps.' His tone was dismissive and he looked at her again with eyes that were dark and cold as the grave. 'You should have left well alone, ignored what you saw. Now I have to deal with the situation you have created.'

'Is that what you said to Jenny when she recognized you?'

'Pah! Jenny was always going to be trouble. She knew that I had sold the business and disappeared. I did not think I would ever see her again. I did not know that she had moved to Woodvale when I bought the Manor House. How could I know that? She was still living in Chesham when I left.'

'You went to London?'

He shrugged again. 'I could be anonymous in the City and there were lots of business interests to keep me occupied while I decided what I wanted to do.'

'So, you grew a beard and changed your hairstyle, along with your surname.'

He smiled. 'And I was reborn. Everything was perfect.'

'Until you went to Jenny's agency in Caulders Lea and she recognized you. You must have been so frustrated to know that she had the power to foil all your plans for an idyllic lifestyle.'

He nodded. 'I admit it, I was shocked, and so was she. Geoffrey was out of the office when I saw her that Saturday morning – I'd gone there hoping to talk to him about a small problem at the Manor, but he'd stepped out for half an hour. She recognized me as soon as she saw me, and threatened to tell the police who I really was.'

'But you weren't going to let her do that, were you?' Sarah was starting to feel shaky inside, her nerves shredded.

'Of course not. I knew I had to act before she could tell anyone. I might have done something about her there and then, but a customer came into the agency to talk to her and she told him that she had to come out to Woodvale to see you. She was already late, she said, but she would phone him at lunchtime from her home. It gave me the opportunity to get my thoughts straight. She left with the client before Geoffrey came back, so I knew she wouldn't have the chance to talk to him. I saw her get into her car and I followed her. While she was with you at the farm, I had time to work out what I needed to do.'

'Things might not have gone to plan. What would you have done then, if she'd had the chance to tell someone what she knew?'

'Oh, I would have finished her off one way or another before that could happen.'

Sarah stared at him. He'd said it without emotion, in a straightforward, matter of fact manner. It made her blood run cold. 'So, you went to her house while she was with me at the farm?'

He nodded. 'I looked up her address.'

It made Sarah feel sick to know that he had been putting his murderous plans in place all the time that she was talking to Jenny. Worse still, he'd come over to the farmhouse and sat having coffee with Sarah afterwards, knowing that Jenny might be drinking the toxic brew even as they'd chatted. 'You knew she had a heart problem?'

'Oh yes.'

'And the comfrey tea?'

'That, too. Back in Chesham, she had a regular routine of going home at lunchtime and drinking the brew. She made no secret of it. And I knew that she grew foxgloves in her garden here... Jyoti asked Geoffrey's advice on how to plant the garden at the Manor House. She wanted a herb garden, so he told her about Jenny's kitchen garden and all the herbs she grew, and her love of cottage garden flowers.' He smiled again, a sickly, horrible smile that curdled her stomach. He was so puffed up with his own guile that he was taking pride in what he had done. 'So, I knew what I would find in her flower borders when I went there.'

'You couldn't have known you would be able to get into her house. It would have been locked up.'

He shrugged. 'It was simple enough. I parked my car around the corner, waited until the cul-de-sac was empty and went down the drive to the garage. I don't believe anyone saw me, but if they did, they might have thought I was trying to sell double glazing or some such. The house opposite was empty, up for sale, so no one there would have seen me, and there are trees screening the drive to one side.'

His mouth twisted. 'It was no problem getting into the garage. All I needed was a length of wire that I could push through the top of the garage door and hook over the release pull on the inside. I found what I needed in my car and hid it under my jacket, and when I came to use it, it took seconds. Once inside, I had access to the house from the side door. All I had to do was pick the lock.' He waved a hand in the air, as though to emphasize his cleverness. 'It was nothing special.'

'And if there hadn't been a side door into the house?'

'I knew there would be. I am familiar with that style of house. But if not, I would have gone down the path at the other side of the building and jemmied a window. I had the tools in the boot of my car. I preferred not to do that, of course – I did not want anyone to know I had been there, but...' He shrugged. 'When you have no choice...'

'Someone might have seen you.'

He shook his head. 'I doubt that. There are fences, pergolas, arches and all manner of shrubs that would have hidden me from view.'

She studied him, upset that she could ever have thought he was a decent man. 'So, what now?'

He stared at her, his jaw clamped in a deadly grimace. 'Unfortunately, Sarah, you know too much. I am going to have to get rid of you.'

Her skin prickled as an icy cold shiver ran down her spine. 'You can hardly use foxglove leaves this time... how are you going to make it look like an accident?'

He moved his head from side to side. 'Perhaps that will not be necessary... you were here alone at the farmhouse when you disturbed a burglar.' He looked around. 'There are some quite nice items in here... those are Wedgwood plates on the shelf, I believe, and isn't that a Waterford Crystal collection in the display cabinet? How unfortunate for you that there have been so many burglaries around the village of late.' Slowly, he drew a long, thin bladed knife from his jacket pocket, and began to walk towards her, menace oozing from every pore.

Sarah stiffened. She was frozen with fear, but her mind was working overtime. Beside her, Lexie seemed to sense her unease, and the fur on her back bristled. As Raj drew closer, Sarah retreated towards the wood-burning stove and reached down to grasp a heavy iron poker from the stand in the hearth.

'Stay back, Raj. You won't get away with this.' She lifted the poker, ready to defend herself. She was filled with a growing anger now, resentment gradually replacing the fear and building up in her – why did he feel he had the right to come into her home and try to attack her? How on earth did he imagine he could get away with it? What kind of man was he, that he could poison Jenny without a qualm?

He laughed as she held up the poker. 'What do you think you are going to do with that? I am taller and so much stronger than you, Sarah. And this...' He looked down at the shining steel blade in his hand, 'this is all I need to quieten you for ever more.'

He lashed out at her and she swiftly sidestepped the thrust, swinging the poker to land a glancing blow on his arm. He might well be stronger, but she was lighter on her feet, and faster than him.

He lunged again, and this time it was too much for Lexie. She growled and snarled, baring her teeth as she launched herself at him in a fury, sinking those teeth into his forearm.

He screamed in pain, dropping the knife, and Sarah's eyes widened as she saw blood begin to seep through the thin suede of his sleeve. 'Get the dog off me,' he howled.

It was her turn to laugh. 'And let you stick a knife in me? I don't think so.' Taking advantage of his temporary distraction, she aimed a kick at his midriff, knocking the wind out of him. As he bent forward from the impact of the blow, Lexie released her hold on his arm, and Sarah followed through with another kick to Raj's jaw, sending him sprawling to the floor. His eyes widened with disbelief.

'They call it self-defence,' she told him, 'and I've been taking classes.' She sent the knife spinning across the room with a flick of her foot. 'Along with fitness training at the gym once a week.'

Raj groaned and tried to get to his feet, prompting Lexie to race over to him and to stand, barking furiously, her teeth just centimetres away from his throat. Then she started to growl, a low, fearsome growl that told him if he made the slightest move she wouldn't hesitate to draw blood again.

'I'd stay there, if I were you,' Sarah told Raj, retrieving her mobile phone from the table and going back to plant her foot on the base of his throat. 'If she doesn't get you, I will.' She still held the poker in her hand, and she rested the tip of it on his rib cage.

She was about to dial the police emergency number when the kitchen door opened and Nick rushed in, looking around as though he expected to find a scene of chaos. 'I heard Lexie barking,' he said in a taut voice, coming to an abrupt standstill. 'I was afraid you might be hurt, or in trouble...'

He broke off, beginning to relax a fraction, a crooked smile coming to his lips as he saw that she was applying gentle pressure to Raj's throat. 'But I see you appear to have everything under control.'

'I do,' she said. 'He came at me with a knife... it's over there by the Aga.'

Nick turned back to the door and beckoned an officer who was waiting outside. 'Help him up,' he said. 'Then cuff him.'

Raj got to his feet and tried unsuccessfully to shake off the officer's hold on him. When Raj was standing upright, his wrists handcuffed behind his back, Nick said, 'Raj Sayed, or Lakuni, you are under arrest for the attempted assault of Sarah Marshall, and the murder of Jenny Carter.'

'What! You cannot do this,' Raj spluttered, his body stiff with rage. 'She attacked me! Her dog attacked me! None of your charges will stick. You have nothing on me!'

Nick turned to the police officer once more. 'Read him his rights, and then call the police surgeon to come to the station. Tell him we need him to examine a suspect who's been injured.' While the officer was doing that, Nick produced an evidence bag and a surgical glove from his jacket pocket and picked up the knife without touching it with his fingers.

Raj was still intent on protesting his innocence, and complaining bitterly that Nick was out of order. 'I have done nothing wrong. You have no proof, no evidence against me!'

'We'll see about that,' Nick said. 'We've obtained a warrant to search your property... and that search is being carried out right now, as we speak.'

Some of the colour left Raj's face. 'You have no right to do that...' he ranted. 'I shall sue for wrongful arrest and invasion of my property. I shall see to it that her dog is put down – it attacked me – it drew blood!'

'The way I see it,' Nick answered calmly, 'the dog was defending her mistress from assault, and that is what I shall say in Court.'

'It will never get to Court,' Raj spat out. 'None of it. It is all lies. The knife fell out of my pocket. It is what I use for cutting fruit.'

'Save your breath,' Nick murmured, and to the officer he said, 'Take him away.'

He glanced back at Sarah as the officer led Raj out to the waiting police car. 'Will you be all right?' he asked. 'You're very pale.'

'I'll be fine,' she answered. Her hands were trembling, but she was stroking Lexie, praising her for helping her out. 'I think I'm just beginning to realize what might have happened.'

'Sit down,' he said, pulling out a chair for her. 'You're in shock. Shall I make you a hot drink?'

'No, really, I'm okay.' She sat down in a chair by the stove and managed a smile. 'How is it that you're here, anyway?'

'After we spoke on the phone, I went to the Manor House to serve the warrant to search the place... and to arrest him on suspicion of fraudulently selling the business – it would have been enough for us to hold him while we investigated other charges. He wasn't there, and his wife said she didn't know where he was – it was unusual for him to go out in the evening without telling her where he was going, she said, so I guessed he might have come after you.' He looked at her searchingly. 'I'm glad you're okay... are you sure I can't do anything for you?'

'No, thanks. I'll be fine... and you have to go back to the station to question your suspect.' Lexie came and sat at her feet and she hugged her. Now that it was all over she was feeling numb inside.

'That's true, and I've a feeling it's going to be a long session. But I could ring your mother – I'm sure she would want to come and keep you company.'

Sarah shook her head. 'No, don't disturb her. It's late and she'll only worry about what might have been.'

He frowned. 'If you're sure... I'll call in and see you sometime tomorrow and let you know what's happening.'

'Thanks.' She glanced up at him, troubled and needing to ask the question that was worrying her most of all. 'Could Raj be right about it not going to Court – about Jenny's murder, I mean? Is there any evidence to nail him?'

'Not yet, but we'll find it.'

There was a determined set to Nick's jaw, and as she watched him leave a few minutes later, Sarah hoped that his confidence was well founded.

CHAPTER FIFTEEN

'**WHY ON** earth didn't you call me last night, Sarah, and tell me what had happened?' Hannah Marshall was clearly troubled when she came into the farmhouse kitchen late the next afternoon. 'Pauline told me Raj went for you with a knife. I was out of my mind with worry.'

Sarah blinked. How did Pauline know what had gone on at the farmhouse last night?

Hannah placed a basket on the kitchen table and sat down. The contents of the basket were covered with a linen cloth, and Sarah was longing to know what was in there, but her mother was cross and upset and so instead of asking she did her best to soothe her ruffled feelings.

'I was all right – I managed to fend Raj off, and Lexie was a trooper. She was magnificent, Mum... you should have seen her. She flew at him as soon as she sensed danger.'

'I should have been here for you. I'd have come round straight away.'

'I know you would.' Sarah frowned. 'How did you find out about it, anyway? How did Pauline know? I haven't told anyone... except for Nick, and of course his police officer knew, but neither of them would have said anything.'

'Good grief, Sarah – didn't you know? There have been police cars outside the Manor House since last night. They're still there this afternoon – and policemen and women are coming and going all the time, as well as the forensic team in their white coverall suits. Half the village knows that Raj has been arrested. Pauline told me when I dropped some books off at the library.'

'Ah... I should have remembered the village grapevine... news around here spreads faster than wildfire.'

'Jyoti was upset. She told her cleaning lady that her husband had been accused of attacking you – can you imagine how I felt when I heard that? I was ill with worry. And as to murder – that's what they're saying - well, whoever would have thought him capable of such a thing? I shan't rest until I know what went on... you have to tell me everything.'

'Okay, Mum... try to stay calm. Everything's under control, I promise you.' Sarah poured coffee and slid a mug towards her mother. 'Here, drink this.' When she was satisfied her mother had taken a few sips, Sarah told her about the events of the previous night. 'But Nick has him locked up at the station, and he'll have a lot of charges to answer, so there's nothing to worry about.' She wasn't convinced that was entirely true, because without hard evidence to connect him with the crime, Raj could still get away without being punished for killing Jenny, but she wasn't going to tell her mother that.

'I hope you're right. I'm so glad Nick came here to check on you.'

'Hmm... apparently they went looking for Raj at the Manor House, and when he wasn't there, and Jyoti didn't know where he'd gone, this was the first place they looked. Of course, they served the warrant to search the place straight away.'

'That's good. At least Nick's on the ball.'

Sarah smiled. 'Yes, he is.' Her attention wandered to the basket. 'So, what's in there, or is it a secret?'

'Oh, I made you a hotpot... something to cheer you up and nourish you at the same time. All you have to do is put it in the oven for an hour or so.' She removed the linen cover, and Sarah peered down at the casserole dish. She knew from past times that it would be made up of tender pieces of meat and succulent vegetables in a rich, tasty gravy, and she could see that it was topped with overlapping slices of potato.

'I'll put it in the Aga now for you, shall I – it should be ready to eat for your evening meal?' Sarah nodded and Hannah switched on the Aga, sliding the casserole dish on to a wire rack and setting the automatic timer. 'There, away we go.' She turned away from the cooker. 'I brought you some crusty bread to serve with it.'

'That's wonderful, Mum. Are you going to stay and share it with me? There's enough here to feed a family!'

'I can't, sweetheart... I wish I could, but I have to go – right now, actually - and meet some friends... we're having a birthday celebration for one of them and I promised I'd be there. I had to come and see you first to make sure you're all right.'

'I am. I'm fine.'

'I'm glad. I feel better now.' Her mother stood up, getting ready to leave, and then hesitated. 'I must say, things are looking good around the farm. I noticed the barn and the new housing for the rabbits, and all the fencing that's been put in place... all Daniel's doing, I guess?'

She nodded. 'Daniel and a friend... yes.'

'Is everything okay with him, now? Has Nick accepted that he didn't do the burglaries?'

'I don't know.' Sarah's mouth turned down at the corners. 'He said he was interviewing a couple of suspects, but I don't know the outcome of that yet.'

'That's such a shame. I hope things turn out all right for him... he's been such a help to you, and if you're going to keep the farm you need good people around you.'

'I do... that's very true.' She studied her mother briefly. 'I could do with your help, too, you know?'

'Really?' Hannah looked pleased. 'What would you like me to do?'

'Well, I'm not sure I ought to be asking this... but have you ever thought about doing something other than catering for private lunches?'

'Goodness! Like what?'

'Did you ever think you might want to cook in a restaurant, or café?'

'You're thinking of starting one at the farm?'

Sarah nodded. 'It crossed my mind. We could position it next to the farm shop.'

'What farm shop?'

'The one I'm thinking of starting.' She was on tenterhooks to know what her mother was thinking.

'Oh, I see... well, yes, that might be quite interesting... I could add my own spin to some of the traditional dishes... home-made soups, lasagne, delicious salads with jacket potatoes, gourmet sandwiches, specialty quiches and tarts.

Oh, yes...' Her eyes were sparkling, her brain ticking over at speed. 'What a brilliant idea. We must talk about it some more.' She looked at her watch. 'But I must go now, or I'll be late.'

Sarah smiled and hugged her mother. 'Enjoy your get-together,' she said.

'I will. And don't you dare not phone me if anything ever happens that I should know about. I'm your mother. I need to know what's going on.'

'Okay.' Sarah was sheepish. 'I will, I promise.'

Matt turned up as Hannah was leaving. He waved to her, saying, 'Hi, Mrs Marshall. It's good to see you,' and then he walked over to where Sarah was standing in the yard.

'Are you okay?' he asked scrutinizing her carefully. 'Are you sure Raj didn't hurt you?'

'I'm okay,' she told him, smiling. 'How did you know?'

'The police surgeon popped into our veterinary hospital to collect his cat. He told me in confidence he'd had to stitch up a wound a suspect received from a dog bite. When I asked why the dog attacked and did it need to be locked up in a secure police kennel he told me she was defending her owner. Then our receptionist told me about all the police activity at the Manor and I put two and two together. I was really concerned, I can tell you. I came here as soon as I could get away.'

'Wow...it's a very small world.' She shook her head. 'No, he didn't get the chance to hurt me because Lexie got to him first.'

'I'm glad to hear it. Is she all right? She didn't suffer any after effects, did she – she's not long given birth, after all?'

'She seems fine. I've been giving her lots of attention to show her how grateful I am. I don't think she's hurt in any way... but why don't you come and take a look at her?'

He nodded. 'I will. I'll go and dress Clover's foot, and have a quick look at the ewes, and then I'll come up to the house.'

'Okay. Will you have time to stay for dinner? Nick said he'd be along soon, so we can all sit and talk. My mother brought round a huge hotpot – it should be ready in about an hour. It's far too much for me to eat on my own.'

'I'd like that, thanks.'

'Good.' Sarah left him to tend to Clover and went back to the house. She couldn't wait for Nick to come and let her know what was going on, how the investigation was going, but he had phoned her at lunchtime to say he couldn't get away until early evening. He'd been busy questioning Raj for most of the day, and fending off counter arguments from his lawyer.

She'd never been good at biding her time, but right now she had no choice. She kept herself busy, feeding the livestock and making sure they were all bedded down for the night, and then she went back to the house to check on the hotpot. An appetising aroma filled the kitchen, making her aware that she had missed lunch while she was working on the kitchen garden, and she was definitely hungry.

'Hi Sarah.' Nick tapped on the kitchen door and pushed it open, poking his head around the edge. 'Is it all right if I come in?'

'Of course.' She smiled, waving him to a chair, and continued setting the table with cutlery, salt and pepper pots and a basket that held the crusty bread her mother had made. 'I hope you have time to stay for dinner?' she asked. 'Or do you have to get back to the station fairly soon?'

'I'd like that, thanks. I can spare an hour before I need to go back... it's turning out to be a long workday.' He sniffed the air. 'It smells wonderful in here. Is this going to be another sample of your culinary expertise?'

She laughed, shaking her head. 'I wish I could say it was mine, but I'm afraid my nose might grow like Pinocchio's if I did that. In fact, this is courtesy of my mother, so I guarantee it will be wonderful.'

'I'm sure it will... her reputation goes before her,' Nick agreed, adding, 'I saw Matt outside in the yard. Is he checking on the animals?'

'That's right. He's going to eat with us. He came to look at one of the goats that had a nasty infection in her foot, but it's much better now. He's been coming over every day to change the dressing, but I doubt he'll need to do that for much longer.'

She was desperate to ask Nick questions about how the investigation was going, but it didn't seem polite to bombard him as soon as he'd come in the door. Instead, she concentrated on serving up the food just as Matt came in from the yard.

'Mm... this looks good,' Matt said, sitting down to eat a minute or so later.

Sarah poured herself a glass of sparkling spring water from the carafe on the table and took a long swallow. Her good intentions fizzled away as the bubbles hit her throat, and she said impatiently, 'Okay, Nick. Out with it. What's been going on with Raj? Has he confessed? Can you pin Jenny's murder on him?

Nick hesitated, spearing a forkful of golden brown potatoes, and then said, 'I'm afraid the answer to that is no, at the moment. He's as wily as a fox and he lawyered up straightaway, which has made life difficult for us.'

She sighed. 'I was so hoping it might be better news.'

'I know... I'm sorry to disappoint you. The attempted assault on you, and the business fraud are enough to hold him, anyway, for now, but obviously we want to get him for the murder. We took his clothes and shoes from the house, and we took his car away for forensic examination. The lab's working overtime to process everything - we put a rush on it. I'm expecting to hear from them any time now.'

Matt helped himself to a chunk of bread. 'Will the charges stick – for the attempted assault and the business fraud?'

'Oh yes. He tried to weasel out of the knife charge, but the knife is evidence. No jury is going to believe him, not when the whole story comes out and they hear about how he stole from his brother and changed his name. He didn't want Sarah telling anyone what he'd done, because that would open up a whole can of worms.'

'Presumably you'll let his brother know that he's been found?' Sarah started to eat, savouring the taste of potatoes, melt in the mouth carrots and onions, all cooked with a subtle blend of herbs.

'We've already done that. I spoke to him myself on the phone. We'll need him as a witness to say they are related and to give his account of how Raj cheated him out of the business and left him virtually penniless.'

'How is he?' Sarah was anxious on Jamil's behalf. 'Is he going to be well enough to testify?'

Nick nodded. 'I think so. He said he's had a lot of physiotherapy and he's managing to walk with a stick, now. The shock of what Raj did set him back a long way initially, but with the help of his family and the medical team he's come through it all.'

'So eventually he should get his money back?' Matt asked.

'After the Manor House has been sold, yes. Raj's assets will be frozen while this is all being sorted out, but in the long-term Jamil should get the money that was stolen, along with interest due, plus compensation, I imagine.' Nick poured himself a coffee from the cafetiere that Sarah had placed in the middle of the table. He offered the pot around, and Sarah held her cup out to be filled. She added milk and sugar and slowly sipped the hot liquid.

'What will happen to Jyoti?' she asked. 'Did she know what he did? She seemed so nice. Do you think she might have been in on it?'

'I don't think she knew what was going on.' Nick was thoughtful as he drank his coffee. 'Raj married her back in London a couple of years ago, so she always knew him as Raj Sayed.' He pulled a face. 'From talking to him, I suspect she was part of the image he wanted to hold up to the world — a beautiful young wife to play hostess when he entertained his business friends at the Manor House.'

'She knew about the car dealership in Hemel Hempstead,' Sarah commented.

He nodded. 'He told her he'd owned it under his uncle's name, and she accepted it without question. She didn't quite understand why he had no contact with his family, but he said there had been a difference of opinion over his ideas for running the business. He had taken on the burden of the day to day running of things, but when there were disagreements he left and went to London. She believed he was a wealthy man, but she didn't have anything to do with the financial side of things, and knew nothing about the sale of the business and the stolen money.'

'I suppose it's too soon for her to know what she'll do?' Matt's brow creased, and Sarah guessed he was trying to work out whether or not he believed her version of events.

Nick's phone began to warble, but before he answered the call he said, 'I expect she'll go back to her family in London. She says she has parents and siblings living there.'

He turned his attention to his phone. 'Hello, Nick Holt here.' He listened attentively to the caller for a minute or two. 'Okay. You did? Yes, thanks for that.'

He cut the call and Sarah and Matt stared at him intently. 'That was the lab,' he said.

'Go on,' Sarah urged him. 'Do they have the results?'

He nodded. 'On the day Jenny died I called the forensic team to collect samples from her garden. They made two casts of footprints in the flower garden and the herb garden. They didn't match any of Jenny's footwear, but they did match shoes that we found in Raj's wardrobe. The forensic team also took soil samples from Jenny's garden. It turns out that she used a special formula, granular slow-release fertilizer for her plants.'

'Was that found on Raj's shoes?'

Nick smiled. 'There were traces on his shoes, and it was also found in the footwell of his car.'

'Did they check Raj's land for the same kind of fertilizer?' Sarah was on edge, worried that something might happen to dash her hopes.

'They did... but they didn't find any.'

She breathed a sigh of relief. 'You've got him, then.'

He nodded. 'I'd say so, yes. The lab also found traces of foxglove leaves in his jacket pocket. He must have stuffed them in there to take into Jenny's kitchen. He was careful to leave no trace that he'd been in the house – he locked up after himself, and didn't leave any evidence of a break-in. I think he wanted everyone to believe it was either an accidental death, or suicide. He thought he'd committed the perfect crime.'

'You've done it! You've got what you need to convict him.' Sarah gave him a beaming smile. 'That's such a relief. I'm so glad you had the forethought to take samples from the garden, bearing in mind your bosses wanted you to leave well alone.'

'I have photos, too... of the torn foxglove leaves in Jenny's flower border. It'll all stand up in Court.'

She was so pleased she could have flung her arms around him and kissed him, but she resisted the urge, conscious that Matt would probably be very put out by her actions.

'What happens now?' Matt asked.

'I'll go back to the station tonight and formally charge him.'

'That's brilliant.' Sarah basked in that thought for a moment, but then another one crowded in on her. She couldn't rest until she knew the outcome. 'Just one more thing,' she said. 'Raj told me he wanted to get rid of me, and that he would make it look like a burglary – which reminds me - you said the other night that you were interviewing a couple of suspects about the burglaries that have been going on. Have you managed to get anywhere with that?'

'As a matter of fact, yes, we have.' He smiled, pleased with himself.

She pulled in a sharp breath. 'Is Daniel in the clear?'

'He is.'

'Oh, thank heaven! That is such good news.'

'As a matter of fact, it was Daniel that provided the clues which led us to the men who committed the crimes. He said his girlfriend had been talking to a man with tattoos one night, and had gone off with him. It turns out that man had been out with his mate burgling a house while Daniel was in the pub with Charlotte. When Rhys had finished, he came to the pub and started flirting with Charlotte, causing the row between her and Daniel.'

'But how did you know it was him?'

'We checked up on people who had done work at the houses – these two men are painters and decorators, and they either worked there or in neighbouring houses, so they could figure out the comings and goings of the people who lived there. We found some of their most recent haul in their own homes – some items stolen from the pensioners the other night. They hadn't had time to move them on.'

'Caught red-handed, then,' Matt said with a grin.

Sarah was smiling widely, too. She didn't like to say that she'd spoken to the man Nick was talking about... she was just thankful he would be paying the price for his criminal activity. 'That was good work, Nick,' she said. 'I'll ring Daniel and tell him he's off the hook.'

'Already done,' Nick told her. 'He's not on bail any more, so he doesn't have to report to the station.' He finished off his coffee and topped up his cup, giving Matt a refill at the same time.

Sarah went to the fridge to fetch a bowl of strawberry mousse that she'd made earlier that day. She served it up into three glass dishes. 'Help yourselves.'

'This has been a really good evening, Sarah,' Matt said, dipping his spoon into the delicate pink dessert. 'Good company, great food, and the knowledge that some people are going to get their just deserts, if you'll forgive the pun!'

'No-o-o...!' Sarah and Nick chorused, laughing.

Sobering, Nick gave his attention to Sarah and said, 'I know how glad you must be that Daniel is in the clear. He's done a lot of work around here... it made me wonder if you were planning on staying on the farm, considering how much effort you've put in to spruce things up.'

'Yes, I've been trying to figure out how I could make a go of it, if I were to stay here, and I think I might have come up with a plan... I'm going to give it a six-month trial to see if I can make it work.'

'Really?' Nick's brows shot up, and Matt suddenly became more attentive.

'Tell us more.'

'Well, first of all, I need to find a way to make this place pay for itself. My grandmother never managed it by running it as a straightforward farm, so I've been thinking maybe I need to do something a little different.'

'Like what?'

'It occurred to me that the children who come here love to explore the farm and help with feeding the animals. They're interested in everything that goes on – so I thought maybe I could turn it into a petting farm. I could get a licence and open it up to the public for days out, school visits, children's parties, and so on.' She looked at both of them, searching their faces for their reactions. 'What do you think?'

'I think...' Nick stopped to dwell on the idea for a moment or two. 'I think that's a brilliant idea.' He smiled at her, and she smiled back.

'Me, too,' Matt said. 'Though, I can't help thinking you're taking a lot on. What will you do about your work at the office?'

'I can only do it if my boss will agree to me working half time – I've spoken to Martin about it and he doesn't think that will be a problem. He says they'd rather have me there part time than not at all. If not, I might have to look for work in another office. And you're right, Matt, it is a big thing to take on. I would need to bring in more staff.'

'And provide food, probably,' Nick commented. 'Most of these kinds of places have a café of some sort, and a farm shop. You could perhaps turn the old stable block into whatever you need in that respect.'

She smiled again, excitement bubbling inside her. 'I've already spoken to my mother about the food side of things. After all, preparing good food is her passion. And the farm shop would sell produce from the farm, along with packets of food granules for the visitors to give to the animals. And even...' She remembered what Daniel had said a few days ago. 'And I could even sell little wooden planters for herbs, to grow on a windowsill... along with other kinds of rustic accessories.'

She was cautious for a second or two. 'But there's the money side of things to consider. I'll need quite a lot of capital if I'm to set things up properly.'

'Well, you do have a flat that you could sell -' Nick and Matt spoke at the same time and laughed. 'Great minds think alike,' Matt said.

'That's true — I'll have to think about that. It's mortgaged... but then again, prices have been rising lately.' She was serious for a moment or two. 'If I did that and things don't work out, I'll have to sell up and find myself another place with the proceeds.'

'I'm sure you'll make it work,' Nick said. 'It's a good plan. I like it, and I'm sure it's what your grandmother would have wanted. She was a very astute old lady – she must have known you would find a way to keep the farm going.'

'Yes,' Sarah murmured. 'I think it's what she was hoping for. She knew I was always happy here. And now that I know you have Jenny's killer safely locked up, I can start to relax and enjoy it.'

Nick raised his coffee cup. 'I'll drink to that!'

'Me, too,' Matt agreed, and as Sarah raised her cup they all clinked the china to make a toast.

'Cheers,' she said. 'Here's to good friends and good times and a job well done.'

*   *   *   *   *

Printed in Poland
by Amazon Fulfillment
Poland Sp. z o.o., Wrocław

55071701R00195